Texas Rein

10 9 8 7 6 5 4 3 2 1

ISBN: 0615803881
ISBN 13: 9780615803883

For more information about the author, please visit her website:

http://brboyette.com/

Texas Rein

By
Becky Rodgers Boyette

Table of Contents

Dedication	VII
Acknowledgements	IX
Chapter One	I
Chapter Two	13
Chapter Three	27
Chapter Four	41
Chapter Five	51
Chapter Six	61
Chapter Seven	73
Chapter Eight	83
Chapter Nine	99
Chapter Ten	113
Chapter Eleven	127
Chapter Twelve	135
Chapter Thirteen	147
Chapter Fourteen	157
Chapter Fifteen	163
Chapter Sixteen	173
Part II: Four Years Later...	181
Chapter Seventeen	183
Chapter Eighteen	193
Chapter Nineteen	201
Chapter Twenty	209
Chapter Twenty-One	221
Chapter Twenty-Two	225
Chapter Twenty-Three	235
Epilogue	243
About The Author	247

Dedication

For my husband, James. You will always be my greatest love story.

Acknowledgements

Whenever I finish a book, there are many to thank, and *Texas Rein* is no exception. I have to first and foremost thank the Lord, and my family and friends for their enduring support. I also must give a nod to my horses, because without them, any attempt at writing an equine saga would ring a little hollow.

Next I must acknowledge my fellow author, colleague, and dear friend, Lamar (L.R.) Giles. Without him I doubt any of my manuscripts would ever have left my hard drive. His unique writing style and creative criticism have layered my work with a richness it never would have attained otherwise. So Lamar, thank you – a thousand times thank you – for all the times you strengthened a sentence, revised a concept, or talked me down off a ledge.

I must also thank Chuck Nesmith, reining horse trainer, and Kay Walker, reining horse exhibitor and owner of Jaz Poco Espejo, former Reserve World Champion Buckskin Reined Cowhorse. Their insight into this fascinating sport fueled my fire and passion for writing *Texas Rein*.

Finally, I thank reining horse enthusiasts and competitors everywhere for expanding the sport beyond the borders of the United States and into international arenas. It is time to show the world what the western performance horse can do.

chapter

ONE

Lightning flashed and thunder rattled the night sky as I trudged through wet pasture with a flashlight, completely inadequate for the task at hand.

I'd searched Dad's hundred-acre spread twice by tractor, accounting for every other animal on the ranch. The cattle sheltered under the woods in the back forty. Boomer and Jack, Dad's riding horses, stood under the overhang in the barn munching hay and watching the rain slide off the roof. Only Prissy was nowhere to be found. Dad figured she'd chosen tonight of all nights to foal. Heaven help me if he was right.

After my patrol in the old blue Ford (which had no umbrella), I realized the mare must be lying somewhere in the ditch that divided the north and south pastures. So much for the superior natural instinct of horses. Prissy's secluded haven would soon fill with rainwater. I parked the Ford near the ditch and hopped down, left with no alternative but to search on foot.

The dark, wet pasture looked vastly different than the sunlit fields I remembered from childhood. As a girl I'd wandered the acreage both on foot and horseback, filling countless hours with shining happiness. Now the same land felt menacing. The threatening weather made me an insecure outsider, no longer a happy girl but a grown woman fumbling her way through what was once familiar.

I slipped and slid to the bottom of the small gully, slopping through the inch and half of water that had already accumulated. I called the mare's name, but thunder and pelting rain drowned my voice. *Drowned.* I pushed the thought from my mind. The mare and her unborn foal were Dad's lifeline, his motivation for recovery. They couldn't drown in a ditch on this grim March night.

I made out a dark shape ahead of me and thought I heard a grunting sound.

"Prissy!"

The mare raised her head, catching the white star on her forehead in the beam of my flashlight. Relief flooded through me. She was alive at least, but her breathing sounded raspy and labored.

I knelt by the struggling horse, patting her sodden neck and speaking to her in soothing tones. She whinnied and nickered, seemingly glad for my company. I shone the flashlight on her bulging belly; the foal hadn't arrived yet. Maybe there was a chance I could convince Prissy to get up, climb out of the ditch and walk to the barn, where she could foal in a warm stall fragrant with pine shavings instead of a muddy ditch flooding with rainwater.

"Come on girl, up!"

The mare heaved with a contraction, and then laid her head down in a puddle. *Oh, no.* Prissy wasn't going anywhere. I watched her quaking abdomen, realizing there was no way she could hoist herself out of the ditch amidst the throes of labor. The foal would have to be born here, or not at all.

All right, then. Nothing for it.

I continued my attempt at equine midwifery. Despite the dismal circumstances, Prissy seemed to be progressing normally. I'd watched cows and mares deliver before, although I'd never stuck my hands inside and pulled out the newborn like Dad sometimes did. I didn't intend to start now.

"'Atta girl, Prissy. 'Atta girl. Keep pushing, come on."

I stripped off my rain slicker and made a tent over Prissy's head, allowing her to breathe without rain pelting her face. She absorbed the encouragement like a sponge, pushing again and again. I rubbed her wet forehead and praised each effort.

With a massive grunt, Prissy expelled the foal. I rushed to her hind end, knowing the equine infant could drown in the inches of water that flooded the ditch.

The flashlight revealed little but a brown blob covered in white film. I found the foal's head and laid it in my lap, clearing away the birth sac and exposing his dainty, velvet nostrils. No air seemed to flow in or out of them. He was still attached to Prissy via the umbilical cord, but he needed to breathe on his own.

I resisted the urge to sob. In the middle of the pasture with no other human being in sight, holding the slimy new foal in my lap, I felt utterly alone and helpless. *God, if you haven't completely deserted me, now would be a great time to help!*

Thunder shook the ground again and a flash of lightning illuminated the pasture bright as day. I caught a brief glimpse of the foal's face, enough to see the streak of a white blaze and two chocolate eyes fixed on me. The newborn looked at me with total confidence, however misplaced.

Without a clue as to what I was doing, I placed my mouth over one of his nostrils, covering the other one with my hand. I filled my lungs and expelled the air into the little muzzle. *Please, breathe.* He responded with what sounded like a hiccup, then a tiny snort. I laughed in relief as warm air tickled my lips.

Prissy grunted again, delivering the afterbirth. Under the circumstances, I had no way to spread it out, make sure it was complete. I took solace in the fact Prissy had foaled seven times previously without complication. She rose and shook herself, then came to inspect her offspring.

I let her have a lick and a sniff as I cut the cord with my pocketknife. Somehow, I had to get the foal out of the ditch and into the safety of the barn. Struggling beneath his weight, all seventy or so pounds of it, I picked him up as best I could, staggering and lurching. Prissy's maternal instincts kicked in and she whinnied and screamed, pawing the ground, demanding the return of her baby.

"We've got to get to the barn, Prissy. You can't tend your foal in a ditch!"

Falling face first into the mud, I managed to climb out of the ditch by slumping over like the hunchback of Notre Dame, burying the toe of my boot into the side of the gully with every step for stability. With a back-wrenching effort, I heaved the foal into the seat of the tractor, climbed aboard, and threw the Ford into gear. Prissy galloped circles around me, neighing hysterics.

The soft lights of the weathered red barn shone like gentle beacons against the violence of the stormy night. I pulled the tractor into its port and switched off the key. The engine roar dwindled, then silenced. Only the sound of the rain and Prissy's anxious whinnies remained.

The sopping wet foal looked at me quizzically, ears swiveling back and forth, as if to say "What next?" The poor thing seemed awfully placid for having suffered such a shocking entrance to the world. I gathered him into my arms and stepped down from the tractor.

Once inside the barn, Prissy recognized my intentions as benevolent, although she hovered like a vulture as I stumbled toward a large corner stall. I entered the stall and deposited my burden into the soft bed of pine shavings, stepping aside for Prissy to join her baby. She gave me a cursory glance, and then proceeded with the business of cleansing the foal's coat with her warm tongue. I paused a moment to enjoy the scene. Even the hardest heart warmed at the sight of a mare tending her newborn.

Dad's words echoed in my head. *Don't forget warm bran for the mare.* As if I were still in pigtails and needed reminding. I entered the feed room, greeted by the thick smell of molasses from the bags of sweet feed. I grabbed an empty bucket and filled it with the textured mixture and two scoops of bran, and then added hot water from the sink. Stirring the concoction into a palatable soup, I caught a glimpse of myself in the tack room mirror. Soaked in rain and blood, I looked like a horror film scream queen. *Mother will have a fit.*

A pile of fluffy towels lay on a shelf next to the sink, and I plucked one from the top. Returning to the stall, I filled the feed bucket with the warm mash. Prissy ignored it, momentarily obsessed with her foal, but I knew she wouldn't let it sit long.

I rubbed her down with the towel, working in circles until the cloth absorbed the bulk of the moisture. Before long her coat turned from sodden black to its usual dark bay. Her foal, too, changed color with Prissy's judicious grooming, from a rather wet, dull brown, to what would certainly prove chestnut in the morning sun. I'd already noted his blaze and four white socks. And *he* was a *he*.

The foal became more animated as I watched, making failed attempts to stand on his spindly legs. For all the ordeal of his birth, he was, in fact, an extremely ordinary colt. He looked about the same as any other quarter horse foal, even his color unremarkable. But there was no denying the charm of the whiskered face or trusting eyes.

At long last he balanced on his limbs, staggering towards Prissy's teats. I waited until he found them and began to nurse, tentatively at first, greedily as he gained confidence. I felt relief, knowing I'd never survive Dad's interrogation if I didn't witness the foal ingesting the precious colostrum.

I struggled with what to call the little no-name after our adventure together.

"Well, goodnight, Splash. I'll see you in the morning. Welcome to the Rocking R."

***

Hank, our blue merle cattle dog, greeted me as I entered the laundry room. He whined and wagged his tail, apparently torn between his joy at my return and his spite that I'd left him behind in the first place.

"Sorry, fella," I apologized, scratching the plush ears. "I would've liked your company, but Mom wouldn't let you back in the house covered in mud."

I shed my clothes, save underwear, and loaded them straight into the washer. Grabbing a dirty towel from the basket and wrapping it around me, I tiptoed into the kitchen, hoping to take a shower before facing the inquisition.

No such luck.

"Mom! Mom! Did Prissy have her foal?"

Sam looked up from his homework on the kitchen table, pushing aside a forelock of blond hair. His blue eyes glowed with excitement.

"Yes, Prissy's foal is here, and no, you cannot go see him tonight."

Sam's face fell, his lips forming a "but."

I cut him off. "Because you have to finish your homework and get to bed. It's after ten, for heaven's sake."

I exited the room before he could argue. I longed to feel steamy water on my back, to smell the fruity essence of sudsy shampoo.

Mother intercepted me halfway through the living room.

"Oh, thank goodness," she sighed, relieved. "You had the sense to leave your clothes in the washroom."

"I know the drill, Mom."

She raised a hand to smooth her perfect gray curls.

"I hope everything went well?"

Mom's voice trembled, not out of concern for Prissy or her colt. Despite being a rancher's wife for forty-plus years, Mom cared nothing about cows or horses, but she adored Dad and knew how much stock he'd put into this foal.

"Prissy and the foal are fine. They're in the barn, safe and comfortable."

"What a relief. You'll tell your father, after you've cleaned up?"

"Of course."

I bolted the bathroom door behind me, shutting out my inquisitive son and nervous mother. My body ached from bearing the foal out of the ditch, and then into the stall. I'd be sore for days.

My wet underclothes fell to the floor and I entered the warmth of the shower. I pulled the scrunchie out of my hair, letting the familiar weight fall around my shoulders. For long moments I stood there, breathing in steam, washing away the grime and blood.

Later, dressed in a thick terry robe, long hair dry and straight, I knocked on my parents' door.

"Come in," Mom replied.

I still hadn't gotten used to the sight of Dad in the adjustable bed, pale and vulnerable. The Dad I knew stood tall and tanned, topped with a cowboy hat, walking with a ground-covering cattleman's stride. I wasn't sure how to deal with this bed-ridden version of my father, except to execute a thin, shy imitation of our former ease.

Dad's eyes lit up; his face looked to me eagerly.

"Your mother didn't get any details." He scowled at Mom, who lay next to him, covered in a long, floral cotton robe.

"Why would she, Dad? It's not like she knows anything about horses."

"Filly or colt?" Dad asked, ignoring my comment.

"Colt. Chestnut with four white socks. He's in the barn with Prissy, cozy as can be. But he was a born in a ditch, so I've named him Splash."

Dad chuckled. "Splash, eh? I guess you had a rough time of it?"

"Did I ever." I regaled him with the heroic tale, sparing no detail of my valiant efforts. But as usual, I received minimal praise.

"Sounds like you did fine. So you'll check on them first thing in the morning?"

I don't know what I expected. It had been that way since childhood. No matter what I achieved or how hard I worked, the praise never seemed proportionate. There was great affection between Dad and me, but also a deplorable lack of kudos.

"Of course I'll check on them in the morning. And I'll bring them round to your window when Splash is up to it."

"Don't tell him that," Mom interjected. "He'll be too excited to sleep."

Dad gave Mom a dirty look.

"What do you think, Cass? Does he look like a futurity winner?"

"Sure Dad," I laughed. "You've got Crimson Commander himself reincarnated out there."

"Oh, get to bed," he growled.

I bid them goodnight and checked on Sam. He lay buried under his covers, the way he always slept, snoring softly. I shut his door, treading down the hall to my own room.

I peeled off the robe and climbed into the same bed I'd slept in since I was three years old.

Right back where I started.

Already the life I'd led in Virginia Beach seemed unreal. I'd thought about coming home to Texas someday – someday *after* I'd created a fabulous new life for myself. A life that included acquiring a handsome husband and becoming some big shot something or other. I'd fantasized about buying property in Pleasant Valley and starting my own ranch raising champion horses. But I'd never wanted to come home like this – thirty years old, broke, an unmarried single mother. I was pretty sure that was the opposite of fabulous.

Not that I'd had much choice. The frantic phone call, Dad's back surgery, this foal of Prissy's, supposedly the culmination of the best Texas reining lines of all time. So I'd returned to sleepy Summerville. Returned to run the ranch while Dad recuperated, *if* he recuperated. I couldn't bear the *if*.

My body ached as I tried to redirect the depressing thoughts. Dad would recover and take up the reins of the ranch again, and I'd return to Virginia Beach with Sam. Maybe get my old job back at Sterling Incorporated, finish up my accounting degree at Old Dominion. I'd pick up where I left off with my single circle of friends, eventually snagging an eligible bachelor at one of the glittering hot spots where wealthy men went to drink beer and close business deals. Dana, my mentor at Sterling, had taught me a lot about snagging rich men. *That* was my future, a fast-paced life at the oceanfront, not wasting away in an East Texas farm town.

Mom would say I should pray for direction. The thought occurred to me, but it had been years since I'd prayed, and I felt certain God had long since tired of my sordid antics. In fact I felt quite certain He'd deserted me the day I ran off with Ronnie at eighteen, heading for the coast in his battered El Camino.

I tossed uncomfortably, drifting into a light and restless sleep.

***

I dreamed of childhood, the smell of coffee and pancakes on Saturday morning. I sprang from my bed with eight-year-old ease, twisting my long hair into two pigtails. Padding down the hall in bare feet, I scampered toward the smell of breakfast. Mom stood in the kitchen, her face fresh and unwrinkled, her back firm and straight.

"Hurry up and eat your pancakes if you wanna go with your father," she winked.

I scarfed pancakes drizzled with honey and crisp, smoky bacon. Then I guzzled milk as Dad, dressed as always in work jeans and boots, took his place at the table and downed his coffee.

"Well, Baby Girl, how 'bout vaccinating some cattle today?"

"Sure, Daddy."

We must have looked like a painting, the little golden girl wearing overalls, Dad in his summer straw hat, working hand in hand in the cattle chute. I ran them into the chute, flailing my arms, shouting "Shoo cows, shoo!" Dad shut the gate behind, closing them in. He measured the vaccines, showed me where to stick, and I expertly delivered the injections. It made for a full day's work. We finished, exhausted but happy.

"Can you grill burgers tonight, Dad?"

"Maybe so, Cass, but we gotta feed first."

Dad fed the cattle while I took care of his horse, Ranger, and my pony, Chico. We walked back to the house, his hand on my shoulder. The best man in the world and his Daddy's girl…

I woke up grudgingly. The sun shone through the window, and the smell of breakfast really was coming from the kitchen. I glanced at the clock. Nine a.m.

I jumped out of bed like a frightened rabbit. *Sam! School!*

I ran to the kitchen to find my mother flipping pancakes over her griddle.

"Mom? Why didn't you wake me? Sam's late!"

"No, he's not. I took him."

I didn't know what to say. Mom had been hard on me since I'd come home, lecturing that Sam was my responsibility and chief priority. "It's not anyone else's job to raise your child," she'd said a hundred times, even though I never asked for help with Sam, and I was, in fact, bailing *them* out by running the ranch.

"Thanks, Mom. I didn't expect you to do that."

"You put in a hard night last night, and you don't ever get to sleep in. I know he didn't say much, but it meant the world to your father. So eat these pancakes, and then go check on that ridiculous horse so your dad will settle down."

"Sure."

Mom and I never enjoyed the easy relationship I had with Dad. Thoroughly domesticated, her life's work consisted of keeping a squeaky-clean house, caring for her family, and serving on church committees. She bore no love for the outdoors or the animals, nor any desire to walk on the wild side like her headstrong daughter. She always did exactly what she should, and harbored strong feelings against those who did otherwise. Myself included.

Things had felt particularly strained since I'd left Ronnie, or he'd left me. Another reason I'd stayed in Virginia Beach so long. Mom thought our split was selfish, unfair to Sam. Not that I'd had much choice in the matter. If only she'd known the truth, she'd have packed his bags herself. But I hadn't told my parents the truth. I figured the dirty details of my relationship were better left undisclosed, and besides, it really wasn't their business.

I ate the pancakes. Not the perfect, fluffy pancakes of my dream, but the heavy, almost chewy renditions produced twenty years later after lack of practice. With a nod of thanks, I washed my plate, loaded it into the dishwasher, and returned to my room to make my bed.

As I opened the pale blue dresser drawer, I laughed at the old specks of pink peeking through the newer paint job. The bedroom set had been mine as a girl, and once sported a startling shade of fuchsia. When I'd left home, Dad had repainted it, but the original color refused to hide completely beneath the tamer hue.

I grabbed a tee shirt and some jeans, shimmying my long legs into the Wranglers. Twisting dark blonde hair into a knot, I glanced at the mirror, sneering at my own reflection. I looked a far cry from the glitzy, made up creature that clubbed at Waterside or took in the occasional show at Chrysler Hall. *Oh, well.* That girl didn't belong here in small town East Texas, mucking stalls and tending cattle on the Rocking R. Without another look, I left the house and made for the barn.

Despite grim determination to feel sorry for myself, I couldn't deny the appeal of the morning. The gentle spring dawn bore no resemblance to the nasty night before. Spring came early to Texas, and late March brought jonquils, bluebonnets, and eighty-degree days.

The sultry air felt ripe with promise, just not for me. I clung stubbornly to my hopelessness. In a way it was all I had.

A familiar blue pickup with the license plate "TXVET" sat parked by the barn. *So Dad already called Guy.* I sighed in disappointment. Forget the fact I'd brought the colt into the world during a horrendous storm, I couldn't be trusted to phone the vet the morning after. Pity replaced aggravation as I realized Dad must've called the vet because it was all he could do, the only way he could participate in the birth of this foal.

And I was probably the only one who knew how much that killed him.

***

"Come on, Guy. You know as well as I do he looks just like any other quarter horse colt."

The old vet chuckled, the wrinkles at the corners of his eyes only emphasizing their green twinkle.

"Don't let your daddy hear you talk like that."

I rolled my eyes. Guy and I stood in the stall with Prissy as her scraggly foal nursed, his fuzzy tail flipping back and forth.

"Don't tell me he's got you on board with this. Surely you realize this is just Dad's late life crisis."

"Girl, your daddy was winning reining championships before you were born. You'd do well to respect what he knows. Look at the hindquarters on that foal, and the legs."

I scrutinized the rounded, well-shaped quarters, and the fine legs.

"Maybe."

"No maybe to it. He picked out a trainer?"

"Bit early for that, ain't it?" I cringed to hear myself lapsing into a twangy Texan dialect. I'd worked so hard to affect a clear, colorless tone to my voice in Virginia.

"The good ones' book youngsters well in advance."

"You recommend anybody?"

"There's only two worth dealing with within two hundred miles of here. Of course you know one of them."

I cringed again. "Cliff Kesterson?"

Guy nodded. "He produced three of the four last futurity winners in Oklahoma."

Hard to argue with that kind of track record, but I dreaded the thought of confronting Cliff Kesterson. He'd been a football-hero-snob in high school, and we'd sort of been sweethearts. When I'd taken up with Ronnie, he'd berated me mercilessly about my poor choice of boyfriend. I couldn't bear the thought of his smug satisfaction at my current situation.

"And the other?" I asked, hopeful.

"Chase Eversoll."

"Never heard of him."

"He's a newcomer, doesn't handle the volume Cliff does. But he brings his horses along sensibly, has a solid performance record."

"I'm sure Dad'll make the decision. I doubt I'll even be here when he starts his training."

"You're not still going on about heading back east, are you?"

"That's always been my plan. This is supposed to be temporary."

"Look, you're a good kid. Always thought so. And we all do some fool things when we're young."

Leave it to Guy to speak plain.

"But you've done the right thing. You've left that bad egg and come home. And your dad's back ain't healing any time soon. You'd better settle in and get used to the fact you're gonna be here awhile."

I sighed. Guy was right and I knew it. I just hadn't been ready to admit it.

"We'll see," was all I could muster.

Guy put a comforting, fatherly arm around my shoulder.

"Cheer up, Ladybug. You've got a lotta' life yet. And you're still just as pretty as the girl that won the queen contest at the Tri-County Rodeo."

"Ugh, that was forever ago."

I walked Guy to his truck, trying to recall those glory days when I'd reigned as rodeo queen and my parents had respected me. The days before I made catastrophically bad decisions, lost my innocence, and packed on ten pounds of baby weight.

Those days were hard to recall, but standing in the warm sun, basking the glow of Guy's smile, I could almost remember.

chapter

TWO

The leather smelled gloriously new and felt butter-soft against my skin. Heaven only knew how much it had set Dad back. The tan outfit perfectly fit my size four frame. Adorned with a pattern of red leather roses and sparkling rhinestones, no rodeo queen could have asked for more. The term "bling" hadn't been coined yet, but I owned it in spades, from the crown attached to my Resistol to the studded spurs on my worn work boots. I pranced around the fairgrounds, flouncing the blonde curls that hung beneath my hat, signing autographs and taking pictures with young wannabe queens.

To secure the title of Tri-County Rodeo Queen, my palomino barrel horse, Trixie, and I had run the barrel pattern in sixteen seconds. The three runners up, my princesses, also paraded the grounds, but their crowns were smaller, their sashes not as grand. Still, they signed the autographs and posed for pictures, only stealing occasional green-eyed glances in my direction.

The cowboys who roamed the grounds in their Wranglers and Justin Ropers eyed me appreciatively. I batted my lashes and smiled. I'd waited for that day all my young life. When other girls had gone for cheerleading and wowed the boys with their short skirts, I'd run barrels with Trixie in our front pasture until we were both sweaty, dusty and exhausted, skills honed to the point we could make those tight turns in our sleep. Now even the cheerleaders envied me in my splendor. Best of all, at the end of the first half of the rodeo, Trixie and I would ride out in the arena with my princesses and their horses, to be formally "crowned" to the cheering of the crowd.

Everyone appreciated my "Queen" status except the annoying Ronnie Baldwin. He leaned against the bleachers, staring at me with a half smirk, half sneer on his face. Once in awhile I shot him a dirty look, but he kept right on staring as he stood there in cutoffs and flip-flops, unconcerned that he looked totally out of place.

The boy had issues.

I considered myself a friendly girl, even when it came to outcasts like Ronnie. I mean, Texans were supposed to be friendly. (The state's name, in fact, was derived from the Caddo Indian word for friendship.) But something about his mocking scowl in the midst of my triumph irritated me. I had to say something.

"What's the matter, Dude? Get lost on your way to the beach?"

"Trust me, Your Highness, I'd be there in a second if I could figure a way out of this stinkin' town."

"Then why are you here?"

Everyone knew Ronnie didn't fit in, and what's more, didn't want to fit in. He'd moved to Summerville six months prior, showing up at school in Hawaiian shirts and shell necklaces. His streaky blond hair looked wild, and he always had a surfboard in the back of his El Camino, although there wasn't a beach within 300 miles.

Teenagers don't tolerate the radically different. While a few girls expressed interest in Ronnie's rebel beach boy ways, most kids at Summerville High treated him like a freak, a surfer hippie in the midst of clean-cut, all-American farm kids. Many treated him downright cruel.

He clicked the heel of one flip-flop against the dusty ground. "No choice. Parents moved. Trust me, as soon as I graduate, I'm outta here."

"I could care less about your post-grad plans. I mean why are you here at the rodeo? This isn't your thing."

"It's the only thing happening in this boring outpost of civilization."

I rolled my eyes, and then ran as Dad called me to get ready for the Grand Entry Parade. I rushed outside the grounds, where horses and riders prepared to enter the ring for the start of the rodeo. Trixie matched me in sparkle, tacked up in borrowed wall-to-wall silver show tack.

"You look great, Baby Girl." Dad beamed like Christmas Town on December twenty-fifth.

"Thanks, Dad." I threw a leg over Trixie's saddle. We followed the other riders into the ring to the cheers of the crowd. I spotted many of my classmates waving and cheering; a few of the boys winked, and I winked back. Ronnie Baldwin still stood against the bleachers, the glow of a lit cigarette between his fingers. He mouthed something, but I had no idea what it was. Nor, I assured myself, did I care.

***

My glorious night ended all too soon. I changed into an ordinary pair of jeans and a horse tee shirt, and Dad and I loaded Trixie back into the trailer. I looked at my sash and crown, stashed in the dressing area. I sighed, wondering what to do now that my moment had come and gone.

"Excuse me."

I heard Ronnie's voice behind me.

"Mr. Roberts, I'm Ronnie Baldwin, one of Cassie's schoolmates."

Dad and Ronnie shook hands and I stared, mesmerized, wondering what on earth he was up to.

"Could I take Cassie out for ice cream to celebrate her big night?"

My mouth dropped open in protest. The rebel-without-a-clue addressed my father in a tone polite and formal enough for the Prince of Wales. Dad turned to me, uncertainty on his face.

"Cassie?"

I looked at Ronnie. "I've got to help my Dad unload Trixie when we get home."

"I can do that for you if you'd like, Cass," Dad said, apparently thinking I might actually want to go. "Why don't you go have fun? But," he looked sternly at Ronnie, "you'd better have her home by eleven thirty, young man."

"Of course, Sir."

I found myself handed over to the likes of Ronnie Baldwin without much in the way of protest. I climbed meekly into the passenger seat of the El Camino as he held the door. He hopped in the driver's seat and sped away from the rodeo grounds.

"So what do you want with me?" I asked.

"I'm a serial killer with a fetish for rodeo queens."

Infuriated, I opened the car door as if to jump out. Ronnie threw his arm over me.

"Whoa! Just kidding. Bad joke, okay?"

"Very bad joke."

"Look, I haven't made any friends since I've been here. You country folk haven't been very welcoming. I thought I'd give this a try."

"How gracious of you," I said in exasperation. I couldn't deny there was something a little exciting about being out with the surfer from California. "Maybe if you'd quit calling us 'country folk' you'd make some friends. Just because we ride horses and have old-fashioned values doesn't make us backwards. And I don't buy the lonesome wolf routine. Why me?"

"Because you looked hot in that leather outfit."

I started for the door again, only half-heartedly. As Ronnie leaned over to prevent my escape, I caught his slightly salty smell, like he'd just come from the ocean. I relaxed into the seat. This felt different from my previous romantic experiences, like the time I'd shared an innocent kiss with Cliff Kesterson at the Sadie Hawkins Dance. This had an edge to it, an excitement and a fear.

"So where are we going?"

"Where do you get ice cream around here?"

"The Tasty Freeze?"

"All right then, Goldilocks, to the Tasty Freeze."

***

The date at the Tasty Freeze turned into more than I'd bargained. After that night Ronnie continued to ask me out, and I continued to say yes, despite the fact that everyone thought I'd lost my mind. I wondered myself.

I hated Ronnie's smoking and drinking, his rejection of all things Texas, his sixties California persona. But he fascinated me. And frightened me. I tried to break up with him once and he went on a certified rampage, calling my friends to rant, throwing things at school, slamming his fists into lockers. Mortified and flattered in an odd sort of way, I repented for trying to break things off and begged him to take me back.

The summer before college, Ronnie planned his escape from what he called "Hickville." My parents and I had dreamed of my future at A & M, and then vet school, but Ronnie had other ideas.

"So explain to me again why you don't believe in marriage?" I asked.

I lay on a towel in the sun, my tan skin greased with baby oil. A motorboat sped by, misting the summer air with refreshing spray. Lake Summerville wasn't exactly the Pacific Ocean, but I thought a day on the lake might cheer the perpetually brooding Ronnie.

"Marriage is so business-like, so contractual. I believe in the free expression of love. I want to be with someone because I want to be, not because I'm contracted."

"But marriage is sacred, blessed by God."

"You know how I feel about that."

"I know, Mr. Atheist. But I believe in marriage. It says you're committed to each other."

"Yeah, until somebody feels like splitting. Then the only happy one is the blood-suckin' lawyer." Ronnie smirked so annoyingly that my hand itched to slap him.

"Well, I'm not going to the coast with you if we're not married. I can't do that to my parents."

"Can't or won't?"

"Both."

"Don't you love me?"

Yes, I do. Or did. I couldn't help it. I knew Ronnie wasn't good for me. But first love is a hormonal, chemical cocktail that stews your brain into bumbling stupidity.

"You know I do, but…"

He shushed me with a kiss, a good, long slow one. I wasn't sure, but it seemed like love, the Romeo and Juliet stuff that drove people half crazy.

"So when do we leave?" I whispered.

"Now that's my girl," he said approvingly, as if he'd just won a surfing championship, and I was the trophy.

My parents barely had time to register the inconceivable. I left my mother crying on her bed and my father looking as pale as a whisper, shaking his fist in anger as we drove down the ranch's long gravel drive. Tears running down my face, Ronnie oblivious, we sped off in that battered El Camino, taking their hopes and dreams, and any chance I had of a future, with us.

***

"Watch me lope, Mom."

"Okay, Sam, but be careful. Look out for holes."

Sam eased Boomer, Dad's plain, brown gelding, into a soft lope along the fence line. Old Bud, our Brangus bull, had pushed the fence down to check out the cows in the neighboring pasture, and Sam and I were on a mission to fetch him home. To Sam it was high adventure, but for me it would mean hours of rough work mending the barbed wire fence, once we got the errant bull back on our side of it.

I watched Sam handle his horse like a natural, heels down, body straight but supple. He'd never had a chance to ride before coming to Texas, but he took to it like a duck to water. In fact he'd taken to the whole of Texas with unbridled passion, and I'd no idea how I was going to get him back to Virginia.

Maybe Guy's right. Maybe we're not going back.

I couldn't face that possibility, not yet. Maybe I'd just have to get Sam a pony in Virginia Beach and board it at a stable.

Are you kidding? On your nonexistent salary?

Fortunately Hank, our cattle dog, interrupted my bleak thoughts. He found the mangled stretch of downed fence and barked joyfully as he leaped over it.

"Slow down, Sam!"

Sam reined in Boomer, and I slowed Jack, hopping off his back. I pulled a pair of work gloves and a set of wire cutters out of my saddle bag.

"Let me clear some of this wire before you try to cross. Barbed wire'll tear a leg to shreds."

I'd learned the barbed wire lesson the hard way. As a thirteen-year-old, before I got my beloved Trixie, I'd owned a fancy blue roan mare that could have gone to the World Show in western pleasure. Unfortunately, the fool horse had an affinity for playing with barbed wire, and she'd pawed at the fence one too many times, finally slicing a fetlock through to the bone. It had become infected, refusing to heal, and I'd cried for weeks after Guy put her down.

"If I had my own Gerber knife, I could help you," Sam offered, ever the opportunist.

"Nice try, but I'll manage."

"Wesley Austin has his own knife."

I was not in the mood to debate preteen weapons ownership.

"Well then, Wesley Austin's parents can cart his fanny to the emergency room when he slices a finger off."

Sam dropped the issue as he watched me struggle with the wire. The boarding stables I'd seen in Virginia didn't use barbed wire. They wisely condemned it as unsafe, but they only had five to ten acres to fence as a rule. No one in Texas spent the time or money to put up a hundred-plus acres of split rails.

I cleared the bulk of the wire and pulled it aside, mentally assessing what might be salvageable. Sam and I rode through the opening, Hank running ahead, scouting the terrain. Before long we came upon our neighbor's herd.

The neighboring pasture belonged to a distant cousin, Norman. He'd phoned Dad that morning to advise him old Bud had migrated into his pasture and ingratiated himself into his herd. Fortunately, Norman had recently auctioned his own bull and was in the market for a new one, so Bud hadn't gotten himself into a brawl over females. And if he happened to sire a calf or two during his visit, Norman wasn't likely to complain.

"There's Bud!" Sam waved his baseball cap, loping Boomer toward the bull.

"Careful, Sam."

He was in no real danger. Old Bud had the patience of Ferdinand and even less energy. He looked up from his grazing as Sam approached, slowly raising his giant, red head. He swung his neck to nibble a fly on his shoulder, slinging slobber from his dribbling mouth in the process. The fly bumbled away, moving almost as slowly as Bud.

Sam came around behind the bull and waved the hat.

"Hiya, Bud! Hiya!"

Bud lifted one trunk-like leg and took a step forward, then another, wiggling his ears as if to say, "Okay, the gig's up." The animal shuffled home as leisurely and meekly as an old man out for a stroll. The cows in Norman's field didn't bother to watch him leave.

***

The task of mending the fence proved monumentally more difficult than the one of getting our wayward bull home. While Sam showered Bud with treats in the form of range cubes, I struggled with hammering three new posts into the ground and re-stringing the barbed wire. After scratching the length of my arm on a section of fence, I sat on the tractor running board, downing a thermos filled with ice water.

I'd wash three loads of laundry for the man who finished this fence. I splashed some ice water on my tank top, and then used it to mop the salty sweat dripping from my forehead. *There is such a thing as man's work and woman's work, to heck with the feminists. And no woman should have to do this.* But there was no male in sight to wield the barbed wire and drive the posts into the ground. Only me.

"Nee hee hee he he!"

I jumped at the baby squeal so close to my ear. Splash had wandered from where Prissy stood grazing nearby to investigate my labors at the fence. When I paid him no mind, he sought to remedy the situation with a high-pitched baby whinny.

"Darn you, Splash!" I dropped my thermos, spilling my ice water, and the fool colt took off at full tilt, thrilled at having scared the wits out of me. Then, changing his mind about fleeing the scene, he sat down on his haunches in an attempt to throw the brakes, sliding about ten feet. Abruptly righting himself, he spun back towards me and trotted merrily, as if nothing unusual had happened.

I wondered if I'd seen right, or if the stinging sweat pouring off my forehead had clouded my vision. That colt had just completed a sliding stop that would have made Skip Real Quick, his reining champion sire, proud. *Great, now Dad's got me seeing delusions of grandeur in a silly colt romping in the pasture. I've got to get out of this place.*

Splash butted me with his impertinent muzzle, and I couldn't help but rub him. He never showed any fear of me, approaching me as easy as he did Prissy. Much to Sam's disappointment, he wouldn't let Sam, or anyone else for that matter, near him. Since I'd been the first to welcome him into the world, I suppose I was accepted.

His baby coat felt soft as a plush animal, no, even softer. Beneath the downy coat his little body stood sturdy and firm. He possessed fine, long legs, and a refined baby head, but he still looked like an average quarter horse colt. His play in the field had been just that, play. Nothing more, no premonition of greatness.

"All right you, move along." I pushed the interloper out of my way and took another go at the fence. Splash refused to leave me alone, making the job three times as difficult with his butting and nipping. I finally called Sam to chase the foal away so I could finish, and the two began an awkward game of tag, Splash keeping a safe distance between himself and the boy.

A couple hours later, long after Splash had retreated to the comfort of Prissy's teats to nurse, I twisted the last bit of wire into place. I must have looked like something out of a refugee camp, sweat and dirt smeared from head to toe, blood caking my arm. I drove the tractor under its port in the barn, and then whistled up Jack and Boomer from the pasture, which brought Prissy on the run as well, little Splash following behind.

"Can I feed, Mom?" Sam had been laying on a bale of hay in the loft, dreaming the afternoon away while I slaved at the fence. I felt no resentment, as there was little he could have done, and I wouldn't have wanted him cut to pieces on that wire.

"Sure. A scoop for Boomer, a half for Jack, two scoops for Prissy."

Dad's barn boasted five horse stalls on one side, the tractor port on the other, a feed room, and a hay loft, with an aisle down the center. The stalls all had two doors, one opening into the barn aisle, the other opening back out into the pasture. We rarely closed the doors. The horses roamed the pasture at will, only entering the stalls during feed time and for shelter in foul weather.

Sam doled out the rations in the feed tubs of three stalls. Each horse filed into his/her own stall without a fuss. During East Texas summer on a hundred acres of lush pasture, there seemed little need to supplement with grain, but the horses had been ridden hard that day, and Prissy was nursing, so I reasoned a bit of sweet feed couldn't hurt. I returned to the feed room to fasten the grain containers tight, discourage mice.

"Hello? Anyone here?"

A man's voice rang through the barn. I couldn't have been more surprised if I'd been caught in nothing but my underwear. Mom and Dad hadn't mentioned anything about visitors.

I stuck my head out of the feed room. There in the barn aisle stood a young, dark- haired version of George Strait. From his straw cowboy hat to his pressed jeans, he could've filmed an after-shave commercial.

I tried frantically to arrange my hair more attractively, but the effect, at best, was minimal. The first real man I'd seen in weeks and I looked like the grapes of wrath.

Sam greeted our visitor. "What can I do fer ya, Mister?" My son's voice reeked of twang.

Sam, will you quit trying to fake a Texas accent?

I stepped out of the feed room. "Yes, what can we do for you?"

Mr. Clean Cut smiled and held out his hand. I laughed, or more like sneered.

"I'm not fit to shake hands. I've been mending barbed wire the better part of the afternoon." I said it accusingly, as if my afternoon's hard labor was somehow his fault. To emphasize, I held out my filthy hands. He grabbed one of them anyway and clasped it in a firm handshake.

"Done my share of mending fences; it's rough work. Your dad ought to get you some help." In other words, I needed a man. I felt miffed even though I'd just been telling myself the same thing.

"How do you know Dad?" I pulled my hand from his grasp and folded my arms. "And I manage just fine, thank you."

We weren't off to a great start.

"Name's Chase Eversoll." The name sounded familiar, but I couldn't place it.

"Oh!" I remembered Guy mentioning him. "You're the horse trainer."

"Yeah, I 'spose I am. Look, your dad called me a couple weeks back, said he had a colt he wanted me to look at. I've just come from a funeral in town. I thought while I was out this way, I'd have a look at the foal, if that's all right. I stopped at the house and your folks sent me out here."

"Oh, I'm sorry. I didn't know…" I fumbled for words, ashamed I'd been flip with someone fresh from a funeral. "Hope the funeral was…nice." I sounded like an idiot.

"It was. Granny wouldn't have wanted any moping or carrying on. She wanted a homecoming party, and that's what Pastor Barry gave her. "

"Pastor Barry? Of Pleasant Oaks Baptist?"

"Yeah."

"Half my family's buried in Pleasant Oaks' cemetery."

"I know. Granny and Grandaddy are buried next to your Great Uncle Monroe and Aunt Ida."

"Wow, small world. Look, I'm usually not so grumpy, it's just been a long day. Why don't my son Sam and I show you the foal? He's in the last stall with his dam."

We walked to the last stall, the three of us. Sam could barely contain his excitement.

"So you're a real cowboy, and you train champion reining horses?"

"I train horses and compete a little bit."

"Grandpa says you've got promise and your horses have spark."

The cowboy laughed.

"I'm honored your grandpa thinks that, Sam."

It hurt me how Sam lapped up the man's attention, as if desperate for male bonding.

We stopped outside Prissy's stall. She'd finished her grain and turned back to the pasture, but stopped at the sight of us, probably hoping for a bit more sweet feed. She walked right up to Chase.

"Well, ain't you a classy lady?" He stroked her glossy bay neck, and then rubbed under her throat. Prissy closed her eyes in bliss, apparently grateful that someone remembered to pay her a bit of attention, not just her mischievous foal.

"That's a nice looking colt."

Splash stood nursing while Prissy enjoyed the stranger's attention.

"Nice legs, balanced build, kind eyes."

"Grandpa bred 'im himself." Sam seemed intent on impressing the stranger.

Chase looked at me, chocolate eyes shining. "Your dad told me he bred this mare from his old Rein Dancer?"

"Yeah, I guess you know Dad and Rein Dancer won at the World Show some thirty years ago? Then he retired him and bred him to our own mares, but never stood him at stud. He sold all Dancer's colts as geldings, kept most of the fillies. None of them ever seemed to meet his expectations, until Prissy."

"He never campaigned her?"

"No, he broke her and rode her around the farm, but never competed on her."

"Hmmm." Chase scratched his chin.

Searching for something to say, I offered, "He's bred Prissy to every decent reining stud in Texas, but the results never please him. He's impossible." I rolled my eyes. "He sold all her other foals. Some of them've made it big in Youth and Non-Pro."

"This foal's by Skip Real Quick?"

"Uh huh."

I didn't understand why Dad put so much stock in Skip Real Quick. He'd only seen him once, at the Fort Worth Stock Show. Apparently that was enough, he'd called the stud's owner the next day and reserved a breeding before the stud ever opened his book.

"Your dad's got an eye."

I turned to Chase, puzzled.

"You sound like you believe this fantasy of his."

"I saw Quick the year he won the Dallas Derby. He had something, something I haven't seen too often."

"What?"

"Oh, I don't know. Call it the eye of the tiger."

Sam slammed his fist into his hand, startling Splash, who stamped his little hoof and whinnied.

"You think he's a winner, just like Grandpa."

"I don't know, maybe. I bet you and that little scamp are fast friends."

Sam shook his head. "Nah, the only one he lets near him is Mom. He does play with me sometimes, though."

Chase turned to me, an appraising expression on his face. He looked me up and down, not like a predator, but like a buyer assessing a broodmare. I felt my face flush.

"Sounds like your mom's a bit of a horsewoman." He smiled at me, more of a smirk. I turned my head, but Chase continued. "I expect you've got some talent with horses as well, Sam. You're just a little wet behind the ears."

I lifted my chin to see Sam light up like a morning sky. He said "Watch this!" and squeezed through the stall rails, running for the pasture. He made kissing noises, urging Splash to follow. The colt took off after him, embarking on a running and bucking spree, coming close to Sam but never quite near enough to touch.

As Sam and Splash played, Splash threw on the brakes, sitting on his haunches in an abrupt halt. I glanced at Chase Eversoll to gauge his reaction. He tried to remain passive, but I caught the slight widening of his eyes.

Splash spun and charged off at full gallop, chasing Sam, who dropped to his knees and rolled. Splash snorted and slid to a stop, legs splayed out. When he stopped, just inches from Sam, he gave the boy's hair a playful snuffle. Sam could have powered an electric plant with his smile.

"He does like me!"

Chase nodded. "He sure does. Thanks so much for your help."

I was dying to know what he thought, but I couldn't bring myself to ask, and he didn't offer. Instead he tipped his hat. *Guys around here still do that?*

"Thank you both for your time, sorry to interrupt your afternoon. I better let you get to that supper your momma's working on."

"Well, okay." I didn't know what to say. "Thanks for stopping by."

He waved at Sam, and then he was gone. Just like that, without another word about the foal. *He thinks he's just an ordinary colt, too.* I felt an odd sense of disappointment.

Splash rejoined his mother. Sam came to me and put his arm around my waist, and I tousled his silky hair.

"He was nice, Mom."

"Yes he was."

"Will we see him again? Will he train Splash?"

"Oh, I don't know. I think he probably came by just to humor Grandpa."

"I don't think so, Mom. When he looks at Splash, he looks the way Grandpa does."

"Et tu, Sam?" I laughed out loud. Sam looked cross.

"It's not funny. Grandpa and Mr. Eversoll know reining horses, and when they watch Splash, they both get that look."

"What look?"

"Like they've just seen something they've waited for a very long time."

chapter

THREE

I ate with half-starved relish. Mom had picked up barbecue brisket from Jake's, along with corn on the cob, fresh rolls, and black-eyed peas. I gulped my sweet tea, and then sandwiched some brisket between two butter tops, dousing the beef liberally with Jake's spicy sauce. I took a bite of the smoky heaven. Delicious.

Mother screwed up her delicate nose in disapproval.

"It's a miracle you've managed to lose weight, Cassie. You've dropped a few pounds here lately, but I can't imagine how, the way you stuff your face."

Sam winced, probably hurt on my account. I bit my tongue, but not enough to withhold a reply.

"It's not hard losing weight around here, Mom, considering you hardly cook anymore. Not to mention I'm working my fingers to the bone running this ranch, with no help from anyone."

I regretted the words the instant a wounded look crossed Dad's face, but I couldn't call them back. Sam affected an "uh oh, now she's done it" expression. Mom's face fell a little as well, but that didn't bother me like it should have. She folded her napkin and lowered her chin.

"I did cook the peas. In fact, I shelled them myself."

That was the extent of her commentary. I muttered a terse "excuse me" and stormed to the back porch. Hank, oblivious to the tension, followed me, tail thumping. I opened the sliding glass door, let Hank through, and closed it behind me. I settled myself into Dad's old rocking chair, fighting tears.

It's time to go home. I'd already stayed longer than planned. If Dad couldn't run the ranch, then maybe it was time to sell. No shame in admitting he's getting past it. One thing was certain, I wasn't going to stay any longer, falling into the same old trap, desperately seeking Dad's approval, while knowing I'd never get Mom's.

I heard the door slide open behind me and caught the whiff of pipe smoke. I'd always loved the smell, rich and reminiscent of leather chairs and studies piled with old books. Dad settled himself in the rocker next to mine, and we looked toward the back pasture, shimmering deep green in the twilight.

"I know I haven't said it often, Cass, but I am grateful for what you've done here."

"I know, Dad."

"My back's still not right."

"I know that, too."

Dad had improved. He attended physical therapy religiously and walked the long driveway to the mailbox at least three times a day. He'd come a long way, but he still didn't have the stamina, strength, or endurance he used to.

"Maybe it's time to sell." My voice trembled.

"Maybe you're right." He sounded stoic, no trace of emotion. "I've actually talked to Norman about it."

I stopped rocking in disbelief, feeling a surprising stab of sorrow. The Dad I knew would never willingly discuss giving up the ranch.

"Did I hear you right?"

"I'm getting old. Sixty-four this year. Too old to be a cattleman, or a horseman. How many more ruptured discs and pinched nerves can I take? Even if I was in perfect health, I don't how much longer I could keep this up."

"But, Dad." I'd just suggested selling, and now found myself arguing against it.

"Norman's willing to buy the cattle and some of the acreage, your mother and I could keep the house and a few acres to piddle with."

I sighed. "That sounds like a good solution, Dad. You could stay on the ranch, maybe even lend Norman a hand. You'd still be a rancher."

"I suppose, not that it matters. Maybe it's time for the Rocking R to stop."

Again, the twinge of sorrow.

"But I need this foal, Cassie. I need your help raising this foal."

"Not the colt again."

"I've waited my whole life for this colt."

"But you won the World Championship with Rein Dancer. You still have that dusty old trophy. What more do you need? And why this colt?"

"I won the championship on a horse someone else bred. This foal is mine, the result of three decades of studying reining horses. And there's more."

"What?"

"Chase Eversoll says reining's becoming a global sport, and might soon be included in the International Equestrian Games."

Again I stopped rocking.

"You're kidding me? A western event in the International Equestrian Games?"

"It's overdue. The US Horse Association already hosts a lot of high profile reining events. Chase says it's just a matter of time."

"And you think this little foal of yours is the first International Reining Champion?"

Dad remained silent, inhaling deeply on his pipe, blowing the smoke out in circles.

"So what do you want from me? I can't stay here any longer; I need to go home."

"To what?"

"To independence."

"Sam's happy here, happier than he's been maybe in his whole life."

"I wish you and Mom would stop talking about how I've failed Sam. Do you know how old that gets?"

I jumped up and paused at the door, wondering where to run next.

"Please sit back down."

With no real place to go, I sat, reluctantly.

"I'm sorry we've been so hard on you. Maybe our expectations were too high, maybe we pushed too hard. I've spent years wondering if we'd done something different, then maybe you wouldn't've run off..."

"I've told you a hundred times that had nothing to do with you or Mom. I made a stupid mistake, an eighteen-year-old girl mistake, and I've never stopped being punished for it."

Dad's eyebrows raised and his expression grew stern, but his voice remained gentle.

"You can't play the martyr for the rest of your life."

"I'm not playing the martyr! I told you it was my own fault."

"You're playing the martyr of your own mistakes, which is maybe the most hopeless kind. Time you stopped wallowing and thought about a future, for you and for Sam."

"I'm not going there. I'm not having this conversation. I've done very well for Sam, thank you."

"You've done a good job with him. But he's found something here - a home, tradition, roots. Let him have that, at least another year or two."

"What are you saying, exactly?"

"Give me two years. Stay here with Sam. Let us watch him grow up. Help me with this colt, and I'll pay you wages for your ranch work, along with twenty-five percent of the foal's future earnings for his lifetime. If at the end of two years you can't see fit to stay, you go back with our blessing, and gratitude."

Two years. My throat felt thick, as if I were choking. Two years here in Summerville. I longed for the salt spray of the ocean, for my own shabby apartment, for nightlife and freedom. I'd be insane to stay here another two years.

I took a deep breath, catching the scent of honeysuckle and rich earth. Lightning bugs twinkled across the pasture, and in the distance, I caught the sound of a high pitched, baby whinny. *Splash.*

To my surprise, I felt torn. Much as I longed for independence, in a way this would always be home. The smell of red earth, the sticky feel of humid air, the sight of chestnut horses in a pasture greener than Ireland. And family. Maybe Dad was right. Maybe I shouldn't deny Sam the chance for a family, a home that didn't rest at the top of three flights of stairs.

I felt tired, soul-deep weary. Dreams of expensively dressed businessmen and cocktails at oceanside nightclubs evaporated with the heat of the day as evening brought the temperatures within tolerable range.

"Okay."

Dad seemed genuinely surprised.

"You all right?"

"Yeah."

"I expected more of a fight."

"I know. I can't manage one at the moment."

"I'm asking you to do this, Cassie, but you're a grown woman. You don't have to."

"No, it makes sense. And you don't have to pay me wages, just the twenty-five percent of the foal's earnings, room, board, and gas money."

"Well, all right then. But you won't work for free, we'll think of something."

"So what's the next step?"

"What do you mean?"

"What's next for the future International Reining Champion?"

"Need to decide on a trainer. 'Bout time we paid Cliff a visit."

"Ugh. I've changed my mind." The thought of Cliff made me ill.

"Can't back out now."

"No, I guess not. For better or worse, you've got yourself a ranch hand."

***

I dreaded the trip to Cliff Kesterson's worse than I'd dreaded childbirth or the root canal I endured last summer. I don't guess anyone particularly enjoys total humiliation, and that's what I was likely to encounter at Cliff's. Perhaps even justifiable humiliation, but that didn't make the pill any easier to swallow.

"So Cliff knows I'm coming?" I posed the question as Dad drove down Highway 58. Bluebonnets decorated both sides of the road, proud and cheerful under the yellow Texas sun.

Last week Dad had finally felt up to driving and started taking spins in his beloved old Dodge. Today he sat tall in the driver's seat, handling the old pickup with care. He turned towards me, his eyes shaded by his summer straw hat.

"Yeah, I told Cliff you were coming. He says it'll be nice to see you. You're making too much fuss about this."

"That's what you think. I bet Cliff can't wait to rub his fancy barn in my face."

"Baby Girl, I hate to tell you, but life went on here in Summerville while you followed Ronnie Baldwin up and down the East Coast. I doubt Cliff's thought twice about you in years."

I wasn't so sure about that. Before Ronnie came on the scene and spoiled it, Cliff and I'd enjoyed a lukewarm high school romance. Nothing much, an ice cream here, a dance there. I didn't recall any great spark, but we were both nice kids, wholesome and ranch-raised. Might've enjoyed a nice future together.

When I took up with Ronnie, Cliff had been the first to try to talk me out of it. When I didn't listen, he started dating the snottiest, richest and perhaps dumbest of all Texas cheerleaders, Mandie Hill. The two of them made a high school career of belittling my relationship with Ronnie. Now they owned the biggest spread in Summerville, while I lived at home with my parents.

We approached a long gravel drive lined in hickory trees. The archway over the drive read "Star Maker Ranch." As we approached the *gi-normous* hacienda-style mansion, I noticed a Cadillac sedan and a 3500 Turbo Diesel Texas Edition pickup parked in the circular driveway. The pastures beyond the house stretched for miles, and the barn and equine complex looked bigger than the Texas State Fairgrounds. *Heaven help me.*

Dad parked our rusty truck behind the silver sedan. I laughed at how ridiculous we looked, Dad and I in our old jeans and beater truck in this high class set out of *Affluent Texan*. I'd deliberately dressed down, not wanting to give the slightest appearance of caring what Cliff thought. Now I second guessed that decision, wishing I'd glammed up a bit more. Maybe a lot more.

We made our way to the door via a terrazzo-tiled walkway lined in potted red geraniums. A wrought-iron Lone Star decorated the solid oak ranch house door. Cliff spared no detail, or expense, it seemed. Dad pushed the longhorn-shaped doorbell, and it chimed "The Yellow Rose of Texas."

Dad shot me a wry grin, and I wrinkled my nose in disgust.

The door opened and Mrs. Kesterson answered. I plastered a bright smiled on my face.

"Well, Mr. Roberts, Cassie, what a pleasure. Y'all come on in."

"Thank you, Mandie." Dad extended his hand.

"Hi Mandie."

"How wonderful to see you, Cass. You haven't changed a bit."

Mandie threw her arms round me in mock friendliness. Or at least what I presumed was mock friendliness. I had to smile as I returned the embrace. There was considerably more of Mandie to hug than when I'd last seen her. The hot-bodied cheerleader had developed a definite middle-aged spread. And yet, to my chagrin, it didn't look bad on her. She oozed expensive clothing, from her linen palazzo pants to her pale blue cashmere sweater. Her glowing complexion and hair evidenced frequent trips to the salon, unlike my own sun-burned face marred by tiny crows' feet and laugh lines, and my home-highlighted messy bun. I mentally confirmed that my "pretend not to care what you think of me" attire had not been the right way to go.

"Please, sit down." She motioned to a luxurious hunk of leather sofa. "Cliff's on a call, but he'll be here in a minute."

The inside of the house appeared no different than expected. Rich leather, cowhide rugs, and bronze Remingtons littered the living room. *Did the Home Furnishings section of Western Couture department store relocate to Cliff and Mandie's?* I half expected a sales girl to show up and ask if I liked the recliner.

Mandie settled herself into a pseudo-antique chair.

"Well, Cassie, it's been what? How many years?"

"I guess a decade or so."

"Hard to believe, isn't it? Do you have any children?"

"A boy, Sam."

"Oh, how wonderful for you. We've got three boys ourselves, what handfuls. So you must have bit the bullet and married your Ronnie Baldwin, then? What an adventure!"

"I, uh, never married."

Mandie's ring-spangled hand flew to her mouth. "Oh! Why, oh, how stupid of me." She looked mortified, but I couldn't tell if she felt truly penitent, or if she took some childish pleasure at my admission.

"It was a logical assumption."

"Still, I shouldn't have assumed. You know what you do when you assume, you make a you-know-what…oh, nevermind…"

Dad stared at some steer horns on the wall, as if trying to avoid the embarrassing conversation.

Cliff at last entered the living room. Like Mandie, he'd packed on some weight, but looked good for it.

"Ah, Mr. Roberts, Cassie. I see Mandie's made you at home."

Yeah, right at home. Maybe I'd enjoy a dip in the pool? Okay, so I felt a little ungracious, even if Mandie had been quite nice.

Mandie stood, excusing herself. "Got some errands to run. So nice to have you home, Cass. You'll have to come back sometime for dinner."

"Nice to see you too, Mandie." I almost choked on the words.

Dad and Cliff shook hands. Cliff nodded towards me. He looked imposing from his towering six-foot four-inch frame, but remained boyishly handsome.

"Well, I expect you two want to see the stables. Let's head out back."

Cliff led us through the house to a set of French doors. The doors opened up into the backyard, where a stunning Mediterranean style pool and more potted geraniums greeted us. Cliff motioned towards a golf cart parked near the pool.

"Hop in." Cliff indicated the back seat of the cart for me, the passenger seat for Dad.

"I don't mind walking." The thought of being chauffeured around the vast property by Cliff annoyed me, but I knew Dad, and his back, probably felt grateful for the ride.

"The barn's three football fields away, Cassie. I think you'd better get in. We built the barn so far from the house 'cause Mandie didn't want any 'horse stench' interfering with her pool parties."

I thought "horse stench" was the best smell in the world. Cliff had, too, when we were kids. But Mandie's money (or rather, her family's money) had built Star Maker Ranch, so I suppose Cliff made concessions to his bride and her financial backing.

Not wanting to upset Dad, I got in the cart.

Cliff sped along the vast green backyard, complete with mini putting course. When we at last approached a large split-rail section of fence, out of nowhere a ranch hand appeared to open the gate. Cliff nodded "thanks." We sped through the opening, and the hand promptly closed the gate behind us.

The equine complex boasted two huge barns connected by an indoor arena. Several outdoor arenas and round pens circled the main structures. Cliff drove to the front of one of the barns and parked. Strangely enough, I had yet to see a horse. Cliff must have read my thoughts.

"Of course the horses are stalled this time of day. Enforced rest after their morning workout regimens."

We entered through a massive sliding door. A large concrete aisle traversed the length of the barn, with rows of stalls lining either side. Gleaming quarter horse heads peered inquisitively out of stall doors.

"Let's step into my office first."

A door to the right before the first stall opened into a vast office furnished only slightly less lavishly than the living room at the house. A huge executive desk dominated the room. Several bookshelves housed volumes of *Quarter Horse Archive* and *Reiner Magazine,* while pictures of Cliff and Mandie posing next to champion horses adorned the walls. Trophy shelves lined one side of the room, where what must have been a hundred gleaming trophies, without a trace of dust, sat on display.

"Quite a collection," Dad commented.

Cliff's chest puffed.

"Nearly every futurity champion of the past five years was bred or trained on this ranch. I've got horses on this property worth upwards of $100,000."

I strained to affect nonchalance, but my eyes flew open wide at the figure. Cliff continued.

"So you think you got something in this colt of yours?"

"I do." Dad's sounded certain.

"Mr. Roberts, I gotta lot of respect for you. You were the best in your day; you paved the way for guys like me. But reining's changed a lot in recent years."

"I'm sure it has, Cliff. But a good horse is still a good horse."

Cliff laughed, and then nodded at me. "What do you think, Cassie? Long time ago you had an eye for a horse."

I wanted to scream. Splash might be an ordinary foal, but I wasn't about to let Cliff belittle Dad's opinion of him, if that's what he was getting at.

"He's got some promise," I said. "Or at least Chase Eversoll thought so."

Dad glared at me. Cliff registered brief surprise, and then a Chessire-cat grin crossed his face.

"Chase Eversoll, eh? Not bad if you wanna win county fairs, but nowhere near world class." Cliff spun around in his throne-like swivel chair.

"Look, Mr. Roberts, I offered my time here today to show you the facilities, give a demonstration. I've got horses here from every big-name ranch in Texas – the Rio Star, Sweetbriar Acres, Gunsmoke Downs. You and Cassie are like family, which is why I'm considering training your colt. You've got to understand the sacrifice I'd be making to devote time to an unknown horse from an unknown ranch. I don't mean to sound condescending, but you're not my usual clientele. So if this is some sort of game…"

"No game, Cliff." Dad stood and squared his broad shoulders. Though not as tall, he managed to appear as substantial as Cliff. "I've got a heck of a nice colt back at the Rocking R. I want to make sure he's in the right hands, same as you're selective about the stock you take on."

"Didn't mean any offense, Sir. Just wanted you know my time is valuable, and I'm paying you respect, is all. Let's go have a look at the horses."

We exited the posh office, entering the stall area. Much as I disliked Cliff, I envied him the glorious creatures that graced his stalls. Rows of glossy-coated animals with perfect legs and enormous haunches nickered as we walked by. Cliff offered tidbits of information about each occupant as we walked the aisle.

"That's Castle Bay of Rimrock Ranch, sired by Spinning Jack. Won the Amarillo trophy two years back…"

"Jet Scout, rode him in the Oklahoma Derby last year, finished second to the chestnut in the next stall, Firestarter…"

I caressed the velvet noses and stroked the satin necks as we walked by. I hadn't envied the monster house, the garish décor, or the fabulous backyard, but I envied this. Judging from the knowing smile on Cliff's face when he peered over his shoulder, he knew it, too.

"This is the training barn; these are all competition horses. The next barn over is the broodmare and foal barn. For now, let's head to the arena and you can meet my stallion."

This can't be air conditioned. That was my first thought upon entering the indoor riding area. The cool of the arena so contrasted with the heat outdoors, I thought it had to be climate controlled. Surely not even Mandie could afford that.

"How do you keep the air so cool in here?"

"There are ceiling fans everywhere, for one thing," Cliff explained, "but the roof is also made of a new state-of-the-art reflective coating, does a much better job of deflecting heat."

"Of course."

Near the entrance of the ring, another wrangler held the reins of a stunning buckskin stallion. The stud, tacked in an expensive reining saddle, probably stood fifteen hands, but his massive musculature made him look much bigger. Which made it made plausible to imagine a man of Cliff's towering height sitting on him without looking silly. The stallion gleamed like spun gold; his black mane and tail shone blue in the indoor lighting. I gasped.

"He's phenomenal, Cliff."

Cliff looked at me with real warmth.

"This is Locomotion, the pride of Star Maker Ranch, and the heart of our breeding program."

"Nice looking stud," Dad offered.

Cliff patted the stallion affectionately, and then swung himself into the saddle. "I'll run a pattern for you."

The stallion galloped to the center of the massive arena and slid at least twenty feet before coming to a halt. He spun to the right, back feet planted, forelegs crossing at incredible speed. Exactly four spins to the right, four to the left. Cliff and the stallion loped a leisurely small circle, then accelerated into a fast circle.

I never saw Cliff move, never caught a flick of the reins or touch of the heel. The stallion slid, stopped, spun, and backed in utter perfection, never placing a hoof wrong, never exercising anything but textbook form. When they finished the exhibition, Cliff rode the stud out of the ring and handed the reins back to the wrangler. He bent over to brush some dust from his jeans.

"Since you two are like family, I'm willing to offer you my services for a substantially discounted rate. There's not an owner in the state that wouldn't jump at the chance to have their colt trained here, but I'm going to do it for you. I'll need the colt as a yearling, of course. We'll get him out here next spring…"

"You haven't even seen the foal yet." I realized Dad wasn't the least bit overwhelmed by the posh surroundings, or the stunning performance.

"I'm gonna trust your judgment that I can make something of him."

"I appreciate the offer, Cliff. It's generous and I might well take you up on it. But I've still got a couple trainers to preview first. Cassie and I thank you for the tour and demonstration."

Cliff looked stunned as if the roof had just caved in. "I know you've been out of reining for a while, but surely you realize that Star Maker Ranch *is* the premier reining horse training facility in Texas, if not the world. What I'm offering you is unheard of, and I urge you, not just as trainer, but as a friend, to take me up on it. This is an unprecedented opportunity."

"I'm not passing it up. I just want to make sure I explore the options for this colt. This is my life's work on the line."

"Okay." Cliff shook his head, apparently dumbfounded by Dad's lack of enthusiasm. "But I'm already booked for next spring; I was going to make a spot for your colt. You wait too long, I won't be able to honor my offer."

"Understood, and I do thank you again."

"Well, then, I've a ranch to run." Cliff grabbed Locomotion's reins from the wrangler. "I'll take him back to his stall. You drive the Roberts back to the house, Miguel."

The ranch hand nodded, and Dad and I were dismissed. I wondered what was going on in that head of Dad's. Much as I disliked Cliff and his snobbery, there was no argument we wouldn't find another facility of this level in all East Texas.

As we bounced along in the golf cart, I whispered in Dad's ear.

"What on earth made you turn Cliff down?"

"I didn't see what I was looking for."

"What on earth are you looking for that you can't find here?"

"I don't know, but I'll know it when I see it."

At that moment I realized my dad was the most impossible person I'd ever met, except maybe my mother. No wonder so much stubborn ran in my blood. I laughed so hard that Miguel, at the helm of the golf cart, probably thought I'd lost my mind.

***

Oddly enough, I happened to answer the phone when Cliff called the next day.

"Oh, hello Cliff, I'll get Dad."

"Wait Cassie, I actually called to talk to you."

Really?

"Okay," I sounded apprehensive, even to myself.

"Look, first of all, Mandie and I both want you to know that we're sorry about all that mess in high school. We were just dumb kids."

"Please, that was ages ago. It's not something I ever think about," I lied.

"Great, just want to make sure that's understood. We never should have given you such a hard time about the Baldwin guy. In fact, I wish we'd been wrong about him."

You're digging a hole. Just stop, already.

"Really Cliff, I'm not worried about it. Let's move on."

"Whew, good. Glad that's behind us. Now, the other thing I wanted to talk about is your dad."

"What about Dad?"

"I'm worried about him. I don't understand his hesitation about the colt. Look, I wouldn't hurt his feelings for anything, but the fact is, very few people in today's reining world even remember who he is, much less the Rocking R ranch.

For a trainer of my caliber take the colt is unheard of, and an opportunity he can't afford to turn down."

"Just what is it you think you can do for Dad that others can't?"

"I can turn some money with the colt, maybe enough to secure him a cozy retirement."

The words struck home. I remembered my conversation with Dad about him selling the ranch. I wondered what he had stored up for retirement. His and Mom's security was important to me, not to mention the percentage of earnings I stood to gain, and if Cliff could deliver that...

"But like Dad said, you haven't even seen him."

"Cassie, my staff and I could turn a mule into a futurity champion. I know your dad well enough to know this colt of his is probably from decent stock."

"But you don't think he's got the potential Dad thinks he does?"

"Probably not. Today's champions come from big-money ranches and new athletic-style breeding lines, not that old foundation stock."

"I thought foundation stock was athletic?"

"Oh, Cassie," Cliff laughed, "you're as out of touch as your Dad. I can bring you both up to speed."

Cliff sounded sweet as pecan pie, and I found his concern for Dad remotely touching, but something nagged at me. I mean, were we a charity case or something? The out-of-touch rancher and his wayward daughter?

"Okay, Cliff, I'll talk to him."

I heard a smile in his voice. "Thanks, Cass. Knew I could count on you. You always were a great girl. We horsemen take care of our own, you know, and I just want to make sure your dad finishes his career on a high."

"Uh, sure. Me too. I'll talk to you later." I hung up the receiver, bewildered. Then it dawned on me.

Cliff wants to train Dad's colt. Why, I couldn't fathom, and he certainly wanted me to think it was out of the goodness of his heart, but every ounce of intuition I possessed told me there was more to it.

I looked out the big window in the kitchen and scanned the pasture until I spotted Splash frolicking in the field. He bucked and played, and then sped across the pasture like a red rocket. *Could that silly colt really be the first International Reining Champion?*

I shook my head. Dad's dream was turning into a swirling vortex of a twister, and I was unwillingly, but surely, getting sucked in.

chapter

FOUR

The rough sand felt glorious between my toes. I basked in the warm sunlight, wondering why the sun seemed like such a gentle entity here, unlike the ball of fire that baked Texas from April through October. An ocean breeze caressed my coconut-oil-drenched skin. I sighed in pure contentment, flaunting my tan legs in what I hoped was an attractive pose. A *Top Gun* style volleyball game played out further down the beach, and I enjoyed the scenery with undisguised appreciation.

Dana lounged in a beach chair next to me, her dark hair pulled back in a sleek knot, apparently absorbed in a glossy issue of *Virginia Arts & Culture.* Only I knew that hidden between the pages of the sophisticated publication lay Darcy Delancey's newest bodice-ripper. I sipped my Coke and snickered. *Now this is living.*

Dad had bought me a round-trip plane ticket to Virginia Beach so I could box up my belongings in storage and ship them back to Texas. I took full advantage of the offer, advising him I needed a week to do the job. In reality, it took less than three hours in the dismal five-by-five foot storage unit to pack up the few things worth keeping; the rest I left for the trash man. When all seven boxes reached Texas, Dad would undoubtedly gripe about the wasted trip. As I lounged under the blue sky, listening to a symphony of crashing waves, I knew there was nothing wasted about it.

I stayed with Dana in her luxury waterfront condo. She'd taken the week off work and we'd run around like two schoolgirls skipping class, instead of two single thirty-somethings. After a spring and summer of grueling ranch work and little company but Sam and my parents, the endless parties and sunbathing felt like a trip to Shangri-La.

One of the volleyball players, a kid no more than twenty, caught my eye and winked. I rewarded him with a sultry gaze, admiring his young, fit physique. The flicker of attention injected me with a much-needed confidence boost. (My new career as Splash's professional poop-scooper didn't inspire much in the way of self-esteem.) I commended myself for splurging precious tax-refund money on a cheap bikini and some tanning sessions at Madame Sunray's.

Dana closed her magazine, her smutty book still hidden inside. The corners of her mouth turned up when she spied the volleyball scene and my attempt at juvenile flirtation.

"Look, Mrs. Robinson, don't forget your date with Garrison tonight. He's a little more your age. That boy might not even be legal."

"Oh please. I've got to squirrel some away for the long dry spell ahead."

"I still can't believe you agreed to that! Two years? Have you lost your mind?"

"It's a family obligation. Can't be avoided."

"You should stand your ground. At our age, you can't afford to waste two years. Garrison won't wait two years."

"I doubt Garrison's waited six months. It was never serious between us."

"It could be. You can't go backwards, Cass. There's nothing for you in Rednecksville."

"I know. Believe me, I've kicked myself a hundred times for agreeing to Dad's offer, but…"

"What?"

Summerville certainly lacked available men and entertainment, not to mention freedom. Mom and Dad knew each time I took a shower, made a phone call, let a curse slip. More intimacy than an adult child cared to share with her parents.

Yet there were advantages Dana would never understand, advantages I hadn't admitted myself. Like summer mornings spent in dew-soaked pastures, when only the horses and I existed. Sitting in church on Sunday mornings listening to the choir sing "Praise to the Lord, the Almighty." Eating at the old catfish joint by the river, getting my hair cut at Laverne's House of Beauty. Simple, homely, old fashioned things by trendy East Coast standards - wholesome, I guess that's the word. I wanted "wholesome" for Sam, maybe even a little bit for myself.

"I need to do this for Sam, and for my dad."

"Don't play the martyr, Cass. You're not getting any younger."

"Gee thanks, Dana. I sure wish people would stop telling me to quit playing the martyr. You sound like my dad. Y'all make it awfully hard to figure my life out."

"I'm sorry, Chicky-poo. Do what you gotta do. But we miss you here at the beach."

"Believe me, I miss y'all too."

Dana spent an hour filling me in on all the latest hookups and breakups among our social circle. Juicy, delicious gossip, another component missing from my life in Summerville. Probably because I didn't have anyone to gossip with. Most of the kids I'd known in high school had either left town for parts unknown, or had become pompous and unbearable like Cliff and Mandie.

Dana finished her chatter with another plea for me to come to my senses, and again I argued family obligation. I had a feeling Dana missed me more as an effective wingman than as a real friend. Funny how I'd never realized that before.

"Well," she sighed, sounding resigned, "if you insist on returning to Hicktown, you've got one last night left in civilization."

"And I intend to enjoy it, trust me. I'm going to savor every moment."

***

Dana loaned me an adorable turquoise sundress from Coco's Beach Boutique and expensive shell jewelry to match. I let my blonde hair fall well past my shoulders, unconcerned with whether or not the length was appropriate for a woman past thirty. I slipped on a pair of high-heeled sandals I hadn't worn since last summer, enjoying the sensation of glamour.

Dana looked gorgeous in a bright pink number, but then again she always managed to look sexy yet sophisticated at the same time. From her French manicured toes to her collagen-injected lips, Dana embodied perfection. She had to. Dana made a career out of dating rich men and reaping the benefits.

My friend's dating acquisitions included a wealth of diamond jewelry, an elegant foreign car, and season tickets to the symphony. Her latest conquest, Roderick Wyatt III, owned Wyatt Staffing Industries, a company that contracted with many local Fortune 500s. Wyatt was a fifty-year-old confirmed bachelor notorious for frequently changing girlfriends, but for the duration of his infatuation, the girlfriends enjoyed lavish pampering. Dana was no exception, judging by the enormous sparkling pendant strung between her cleavage.

Her doorbell chimed twice in plain bell tones.

"Cass, can you get that?" Dana struggled with a fake eyelash in front of her bathroom sink. "Wyatt and Garrison must be early."

I opened the door, recognizing Wyatt from a brief introduction at an art exhibit gala, and from pictures in the Virginia Beach paper. He reminded me of George Hamilton with his tanned skin and gleaming teeth.

"Hello, Wyatt. You probably don't remember me."

He turned on instantaneous plastic charm, throwing his arms open wide.

"Why of course, Cassie. How great you look! Living rough must agree with you, eh, Garrison?" Wyatt elbowed Garrison, who stood behind him, grinning, while the older man embraced me.

"Yeah, just call me redneck chic." Both men laughed as if I were the wittiest person on the planet, or perhaps the universe. Their laughter ended abruptly when Wyatt turned me loose so Garrison could stake his claim.

"Hello, my sweet." Garrison wrapped his arms around me. He smelled of L'Homme, an expensive men's fragrance found only at Pierre's Discriminating Male. His gym-toned biceps felt incredible, like croquet balls wedged beneath the flesh of his upper arms. We'd seen each other most nights that week, but I still drank in the sensation, having felt deprived during my months back home, knowing deprivation would soon again follow.

"Hi Garrison." I kissed his mouth and tasted strong mint.

Dana emerged from the bathroom clutching a tiny, useless purse.

"Now Wyatt," she teased, "haven't you learned not to rush me? This degree of beauty doesn't come without prep, you know." She popped him with her overpriced mini-bag.

"If we want to make our reservation at Mahi's, we need to get moving. It's Saturday night. They might not hold a table, even for me."

The threat was empty and we all knew it. Roderick Wyatt would have a table regardless of when we arrived. Nonetheless we allowed him to cajole us out the door.

The backseat of Wyatt's Jaguar didn't prove the roomiest of rides, but Garrison and I lounged against one another, anticipating the night ahead with pleasure. *How hard it will be to give this up.*

I liked everything about Garrison, from his ostrich-skin loafers to his sporty business savvy. He was a self-made man, having invented a new type of ping pong table at the ripe age of twenty. He'd launched the table as part of a college marketing class, capturing the interest of a big-name sports equipment manufacturer. The royalties on the patent sale paid for his current beach chic lifestyle.

Yes, I liked Garrison quite a bit, but for some reason couldn't seriously contemplate a future with him. The very idea seemed preposterous.

He caressed the back of my neck, knowing the sensation sent shivers of delight down my spine.

"So you're really off again to your Texas boys, leaving me lonely?"

"I highly doubt you'll be lonely."

"But I will. I think you've found yourself a cowboy out there. Do I need to come to Texas and rough him up?" He gave me an adorable blue-eyed pout. I laughed at the idea of Garrison in Texas, much less Garrison beating up a fictitious cowboy.

"No cowboys, I promise." I thought of my ill-fated meeting with Chase Eversoll, and the afternoon at Cliff's. Those were the closest encounters I'd had with men in Texas.

Wyatt turned the Jag into Mahi's parking lot. Mahi's sat on the edge of an inlet and prided itself on the view; the restaurant also offered the freshest, most delicately seasoned seafood at the beach. The valet recognized Wyatt's car and opened our doors the moment the Jag stopped. Garrison nodded thanks and guided me into the restaurant with his hand on the small of my back.

Dinner turned into a delicious, boozy affair, with sparkling champagne I pretended to enjoy, though its expensive, dry tones contrasted with my cheap, sweet preference in wine. I did genuinely enjoy my scallops and grilled tuna, prepared perfectly and served with lemon butter. Wyatt and Garrison, well practiced in the art of entertaining the feminine persuasion, kept Dana and I in stitches. Memories of blinding Texas heat, back-breaking ranch work, bickering with Mom, and even my sweet Sam, all faded into oblivion. Only the opulence of the glamorous evening remained.

After dinner we strolled through the nearby marina, watching the moon rise over the inlet. Quite romantic, especially when Dana and Wyatt ducked into the cabin on his sport boat, leaving Garrison and I alone on a starlit deck. Garrison kissed me with no small amount of expertise. I relaxed into the kiss and the stars began to dance, but then he pulled away, I presumed to catch his minty breath.

"You can't go back," he said. I assumed he was teasing, but he rambled on.

"Cass, I know we've kept this on the light side, but we've got something going here. You've done your family duty, and I respect that. But it's time you got back to your life."

"You've been talking to Dana."

"You should listen to her. And to me."

"I can't run out on my dad."

"You've been playing cowpoke for six months, that's hardly running out. They can't expect you to give up your future."

"And just what am I giving up?"

"Me."

I didn't want to think about anything beyond the night. I wished Garrison would just shut up and keep kissing me. I ran my fingers up and down his tight chest, trying to get him back in the game.

"I never had you, Gare. Really. I'm just one in a long string of blonde girlfriends who look good in your red convertible."

"Not true."

I tried to make a joke of it.

"That's right. I'm older than the women you usually date."

Garrison's voice began to sound irritated.

"I'm not playing games with you. You're different than the women I usually spend time with. You try to come off cool and cultured, but there's more to you. It's almost like you try to be phony, but can't pull it off, because deep down, you care too much about people."

Between Garrison's babble and the champagne, my head spun.

"Garrison, would you please shut up and kiss me? We don't have much time."

"But we could. Just call off this stupid Texas thing, go get the kid, and come back."

The shimmering romance of the evening dissolved into focus like a mirage gone bad. I stiffened in Garrison's arms.

"The kid?"

"You know what I mean, go home and get ...oh, you've just got me flustered, I can't think..." No matter how hard he fumbled for Sam's name, he couldn't come up with it. He'd even attended one of Sam's school plays a month before we'd left town, but he couldn't remember his name. He couldn't remember my son.

I disentangled myself.

"Gare, I've got an early plane to catch. This has been a magical week, but I think you better take me back to Dana's."

"Cassie, please."

"Wyatt said you left your car in Mahi's parking lot, in case we wanted to leave separately. So please take me back. Now."

I threw up promptly upon reaching Dana's bathroom and felt like crying, but didn't. Garrison sped off in his convertible. "You won't get another opportunity like this," were his parting words, as if I'd blown a big business deal. *Or turned down a hotshot horse trainer.* I sprawled on Dana's couch, clammy and disoriented.

When Dana returned, hours later, only slightly disheveled from her rumble in Wyatt's boat, I relayed the saga of the sort-of-break-up.

"You're insane, Cassie." She brought me some aspirin and a bottle of water, supposedly from a spring in Canada. It tasted like tap.

"Maybe you're right."

"You call him tomorrow morning." It was a command, not a suggestion. "Apologize, grovel." She ran her hands through her hair, apparently more upset than I was. "Maybe he even meant to propose?"

"He couldn't remember Sam's name."

"Cassie..."

"It's over, Dana. The thing with Garrison, Virginia Beach. I'll miss all of you terribly," I finally teared up, "but I'm going home."

***

My head reeled as the puddle jumper flight from Dallas to Summerville bucked during the landing approach. I gazed out the window during the bumpy ride, nothing but green fields as far as the landscape stretched. I was home, all right, not an ocean in sight, or civilization to speak of. I thought of Dana and Garrison, probably out enjoying the Sunday East Coast sun, last night just an unpleasant memory. I felt a pang of sorrow, but not regret.

The sorrow eased as I climbed down the ladder of the little plane and crossed the tarmac. Sam raced to me as soon as I entered the non-secure area of the tiny regional airport.

"Mom!" His sturdy, suntanned arms held me tight. I ruffled his hair and hugged him.

"Oh, I missed you, Sam!"

Dad gave me a brief hug and went to collect my luggage.

"Dad, you shouldn't lift that…" I shushed when he snarled.

We exited the airport, and he dumped my bags in the back of the pickup. Sam squeezed between me and Dad in the cab; the radio thrummed to life as Dad's keys hit the ignition. George Strait belted "All My Exes Live in Texas…"

Not my exes. Mine live in Virginia Beach. Most of them, anyway.

"Mom, you gotta see what me n' Grandpa've taught Splash. We worked with him the whole time you were gone."

"Is that right?" Dad looked sheepish as I raised my eyebrows.

"Well, Sam did the legwork. Mostly I sipped iced tea and barked orders, didn't I, Sam?" Sam nodded. It was a conspiracy.

"I can't wait to see what you've done with him. I'm sure you learned a lot with Grandpa teaching you."

Dad settled his ball cap more firmly on his head. "So, you get your stuff all packed up?"

"Yeah, should arrive sometime this week. Shipped it ground."

"Mmmm. Good. We've got an appointment with Chase Eversoll tomorrow."

"Really?" My stomach still felt queasy from the night before, so the thought of the handsome cowboy stirred little enthusiasm. In fact, I'd had enough of men for awhile.

"Yeah, I need to decide on a trainer before we go any further with Splash."

"You expect much from Eversoll?"

"I reckon we'll see." Typical Dad, ever ambiguous.

Mom hardly looked up from the stovetop when we trundled into the house, and I smelled some sort of casserole baking in the oven.

"Hello, Cassie. Welcome back."

"Thanks, Mom. Something smells good."

"King Ranch chicken."

"Wow."

The casserole melted in my mouth. We all ate heaping helpings. After a week of chic beach cuisine, the simple chicken, cheese and green chili casserole tasted like heaven. Sam drug me outside the instant I cleaned my plate.

"Sam, we can't, we have to help with the dishes."

Mom motioned us outside. "You go on, that child's waited a week to show you that fool colt."

We ran through the pasture to the barn, where Sam made me stand outside Prissy's stall and close my eyes.

"You wait here, and don't peek."

I waited for what seemed an eternity. I heard a cat rustling in the hayloft and the sound of the cattle out in the fields. Finally, the tiny clip clop of hooves.

"Okay. Open your eyes."

Sam stood proud as punch at the end of a small lead rope. At the other end, Splash sported a baby blue foal halter.

"Why, you've got a halter on him."

Sam screwed up his nose. "Mom, that's not the half of it. Watch this." He turned Splash around and led him out of the stall. He led the colt in a circle out in the pasture, and then made a kissing sound. Splash picked up a prancing little trot, Sam jogging at his side. When Sam returned to a walk, Splash followed suit. Sam led him back into the stall.

"Impressive. He walks on a lead better than Hank."

Sam beamed. I entered the stall and Splash shied away, snorting.

"Oh come on now, I haven't been gone that long. And I'm practically your mother."

Splash seemed to agree, nuzzling my palm with his whiskered muzzle.

"He's pretty great, isn't he, Mom?"

"Yeah Sam, I guess he is." We stood there fussing over the colt as the smell of honeysuckle drifted in from the pasture. I breathed in the sweet air, stroked Splash's soft coat, and basked in Sam's smile.

Maybe it's not so bad to be home.

chapter

FIVE

Chase Eversoll lived off County Road 1432, ten miles from the nearest Wal-Mart. After three wrong turns and two stops at Terry Don's Country Store for directions, we finally found Chase's modest sixty acres. He lived on a beautiful plot of land with a huge stock pond and lots of trees. Horses dotted the pasture, mostly grazing, some wading in the pond up to their knees to escape the afternoon heat and flies.

We parked the truck in front of a small but tidy house trailer. Chase emerged from the redwood trailer deck, looking about like I remembered from our brief first meeting. He wore his brown hair cut short and crisp, a "Cowboy Church" tee shirt, dark jeans and durable work boots. I still thought he belonged on a country album cover.

I'd learned from the trip to Cliff's and taken pains with my appearance this time. No scrunchie today, my hair hung long and straight. I wore a tight pair of embellished jeans, a studded belt and a tank top with "Cowgirl Up" spelled in rhinestones across the top. My unusually fancy get-up didn't escape Dad and Sam.

"Wow. You sure look sparkly, Mom."

Dad stifled a laugh, and I ignored the both of them.

"A girl has a right to clean up now and then."

When Chase opened the truck door for me, trying to look like he wasn't ogling, I decided the result was worth the ribbing. He offered a hand to help me out, and I took it, even though I'd climbed out of the big old truck hundreds of times without assistance. I stood to my feet and Chase towered well above me, nearly as tall as Cliff Kesterson.

"Nice to see you again, Cassie. Hope y'all made it here okay."

"Not exactly, but we're here, thanks to the clerk at Terry Don's. Don't know how UPS and FedEx ever find you."

Dad and Sam popped out the other side of the truck and converged on us.

Chase held out a friendly hand to Sam. "Hey there, Sam. How's that colt of yours?" Sam shook his hand and began chattering about Splash. Chase grinned and clapped Dad on the shoulder.

"Welcome to my place, Mr. Roberts. I hope you weren't expecting the Rio Star. I'm a humble operation."

Dad surveyed the green fields, the red barn not unlike our own, and the no-frills but functional riding arena. "Seems like a fine place to me."

Chase led us inside the barn, which was old but neat as a pin. A solitary horse poked his head out of a stall; otherwise, the barn stood empty. Chase grabbed a rope halter and put it on the stalled horse.

"This is Stetson, from the Flying J Bar. Took him on last spring. Ought to give you a good idea of my work."

The horse was nice looking but not as impressive as Cliff's stallion. He sported clean legs, plenty of rump and a pretty head. Chase brushed the sleek gray coat, stirring up tiny tufts of dust. Sam patted the young stallion while Chase threw an old saddle over him. I noticed he took great care with the cinch, making sure it didn't pinch or bind. Then he stretched the colt's forelegs. Dad nodded in approval.

"Come on out to the arena." We started sweating outside the barn as the afternoon sun bore down on us. Wet marks soon decorated our shirts. I felt my makeup melting, along with my attempt at looking cute.

Chase warmed the stallion up for several minutes, bending at the walk and loping in lazy circles. Then he urged the horse into a faster, ground-consuming stride. The pair worked well together, the animated stallion and the giant cowboy.

They sped around the ring, boldly at first, then slowing and executing a collected, smaller circle. The horse swapped leads in the center of the arena and completed similar circles in the opposite direction. Chase halted the stallion, backed about ten steps, then spun around and fired off like a shot. After racing the length of the arena, Chase mouthed "Whoa" and the gray threw the brakes. The horse sat deep on his haunches, sliding impressively, and then switched gears to reverse for a rollback. The fresh young colt seemed eager to show off.

Chase brought the stallion to a stop. A slight twitch of the reins and he spun right, drilling a hole in the arena floor. He halted, and then Chase twitched the reins in the other direction. The colt became excited spinning to the left, stumbling as he crossed his feet one over the other, but the speed of the spin defied belief.

After completing his spins, the stallion loped prettier than most pleasure horses, then galloped a large circle like he'd just eaten jet fuel. Chase halted the horse and stroked his shoulder, murmuring sweet nothings in the colt's ear. Despite the heat and the demanding maneuvers, the animal seemed fresh as when he started. Chase brought him back to us at an easy walk.

"Nice," Dad nodded. "That the colt that won the Four States?"

"Yeah, he did pretty well last fall. His owner took him to service some home-bred mares this spring; I just got him back last month. I'll probably campaign him come September, run the fair circuit. Did you want to see more? I don't usually school in the afternoon heat, but I'll be happy to run another pattern if you like."

"No, that's fine. I saw what I needed to see." Dad turned to Sam. "Sam, why don't you help Mr. Eversoll untack that stallion?"

"Sure, Grandpa."

Chase turned to lead the colt back to the barn. "C'mon then, Sam. Once we get this fellow untacked, we'll all take a stroll through the pasture to meet some of the other horses."

Dad and I found a shade tree and stood beneath the sheltering leaves. I pulled my hair up off my neck, wishing I had my faithful scrunchie to twist it into an unattractive, but much cooler, bun.

"Okay, Dad, I'm curious." I fanned myself with my other hand. "Your reaction at Cliff's surprised me. Cliff ran a perfect pattern and you weren't impressed. So I'm dying to know what you thought of Chase?"

Dad pulled a bandana out of his pocket and dabbed his forehead. "I was about to ask you the same thing. Or did you even notice the horse?" He cut his eyes at me and winked. I glared at him.

"Daddy! Stop it!" Then, hesitantly, "Was I that obvious?"

"No more obvious than he was, Baby Girl. But he seems like an all-right fellow. Has a reputation not just for being a good horse trainer, but a good man. Anyway, tell me what *you* thought."

I leaned back against the tree, resting against the rough bark. "Well, Chase's pattern wasn't as perfect as Cliff's. His horse isn't as seasoned."

Dad scratched his chin and nodded, but he remained silent.

"At the same time, the colt and Chase had a connection. The horse wanted to work for him. I'd say the pattern wasn't as good as Cliff's - Chase's aids were more obvious - but it had…well…something more."

Dad placed a gnarled hand on my bare shoulder. "You've always had a good eye, even Cliff was right about that. You're exactly right. Chase and that colt just had…more. That's what I'm looking for, and that's why he's going to train Splash."

I remembered Cliff's phone call and felt a twinge of guilt. After all, I told him I'd talk to Dad. At the same time, Dad's decision made me happy. I'd never felt real cozy about the notion of Cliff controlling Splash.

Chase and Sam emerged from the barn, Chase leading the stud by a rope halter. He turned him loose in a field with a couple other young stallions, duplicating a "bachelor band" like wild horses sometimes formed. I nodded, pleased. Some horsemen isolated young stallions; others believed they needed social interaction with other horses. Chase seemed to be of the latter opinion. I liked that. Chase and Sam walked over to our shade tree.

"If y'all are up for it, I'll walk you through the mare and gelding pasture, show you around."

Dad nodded and ambled after Chase. I watched Dad for signs of pain, but he'd grown stronger and I couldn't detect any hesitation in his long stride. Chase led us through two sets of gates and fences, which separated the stallion pasture from the others, into the field with the stock pond. Sam eyed the pond, and hot as the day was, I couldn't blame him. Still, the mother in me prevailed. "Sam, don't even think about it."

Chase turned and grinned. "Tell you what, Son, see the water trough in the stallion pasture? The big galvanized one? That water's fresh and cold, and a lot cleaner than this pond. Maybe your mom won't mind if you strip off and dunk in that."

"Can I, Mom? Please? I'm burning up."

"All right, go ahead. Just keep your eye on the stallions." Sam raced for the tank. Horses began circling us, approaching Chase, clearly expecting a rub or a treat. Chase introduced them as they came forward.

"This is Mollie, the first horse I ever trained. Now my young cousin shows her in Novice Amateur. The black horse is Jaybird, Jack Clinton of Sugar Springs owns him. He can spin like nobody's business, but I've never gotten a stop out of him more than fifteen feet. That's Gold Rush in the pond."

We fussed over the sleek horses as they nuzzled and nudged us. These were real horses, not show machines. They all looked healthy and content, except for a thin buttermilk-colored mare that stood apart from the others. Little more than skin and bones, she gazed at me from a pair of enormous, gentle eyes. I wandered over to her and stroked her rough, dull coat. She thrust her muzzle in my hand, making me wish I had a carrot. I wondered why Chase had allowed this particular mare to suffer such poor condition, while the others looked like pictures of prosperity? My eyes narrowed in anger.

"That's Tinkerbell." Chase must have read my accusing look. He walked over to me and the skinny filly. "Believe it or not, her bloodlines go back to Impulsive."

"Then why does she look like this?" Emotion choked my voice. I had a soft spot for horses and dogs, and couldn't stand to see one neglected or abused.

"A good friend of mine works for Equine Rescue in Colorado. He saw this little mare at an auction, on her way to a Canadian slaughterhouse. He read her papers, saw the likes of Impulsive and Feature, and called me up. I told him to buy her and ship her here; she arrived a week ago. Believe it or not, she's only three."

Dad shook his head. "What's a filly like that doing at a meat auction? With those papers?"

"You wouldn't believe some of the horses that go to slaughter, according to my friend Tom. Plenty with registration papers. Just too many unwanted horses, I guess. Judging by this filly's condition, she was likely a victim of abuse and neglect. Poor little girl never had a chance."

I hugged the filly around the neck. "She does now, don't 'cha girl?"

Dad smiled at Chase. "Seems my daughter's found a friend."

The mare leaned into me, accepting my affection. A crazy idea hit me. "Is she for sale?"

Chase's face registered surprise. "I'd never sell a horse in this condition."

"I'm not looking for a world champion reining horse. I just want this filly."

Dad looked as shocked as Chase. "Cassie, honey, what on earth would you…"

"She reminds me of Trix, Dad."

I buried my face in Tinkerbell's scruffy mane, and she craned her neck protectively around me. I felt embarrassed by my display of emotion, but somehow determined to leave Chase's farm the owner of the filly.

Dad, bewildered, shrugged and looked at Chase.

"Would you consider selling?"

Chase pointed towards the trailer. "Let's head back to some air conditioned comfort and talk it over."

***

Chase's trailer looked about like what you'd expect from a horse trainer bachelor pad, except neater. Simply furnished and utilitarian, the trailer's decor consisted of scattered horse magazines and family photos. I recognized a picture of his grandmother, realizing I'd seen her at church.

"Mrs. Emmeline was your gramma? But I knew her, she used to teach my Sunday School class when I was like, five."

"Yep. I told you it's a small world. My great aunt and uncle lived out your way, too. Pretty ironic we never crossed paths."

"I don't think I ever met your folks, though." Dad eyed a picture of a handsome couple in their Sunday best.

"Mom and Dad live in Tyler, now. Dad used to have a cattle ranch, but he gave it up a couple years ago. Mom wanted to retire on the lake in Tyler, surrounded by roses."

"Your dad miss the ranch?"

"Yeah, he misses it, but it's a relief, too. He was getting past it."

"I know how he feels. We old men have no business messing with cows and horses, at least that's what my wife tells me."

Chase pointed to a small, immaculate kitchenette.

"Cassie, would you mind grabbing some sodas out of the fridge? Should be a Coke or two in there. I'll dig up the papers on that filly."

Chase wasn't kidding about the contents of the fridge. The fridge contained, precisely, two Coca-Colas, a bottle of Tabasco and some ketchup. My curiosity aroused, I snooped in the pantry as well. Just a few cans of ranch-style beans and a jar of salsa.

I popped the top off one of the Coke cans and walked it to Dad in the sitting room. I left the other can intact in case Chase wanted it, but I craved the bubbly refreshment after suffering the afternoon heat. My Virginia years had turned me into a wimp.

Chase emerged from the back room with a notebook filled with plastic sheet protectors. He sat next to Dad on the beige sofa, opening up the book. I handed him the Coke, but he shook his head.

"Sorry, I'm a bad host. Should've stocked up on drinks and snacks. You take the soda."

I couldn't hold back from commenting on his kitchen contents, or lack thereof.

"What do you do for food? A roach couldn't make a living in your pantry."

"Cassie!" Dad's tone indicated I was being rude. Chase laughed.

"No, she's right. I'm the most pitiful of all things, a confirmed bachelor who can't cook. If you look in the freezer, you'll see Tupperware containers full of home-cooked meals packed by my mother. When I run out, there's a Mickey D's down the road a few miles, and a hole-in-the-wall Mexican restaurant with the best chile relleno."

"Good grief! Do you know what you're doing to your insides? What about fruits and veggies?"

Chase shrugged and grinned.

"You sound like Mom. Anyway, about the papers on that filly..."

The filly's papers read like the "Who's Who" of foundation quarter horses. Dad read the registration, tracing the names of the mares and stallions with his finger. He looked at me with raised brows.

"You serious about this, Cass?"

I nodded. Dad turned to Chase.

"Would you sell?"

"I bought the filly to save her life. I never intended such a quick resale."

I stared hard at Chase, fluttering my eyelashes.

"But with your daughter boring holes into me with the bluest eyes in Texas, I don't see how I can keep the filly. And I can't profit off a horse in that condition. I'll sell her to you for what I paid the auction, plus the transportation fee to get her here. I expect she's green broke, but I haven't had the heart to put a saddle on her."

It didn't matter. None of it mattered. I just wanted to take the scruffy, ill kept filly and make her beautiful again.

"Deal!" I felt triumphant, at least until I remembered I had no money. I turned to Dad. "Deal?"

"Well, I told you I'd give you something in lieu of wages, although this is the last thing I'd expect you to want."

"She might make a nice filly for Sam." It sounded plausible as anything. Dad fumbled for his checkbook.

"Well, Mr. Eversoll, I suppose we've bought ourselves a rescue filly. Now if my daughter wouldn't mind terribly, can we please get to the business of my colt?"

I grinned at the both of them.

"You two go right ahead. I better fish Sam out of that horse trough, if he's not turned into a prune."

I found my son lounging in the horse tank, the young gray stallion drinking from the same water Sam bathed in. The horse looked at Sam, obviously wondering why a human inhabited his drinking water. Then he decided to make a game of it, snaking his nose back and forth, splashing water in Sam's face. Sam laughed and splashed back, which sent the stallion off running in a huff. A moment later he stopped and spun around, then trotted back and dipped his nose in the tank again, asking for more.

"That's quite a display."

Sam smiled a guileless smile. "I like Stetson, Mom, he's a smart a…, I mean, wise guy, like me."

I tried to look stern. "Nice save. Anyway, 'wise guy,' you need to get out of that trough. Grandpa's almost finished with Mr. Eversoll, and have I got a surprise for you."

"A surprise?" Sam swung a gangly leg over the side of the silver tub. He was soaked to the bone, wearing nothing but his boxer shorts. "How'm I gonna dry off?" He eyed his dry but dirty clothes, piled in a heap on the ground next to the water trough.

"Just carry your clothes and boots up to the trailer. Mr. Eversoll doesn't have much in the way of domestic trappings, but I expect he's at least got a towel."

I left Sam, still dripping, on the porch, quietly opening the trailer door in case Dad and Chase were still talking business. They were, and I needn't have bothered. Neither man took any notice of me. Dad leaned toward Chase, his shoulders square, his face intense.

"...so you're really suggesting we skip the two-year-old futurities?" Dad sounded incredulous.

Chase, on the other hand, seemed cool as a breeze. "I'm not suggesting, Mr. Roberts, I'm insisting."

Dad shook his head like he couldn't take it in, as if Chase had just suggested he walk through the Dallas Galleria butt naked.

"Mr. Roberts, I understand your gut reaction. Us Texas quarter horse men, we've bred horses to mature young and compete as two and three-year-olds so long it's all we know. But if your dream is the International Equestrian Games, you gotta think like the US Horse Association."

Dad shook his head. "Maybe I have been out of this too long."

"Nonsense. You just gotta change your way of thinking. Reining is going global, sooner rather than later. But if we want in, we have to play by the USHA's rules, and the USHA doesn't allow horses in sanctioned events until the age of six."

Six? A warmblood eventer might be considered green at six, but quarter horses were practically senile by then. Well, not exactly, but most of them would be past peak performance. No one, for instance, began training a western pleasure horse at six. By six the horse had likely shown the futurities, retired open competition, and been sold to an amateur or novice to show at lower levels.

Chase continued despite Dad's dropped jaw.

"This is gonna be a great thing for quarter horses, and quarter horse sports. Think of what we do to our horses now. We start them as long yearlings, put guys like me at six foot two, two hundred pounds on top of them. We stress their joints and ligaments, not to mention maturing bones. How many horses do you see at top form in their later years? A dressage horse is just getting started at ten or so, same with eventers. By then our quarter horses are over the hill.

"If we bring them along slowly instead, they'll have longer careers, live happier, healthier lives and increase in value."

Dad scratched his chin, scowling. "I can't quite wrap my brain around it, but I suppose there is a sort of logic. I always thought we started colts too young, thought I was conservative waiting for 'em to turn a full two."

"I'm not saying we won't begin groundwork and that we won't back him at two. Although I'd rather you or Cassie back him, as opposed to putting my weight on a young, immature horse."

Dad nodded. "That I understand. Why do we always pack big ol' boys on these compact models? You and Cliff Kesterson are the only trainers I considered, and you're both strapping fellows. I'll tell Cassie she's been drafted."

"We'll cross that bridge when we get there. I thought it was only fair that I lay this out now, so you can take or leave it. If you want a flash-in-the-pan futurity champion, I'll try to get him there for you, but if you're aiming for the International Equestrian Games, it's slow and steady from here on out. You'll have to tell me which way you want it."

I wondered as much as Chase what Dad was going to say next.

"Okay young fellow," he clapped Chase on the shoulder, "I'm gonna defer to the younger generation on this one." Dad grabbed his hat from the coffee table, plunking it on top of his head.

"Just hope I don't live to regret it."

chapter

SIX

Of course I wasn't home when Chase delivered Belle. That's what I nicknamed my filly, Belle, hoping once her dull coat shed out and she packed on some weight, she might live up to it.

I'd hung around the farm for days, afraid to venture out for fear of missing the delivery. The weekend passed with no sign of Chase or the filly, as did Monday, Tuesday and Wednesday. My mood soured, but I couldn't bring myself to ask Dad to call. He'd see straight through me and I wasn't up to more ribbing. At the same time, I had a list of errands piling up that required leaving the premises.

On Thursday I drove Sam to orientation at Summerville Middle School. We spent at least two hours meeting teachers, selecting classes, finding lockers and listening to lectures on hallway and lunchroom etiquette. When we returned and pulled into the ranch's long gravel drive, I spotted my new filly in the field to the left of the house, grazing.

Figures.

"Mom! It's our horse."

"Yeah, Sam, looks like Mr. Eversoll dropped her off."

My heart quickened as I scanned the drive for Chase's truck and trailer, but only Dad's "old blue" and Mom's sedan sat parked in front of the house. *Just as well.* No point adding Chase to a long list of failed romantic entanglements, regardless of what he looked like in snug jeans.

I parked my old SUV and toddled toward the pasture in the high-heeled sandals I'd worn for Sam's orientation. My heel caught a hole and I stumbled, nearly turning my ankle. Sam offered his arm to steady me, and we walked toward the fence together. After the initial let down of missing Chase, I felt excitement that my filly, at least, was here. I opened the gate to the side field, an acre of solitary pasture used to isolate new or sick horses or cattle, and whistled.

Belle perked her ears up and floated to us in a lovely trot. She nuzzled Sam and I in turn, and we petted the rough coat.

"When can we ride her, Mom?"

"Not til she's picked up some weight. I expect she needs almost a hundred pounds. Then we'll see what we've got. You like her?"

"Uh, yeah." Stupid question.

I eyed the thin filly, the color of dirty string, wondering why on earth I'd spent my future earnings on a rescue horse. What difference would one rehabilitated horse make in the grand scheme of things? Belle rested her head on my shoulder. *It will make a difference to me,* she seemed to say. I couldn't argue with that.

I heard the back porch door creak open, and Dad lumbered out to the field. I smiled as I watched him stride in a true leggy, cattleman's fashion. Maybe not quite like he used to, but certainly much improved, more reminiscent of his former self. He waved his straw hat toward the filly.

"I figured I'd keep her out here 'til you got home, didn't want any trouble with the other horses. I expect she'll be low on the pecking order."

"You're probably right. I can't imagine she's got much energy to assert herself. Prissy'll rule the roost. What do you think about the geldings?"

"Aw, Boomer 'n Jack won't pester her too bad. They're too old for that nonsense."

"Eversoll brought her papers and everything, then?" Maybe he'd forgotten something, would have to come back.

"Papers, vet record, and a bag of the feed she's been eating."

"Oh." I buried my face in the filly's neck so Dad couldn't read my expression. I guess I'd just imagined interest on Chase's part. Surely if he liked me even a little he would've stayed until Sam and I got home.

"...said he's bringing his folks to the barbeque up at the church Saturday. In fact, he must've mentioned it ten times."

"Oh really?" I peeked out from under Belle's mane. Trying to change the subject, I commented, "I haven't been to that barbecue since Uncle Monroe died."

"It's past its glory days, though we still draw a crowd."

My great Uncle Monroe, throughout his living years, had presided over the church's annual barbeque, masterfully manning the massive smoker, turning out vast quantities of delicious brisket and chicken. People came from miles around to buy a plate of Monroe's smoked meats, filling the coffers of Pleasant Oaks Baptist Church's cemetery fund. Since Uncle Monroe passed away, no one had emerged a worthy successor to his smoker. Dad and some of the other church leaders took turns at the helm, with satisfactory results, but the meat never tasted quite the same, or so I'd heard.

"Who's smoking the brisket this year?"

"Marty Jones." Dad rested his arm on my filly's back, and she seemed to bask in the newfound attention. "You know, Marty, your third cousin on Gramma's side? He'll do all right, but it'll never be like it was before. In Monroe's day, we took orders weeks in advance."

My mouth watered remembering Monroe's brisket, so tender it fell apart and full of rich flavor that saturated the meat. Never dry, always juicy.

"Why can't anyone barbeque like Uncle Monroe?" Sam asked, turning his attention from the filly to Dad. "What made his so good?"

"Now if I knew the answer to that, I'd be onto somethin'. Nobody knows exactly. But it's the same as anything else, Sam, time and experience. Monroe never rushed the meat, never cut corners. And," Dad tousled Sam's sunbleached hair, "never gave away his secrets. I don't think even Aunt Ida knew."

"So are we going to the barbeque?" I tried to sound casual.

"Now that's a silly question. We go every year."

"Did you tell Chase we'd be there?"

"I told him we'd all likely go."

"Hmmm." I took a mental walk through my closet, trying to pick a dress.

"Awesome, we'll get to see Mr. Eversoll." I marveled at Sam's optimistic spirit, wishing we shared that particular trait. The corners of Dad's mouth turned up, and I wished he'd stop smirking.

"I suspect your mom's pleased about that too, Sam." Dad turned and pointed to the barn. "But that's enough of that. Why don't you fetch the halter your mother bought at the feed store, and we'll see how this filly does in the big pasture."

Sam took off at a trot, floating across the field almost as pretty as Belle.

***

The scene at the country church mimicked the crowd at a fifties show in Branson, gray-hairs gone wild. While a normal Sunday at Pleasant Oaks saw a crowd of a hundred or so, there must have been at least twice that occupying the picnic grounds, roaming the cemetery and filling the social hall with chatter and merriment. They reveled in shooting the breeze with old friends, guzzling gallons of sweet tea and downing plates of inferior barbeque. It was, in fact, the senior social event of the season.

I felt almost as young as Sam by comparison. There were children running amuck, most likely grandkids of the barbeque-goers, but very few young parents or thirty-somethings. Sam joined ranks with a pack of boys playing baseball. He wasn't very good at it, but it didn't seem to matter, and the boys welcomed him.

The old people smiled and greeted me warmly, most of them I'd known since childhood and shared some distant kinship. A lady in a flowered hat grabbed Mother to serve homemade cakes; the men recruited Dad to stir cowboy-style beans. I found myself left quite alone, amused that against the odds I'd conquered the cliquey Virginia Beach social scene, but here at the Pleasant Oaks End of Summer Smokeout, I was a total non-entity.

I felt a strong hand on my shoulder and turned. Two dark, twinkling eyes, set by a handsome face, stared back at me. *Chase.*

"Hi Cassie."

"Hi Chase." I discreetly licked my teeth to make sure no lipstick smeared them. I felt a blush creeping into my cheeks, wondering what it was about this man that turned me into an insecure teenager. I straightened the skirt of my red, daisy-patterned sundress. I'd pulled my hair up in a French twist, and I fiercely hoped that the exposed skin on my back appeared smooth and inviting.

He grinned at me. "I hoped I'd see you here."

"Really?"

"Yeah, I wanted to find out how Belle's settling in."

Oh, that's all.

He put his hand on the small of my back and steered me away from the crowd. "Why don't we sit down? We'll never get through the brisket line right now." I looked at the mile-long line of seniors with paper plates and nodded. We found an empty corner table in the back of the hall.

Chase looked out of place. Instead of his usual cowboy get-up, he wore a polo shirt and a pair of dress shorts. His legs glowed stark white compared to his deeply tanned arms and face, and somehow those pale legs bolstered my flagging confidence. He tucked me into my chair and took the seat across from me.

"Sorry I missed you the other day."

I waved my arm, shrugging it off. "No problem. Belle's doing great, except Splash is in love with her. He drives her crazy with his nipping and teasing."

"I figured he'd consider her his own personal playmate."

It was hard to hear each other over the roar of the gray-hairs' festivities, so we leaned closer over the checkered vinyl tablecloth. I rested my elbows on the table and felt gritty spilled salt rub my skin. Smoke drifted in from the barbeque, casting a haze over the room.

"Looking forward to the brisket?"

"Huh?" He leaned in even closer. I felt warm and clammy as I repeated the question.

He winked at me. "Since you know what's in my fridge at home, you can probably guess the answer to that. Not that the brisket's been the same since your Uncle Monroe passed."

"Yeah, we had a big family discussion about that. Sam's intent on finding the secret to Uncle Monroe's recipe, but he didn't leave much of a trail."

"You know that my great Aunt Clara was good friends with your aunt and uncle?"

I still had to raise my voice to be heard above the tumult. "Yeah, like we said before, it's surprising we never met."

Chase shook his head and stood up, grabbing my arm and tugging gently. He pulled me to his side so he could speak in my ear. His touch was firm, his body muscular. I quivered as his breath tickled my ear.

"This is no good, these old folks are giving me a headache. What'd ya say we go outside, walk through the cemetery?"

I agreed. Walking through a cemetery might not constitute a traditional romantic pastime, but I felt game. He steered me through the benign, beaming crowd and out the door, and then removed his hand from my back, severing the physical connection.

Hot, yellow sunlight shimmered through the dusty trees. They still wore their summer green and would for another few months, but their leaves had changed from the bright vigor of spring to the faded hues of late summer. One didn't endure months of Texas heat without evidencing some wear and tear. Still, I found the leaves all the more beautiful, because autumn would eventually come and strip them, and I hated winter bare trees. Summer was much more to my taste, despite its blinding sun and intense heat.

We strolled past the picnic area and the field where the boys played baseball. Sam spotted us and waved, apparently torn between joining us and continuing his fun. Chase waved and smiled.

"Hey Sam, we'll catch up with you when you've finished your game." I wondered where Chase got his intuition, which worked as good or better on people as it did horses.

The black iron gate to the cemetery stood open, and many of the seniors roamed the grounds, stopping by gravesites, exchanging anecdotes, leaving flowers. I thought it strange that I noticed few tears or expressions of sorrow. Maybe after enough time only the sweetness of the memories remained.

Without thinking I headed straight for my grandparents' grave. Chase followed. Fresh garden-cut roses adorned the site, so I knew Dad had been there preparing for the day's visitors.

"Hi Gramma, Grampa," I said without thinking, for once almost forgetting Chase's presence until I felt his hand on my shoulder.

"My Mom and Dad told me your grandparents were the salt of the earth."

"They were."

I traced one headstone fondly. *John Green Roberts.* I remembered Grampa's towering height, rich voice, gentle touch. *Ethel Rose Roberts.* Remembered Gramma's pecan pie and hand-sewn Barbie doll clothes. Tears welled in my eyes, and I said out loud, "I seem to be the only one in this cemetery crying."

Chase took my hand in his firm grasp. "Then let's walk together, because I'm bound to shed a tear, too."

We walked past the graves, most of them relatives, and wondered about the head stones, some ancient and simple, some ornate. Some of the graves were lush with flowers, others bare. We reached a newer grave that hadn't quite grown over with grass, and I realized it belonged to Chase's grandmother. She lay next to his grandpa, and we stopped reverently. Chase's grip on my hand grew tighter, and his square jaw seemed clenched, but I didn't see the promised tear.

"You and your grandma were close?"

He nodded. "I was her baby. Besides being older, my brothers grew up quicker than I did. I was what you call a late bloomer, so Grandma fussed over me longer than she did the others."

We strolled through the cemetery in the sunlight, hand in hand. Other cemeteries felt creepy to me, but never this one, filled with the remains of friends and family. Here I felt comfortable and somehow whole, as if taking my place in the circle.

Toward the back of the property stood a massive monument of glossy granite. An artist had etched a likeness of the deceased in the stone, along with images of horses, deer, saddles and other cowboy insignias. The marker read *Cecil Ray Counts* and listed a plethora of his accomplishments. I'd never heard of the guy, but apparently he'd died at forty and was a rider of some renown about twenty years ago.

I turned my face toward Chase. "Do you know who this guy was? I've never wandered this far back before."

Chase eyed the monument, reading the epitaph. "He was a rodeo cowboy, pretty successful at roping and bull riding. I think he was killed in a car crash." I looked at the face on the monument, young with bright eyes and a dashing moustache.

"Would you want a grave grand as this?"

Chase shook his head and chuckled.

"Nope. Pine box, simple stone, and 'Just As I Am.' That's how I wanna go."

Somehow I knew he'd say something like that. "So you're a believer, then?"

"Have been since seventeen, when I hit the altar at Mom and Dad's church. How 'bout you?"

"I believe in God, but I haven't given Him much reason to believe in me."

"You don't give Him enough credit."

"You don't know how mangled my life is."

"Don't have to. Just lay it down, Cass."

He called me ' Cass.' I was particular about who shortened my name, and I didn't mind Chase using the more familiar form.

"Lay what down?"

"The weight of the world you're carrying on your shoulders." He pinched my shoulder with his free hand for emphasis. We laughed out loud in front of the elaborate grave. A lock of hair escaped its twist and fell in my eyes, and Chase brushed it back, caressing my face. I thought he was going to kiss me and he did, brushing his lips against my cheek.

"Let's go find my folks. That line's bound to be shorter by now, and I'm starved."

We found Chase's parents at a picnic table outside, enjoying plates piled high with barbeque and all the fixin's. Chase spotted them and made a bee-line; they stood courteously as he introduced us. I offered handshakes, but both Mr. and Mrs. Eversoll insisted on hugs instead, which suited me fine. They looked youthful and fit, both of them, exuding friendliness and good humor.

"So nice to meet you, Cassie." His mother gushed, her face beaming. "We've known your family for ages."

"So I've heard." I nodded. "We keep talking about how it's amazing we've never met, but then again, when I was little, we went to First Baptist in town."

Chase's Dad, who looked more natural in dress shorts and loafers than his son did, put a fatherly arm around Chase's shoulders. "And we've always lived out in the styx, haven't we, Son?"

Chase laughed. "That's an understatement."

His dad's eyes shone a pale blue, so Chase must have gotten his doe eyes from his mother's warm brown.

His dad continued. "For years we farmed land originally deeded to my great grandfather, David Henry Eversoll, from the Republic of Texas. The fledgling republic couldn't afford to pay much in cash, so it paid soldiers in its most abundant currency, land.

"We raised cattle and a few crops, and I worked as a rural mail carrier. I delivered mail to every back road in this county. Chase's spread is actually part of that original acreage. We parceled the rest out and sold it to an oil company to finance our retirement. Which worked out great for Chase, because the oil company owns the surrounding land, but hasn't bothered to develop the property."

"So you gave up farming, then?"

Chase's mother laid a beautifully manicured hand on my arm. "I insisted, dear." She elbowed her husband. "Old man was getting past it."

Mr. Eversoll scowled at his wife, but he smiled as he winked at me. "She's right, it was too much, don't know how your dad manages to run cattle at his age. Though he's got some fine ranch hands, I hear." He glanced in Sam's direction. "We met your boy a few minutes ago, when his baseball landed in my smoked chicken."

My hand flew to my mouth. "Oh no! I'm so sorry; his aim's not very good."

His parents laughed. "It was actually a heck of a throw. He was real polite about it, apologized and offered to get me another plate. Very respectful, your boy."

They nodded at me approvingly, and I drank it in. My own parents never seemed to think I was very good at mothering.

"So y'all live in Tyler now?" I remembered Chase talking about their lake house.

"On the lake. It's quiet, peaceful and I don't have to drive forever to get to a Piggly Wiggly." I enjoyed his mother, a vivacious chatterbox of a woman. We talked a few moments, and then Chase grew impatient.

"I'm starved. We'll go get some food, and then bring our plates out here to join you."

As we walked toward the entrance of the social hall, a spanking-new blue pickup pulled up to the church. My stomach lurched when I saw Cliff in the driver's seat and Mandie riding shotgun, untying the old-fashioned silk scarf that secured her expensive coiffure. Cliff's head snapped in our direction and a scowl crossed his features. Chase reached for his hat to tip, and then seemed to realize he wasn't wearing one. He waved instead, muttering under his breath, "well, if it isn't Showboat."

"What?" I asked.

"That's what we call your buddy Cliff Kesterson on the circuit, Showboat. Everything that boy does is for show."

Cliff and Mandie got out of the car and headed our way. I tugged on Chase's arm to go inside, but the effort came too late. Cliff, decked in pressed jeans and ostrich boots, zeroed in on us with Mandie in tow.

"Well, hello Cassie."

Awkward didn't begin to cover my emotional state. I knew Dad had called Cliff and informed him about his decision to go with Chase, and I was pretty sure there'd been a ruckus over it. I felt like a traitor, although my conversation with Cliff had hardly been committal.

"Hi Cliff, Mandie."

Cliff tipped his hat to Chase. "Eversoll."

"Hello, Cliff. Good to see you. Sorry about Fort Worth, heard your colt stumbled. Too bad, that was a big purse. You have my condolences."

Chase sounded sincere enough, but for some reason I doubted he felt any real sympathy for Cliff. The two men glared at each other like two pit bulls.

Cliff laughed, but it came out more like a sneer. "Well, we all have our days, kinda like when that black horse of yours refused to spin at the derby."

Point, Cliff. Now they were even. Mandie and I exchanged helpless looks.

"Yeah, that was the rookie's first time out. How many times have you competed on that bay colt from Sweetbriar?"

"Enough!" I jumped in before Cliff could answer. Obviously there was a deep-seated rivalry between the two trainers, and the testosterone level was rising a trifle high for my taste. They might have been joking, but the cuts had an edge.

"Nothing to worry about Cassie, we're just blowing smoke. It's part of the game. Cliff here'd be offended if we didn't trade some insults, wouldn't you?'

Chase, you idiot. You just opened the door a mile wide. Cliff took the bait.

"Speaking of which, I should congratulate you on getting the Roberts' training job. Of course, I guess now we know how you got it. Hope he at least brought you flowers, Cassie." He elbowed Chase in a none-too-friendly manner.

"Cliff…" I began.

Even Mandie rolled her eyes. "For goodness' sake, Cliff. This is too much." She looked at me and mouthed "I'm sorry."

Chase took my arm and tried to lead me inside. Cliff tugged on Chase's arm again.

"It's no sweat off my back, Eversoll. Glad you got the colt instead of me. My barn's full of top-notch futurity hopefuls, I'm short on time as it is."

"Well, I have no such trouble, Cliff. I consider myself lucky to be handling a colt for the likes of Marvin Roberts. Now if you'll excuse us." We turned to go but Cliff grabbed Chase's shoulder this time, forcing him around.

"I guess you two deserve each other, then. You probably heard about Cassie's reputation, made it real easy for you get the training gig and some fringe benefits on the side."

Mandie's mouth flew open in shock and she whacked Cliff hard with her designer tote bag. "Good God, what's gotten into you? You're embarrassing me!"

He's embarrassing you? I'm the one he just labeled a tramp in front of the entire Pleasant Oaks Baptist congregation. Fortunately, it was unlikely anyone had heard Cliff above the general hubbub.

Chase wasn't quite as tall or solid as Cliff, and in his picnic get-up he hardly looked imposing. But there was no mistaking the steel thread in his voice.

"Kesterson, we're entering the house of God and among gentle company, so I'm not gonna lay you flat right now, but with God as my witness, if you insult the lady again, I *will* take you out."

No one doubted it, not even Cliff by the look on his face. Chase had hardly raised his voice about a whisper, but there'd been no mistaking his conviction. Cliff backed down, raising his arms in mock surrender.

"Okay, settle down. I took our sparring match too far, is all. Sorry, Cassie. You know I didn't mean that. Just got caught up in the moment. You two go get some iced tea and cool off."

Which we did. Chase squirreled me away to the corner of the hall farthest from Cliff and asked if I was okay. I nodded my head, but didn't trust myself to comment.

"You don't look okay."

"You baited Cliff into that, and you used me and my father's training job to get under his skin. I don't know why you wanted to cause a scene."

"I did bait Cliff, and I'm sorry. He gets on my last nerve, and I saw a chance to take a dig at him, which was totally unfair to you. Forgive me?"

His honesty surprised me, and he melted me with a look of concern. Then he put his arms around me and held me tight. I wondered if this was how he'd settle a nervous horse. He tilted my chin up and kissed me lightly on the lips, not enough to cause another scene, but enough that a delicious shock registered throughout my body. "You sure you're all right?"

"I am now." And I meant it.

***

The Kestersons left after a token appearance. Mandie must have drug Cliff home for fear of another scene. I hoped she tongue-lashed him all the way back to Star Maker Ranch. I breathed easier after they sped off in the shiny pickup.

We enjoyed our dinner with Chase's parents and Sam, who finally gave up playing baseball. Chase's Aunt Clara, who I recognized from the senior choir, sat at a table nearby. After we ate, we wandered over to chat with her. She took a fancy to Sam and told him he looked a lot like his great, great Uncle Monroe.

"You knew Uncle Monroe?"

"Knew him?" The old lady scoffed. "I dated him. He was quite the catch. But we were fool kids and broke up in a spat, and then I married my Walt and he married your Aunt Ida. God knew what He was doing all along. Years later we all became great friends."

Sam looked troubled.

"What is it, child?" Ms. Clara asked kindly.

"I want to figure out what Uncle Monroe did to make his brisket so good. It's a family tradition, except it's not anymore, because no one knows his secret."

The old lady's face broke out in a wrinkled smile. "Why young man, you've come to the right place." Sam, Chase and I all looked at Clara in disbelief.

"Surely you don't…" I began.

"But I do." She looked smug as a persian cat with a jug of cream. "Monroe and I were dating when he perfected that recipe from his Uncle Joe - your great, great, great Uncle. In fact, I was his taste tester. He swore me to silence for as long as he lived."

Sam dropped to his knees and folded his hands in an exaggerated plea. "What is it? You have to tell me!"

"Well of course I'll tell you. With Monroe gone, God rest his soul, it's about time someone took up the mantle. The secret is fresh Hickory wood, cut from the tree, not those chips you get in bags. And you have to soak it in a bucket of iced tea. Oh, and he rubbed the meat with Stutgard's rub, which you can only get at Dale Earl's butcher shop on Pine Street. They've carried it for seventy-five years."

You could have blown us all over with a feather. I couldn't wait to tell Dad. All these years, and the secret was alive and well with Chase's great aunt.

"Why haven't you told anyone?" I asked incredulously. Ms. Clara stared at me as if I were an idiot.

"Why, young lady? Because I've never been asked!"

chapter

SEVEN

I didn't walk through the pasture - I drifted, dreamy-eyed and content. *Next thing you know, I'll be singing Disney tunes.* In fact I tried to remember the words to "Once Upon a Dream," but couldn't, so I settled for *The Little Mermaid's* "Kiss the Girl." An animated crab with a Jamaican accent didn't seem out of place in my new sugar-coated world. Because after that chivalrous defense at the senior-fest, and that sweet-but-electric kiss, Chase would certainly call me. Soon.

I couldn't fathom why Chase Eversoll produced this soul-stirring effect on me. A simple country boy from my neck of the woods, he lacked both Ronnie's rebel-without-a-clue allure and Garrison's urbane, sophisticated charm, yet my response to Chase was anything but lacking. There was something wholesome (that word again) about him.

My parents even liked the guy. I couldn't help wondering if Chase was the type of man I should have dated all along. Maybe if I hadn't run off with Ronnie, I'd have crossed paths with Chase sooner and saved myself a world of heartache. But then Sam wouldn't have existed, which was unthinkable. My thoughts raced a mile a minute, trying to unravel the puzzle of my life, but one theme dominated the rest: *Maybe it isn't too late.*

I envisioned a small country wedding at Pleasant Oaks, starring me in a simple white dress (yes, I'd wear white, regardless). A harpist would play Canon in D, and I'd cover the church in gardenias. Chase would look dashing in his tux, and Sam would shine as ringbearer. I'd revel in all the nuptial frills I'd scorned as cliche because I couldn't have them before. Maybe I'd compose a heart-wrenching email to that celebrity wedding planner on cable television, and he'd feel so moved he'd do a show on Chase and I....

Whoa, girl!

I tried to restrain the runaway freight train chugging through my brain. *You'll send Chase running for the hills.* I knew this was the kind of thing men hated, visions of weddings and altars, and we hardly knew one another. *But all women do it, right?* Some primordial need to secure commitment before the man got away.

"Mom. Earth to Mom." I snapped to attention and remembered the lead rope in my hand, and Sam walking by my side. "We passed the barn. Where are you going?"

I shook my head. "I don't know, Sam, I guess I'm not thinking straight today." I turned around and led the palomino filly back to the barn.

I fastened the horse into a stall and sent Sam for a box of grooming tools. We worked the filly's coat in tandem every day, and a lot of the dull, rough outer coat had come loose with the scrubbing. She still wasn't much to look at, sort of cream-colored and too thin, but in just a few days' time she'd shown much improvement.

Sam worked her over with a dandy brush using a circling motion, sloughing off dead hair. I combed her mane, which I'd pulled to a neat, short quarter horse length, and her forelock, which I'd left long. I wanted to see Chase, but in a way I hoped it would be another few days, because I wanted to surprise him with the filly and her progress.

"When we can ride her?"

I eyed the filly's barrel, which had already begun to fill out. We'd limited her pasture to keep her from founder, but she'd still packed on a little weight. Her ribs, which had jutted so prominently just a week before, were now less visible.

"We'll start longing her next week. I think some work at this point would be good for her. If she knows what she's doing on the longe, we'll try a saddle and go from there."

"I wanna ride her first."

"We'll see, Sam. I'm not even sure she's broke. I don't want you getting hurt."

Sam threw his arms around the filly's neck. "Belle wouldn't hurt me."

"She wouldn't hurt you on purpose, but we don't know what she's been through. It's amazing she trusts humans at all, much less seems so fond of us."

Everything about the filly radiated kindness. She seemed to prefer our company to the company of the other horses, always standing at the fence nickering, begging attention. She received attention in spades from Splash – the foal was besotted with her – but she told him plainly with bared teeth and flashing hooves that she had no interest in his immature antics. Still the persistent red colt followed her, nipped at her, and pleaded with her to join in his games. Prissy occasionally spared Belle a sympathetic look, as if to say, "Now you know what I have to deal with."

I patted the filly on the shoulder and told Sam to fetch a small measure of sweet feed. Belle politely waited for him to dump the food into her bucket before submersing her muzzle into the molasses-covered grain.

"I expect you're right, Sam. We'll err on the side of caution, but I don't think this filly would hurt you."

A week passed and true to my promise, we started longing the filly. Still no call from Chase. I waited anxiously as the days came and went, jumping every time the phone rang, scanning the kitchen counter for messages. I must have chewed out twenty telemarketers in frustration. I didn't worry too much at first, but after a week rolled by, I began inventing explanations for his lack of communication.

As I showed Sam how to keep the filly at a steady trot with a shake of the longe whip, I wondered if I could've possibly mistaken Chase's actions at the barbecue. The possessive touches, the chaste kisses, those furious words with Cliff, a woman doesn't misjudge things like that. And Chase was no idle flirt. *So why hasn't he called? Could he be shy? Afraid I don't feel the same?*

"Like this?" Sam stood in the circle of the round pen, holding the whip aloft, shaking it ever so gently when the filly dropped back to a walk. When he shook the whip, she shuffled back into a pretty western pleasure trot, mild as a lamb.

"She looks great, Sam. Try a little canter." He made kissing noises with his mouth, moving the whip with greater animation. The filly stepped into a lope, but on the wrong lead. Sam got in front of her, slowed her to a trot, and asked for a canter again. This time the little mare loped out on the correct lead.

"Great, Sam. That was perfect. You caught the wrong lead and corrected it." Sam flushed with pride. Maybe it *was* time to let him ride her.

I couldn't get Chase out of my head. I figured he must be waiting for a sign from me, a show of interest on my part. That had to be it. All I needed to do was give him a reason, flash the green light. I'd learned enough from Dana's bag of tricks to play the game.

I waited until nine o'clock, when I figured he'd be finished with barn chores. Mom, Dad and Sam were busy settling in for the night, taking baths and putting on pajamas. *Good.* I didn't want an audience for my phone call. My stomach turned back flips as the phone rang once, twice, three times. Just as I thought voicemail would pick up, I head the familiar voice, "This is Chase."

"Chase, uh, hi. It's Cassie."

"Hey, Cassie, what a nice surprise." *Really?* His tone sounded courteous, polite, formal. As if he really hadn't expected to hear from me. I felt absurdly uncomfortable, but there was no backing out now, I had to go through with it.

"Sorry to bother you, and to call so late. Sam and I've been longing the filly; she's doing great and seems quiet. Sam wants to ride her, so I thought I'd let him try it. I wanted to see what you thought." For an instant, it worked.

"Hmmm, well sure. Maybe I could…" *Yes, come over!* His tone abruptly changed. "No, that won't work. Look, I'm swamped with state fairs right now, got three colts I'm campaigning, otherwise I'd love to help you out. If the mare's been nice and quiet, I don't see why you and Sam can't throw a saddle on her and see what happens, just take it slow and easy, and let her go at her own pace."

"Sure. Okay. We'll try." I was glad he couldn't see the color drain from my face or read the disappointment in my voice. There was a moment of silence on the phone, and then finally he replied.

"Let me know how it goes. I probably won't be out there again until spring to start Splash's ground work, but you can always give me a call."

"Yeah, I'll do that." *Not.*

I hung up, not knowing or caring if he wanted to say anything else. He'd made his point; he had no plans of calling or any notion of seeing me outside Splash's training. Apparently I'd misread him, or maybe I'd just played the pawn in his one-up game with Cliff.

It stung as bad as the time I stepped on a bee in the church parking lot. The bee had wedged itself between my foot and my delicate sandal, and the sting had been sharp and unexpected, leaving me howling in pain. I didn't howl after the call with Chase, but I felt the sting. I stung with something akin to hopelessness.

***

That night I dreamed of Ronnie. Not so odd, I guess, since I went to bed feeling bitter and disappointed, two words that encapsulated my emotions concerning my ex.

In the dream I was pregnant with Sam, heavy, eight months along. I turned the key to our meager apartment but needn't have bothered; the door swung open. Thick smoke filled the air, sending me into a coughing spasm.

At least five of Ronnie's close personal friends inhabited my living room, beer cans littering every available space on the coffee table and spilling onto the floor. A women's beach volleyball game loomed life-size on our theater-wide television, the most expensive item we owned. Or pretended to own, as it was bought on credit. The rectangular monster looked ridiculous in our humble apartment, taking up a full half of our living room, but neither Ronnie nor his friends seemed to care.

"Babe!" he called from his position of honor in the recliner. "How 'bout whippin' up some eats? The boys are hungry." The "boys" were always hungry. Ronnie dragged them in from the surf shop where he worked. They were all just like him, overgrown kids who drank, smoked and surfed, in that order. No thought for anything but the next bottle of beer or the next wave, certainly no desire for responsibility or permanence.

Ronnie'd been furious when I got pregnant, as if the whole thing had been my fault. After living a nomad's existence up and down the East Coast, we'd finally landed in Virginia Beach. Since Ronnie's employment was sporadic and we needed every cent of my paycheck, I didn't have insurance for proper medical care or check-ups. Foolish pride didn't allow me to wait in line with the women at the free clinic, so without birth control pills, nature had taken its course.

Ronnie'd lectured me endlessly about how my pregnancy didn't fit with his plans or life goals, and how he hoped I understood I was taking full responsibility for the baby. He wasn't going to be inconvenienced by my lapse in precaution. Out of the goodness of his heart, though, he wouldn't kick me to the curb. He seemed to forget his modest income from the surf shop barely covered the alcohol tabs for him and his friends; my job as payroll clerk for Sterling Incorporated put food on the table and paid the rent.

Of course I never painted this picture in my letters home. My letters contained vignettes of domestic bliss, Ronnie helping me shop for baby clothes and a crib, Ronnie faithfully attending my doctor's appointments. Pure fantasy. Mom and Dad's letters in return always posed the same questions, "When are you getting married?" and "When are you coming home?" I left those questions unanswered.

I went to the kitchen, grabbed a couple cheap frozen pizzas from the freezer and turned on the oven. While it heated, I took a garbage bag and began collecting beer cans. Most of Ronnie's friends paid me no mind, but one said, "You got her trained well, eh Ron?"

"Well, I learned one thing from my time in Texas. Dismal place, but they do know how to raise women. In Texas ya get 'em young and train 'em up like good huntin' dogs." He affected an exaggerated Texas twang and his friends reeled. I sputtered as the smoke choked me, but otherwise silently picked up more trash.

The image became cloudy and faded. Like I'd pressed fast forward, my dream skipped ahead two years. Same grungy apartment. This time I wasn't pregnant, but in the throes of a severe sinus headache. I'd had to leave work early due to the unbearable throbbing, and my head bordered explosion. I needed antibiotics, but we still didn't have insurance. I gripped my head in one hand while I tried the door with the other. Locked this time, which was strange since Ronnie's Camino was in the parking lot.

I opened the door to moans from the television set. My vision blurred as I tried to process the images on the screen. Despite running off with Ronnie at such a young age, I was still naïve about things like pornography. Nothing could have prepared me for the repulsive images on the screen, images which had nothing to do with love or respect. But then again, little in my life with Ronnie had much to do with love or respect.

I didn't see Ronnie anywhere. I felt like throwing up as I turned off the TV, trying to erase the sordid pictures from my mind. The moans continued, at first I thought just in my head, but then I realized they weren't coming from my imagination.

They were coming from my bedroom.

I stumbled toward the noise and into a reenactment of the scene I'd just watched. Ronnie and some cheap, redhead girl with a butterfly tramp stamp on her fully-visible lower back played the starring roles. I must have stood there, mouth open in mute horror, for at least five minutes.

Finally the girl noticed me and squeaked, burying herself in the covers, clinging to Ronnie and giggling. Ronnie looked stricken for a moment, but quickly recovered. "Babe, it's not what you think. We're just playing around. You're so busy with the kid you don't have time."

"Leave."

"Babe..."

"Get out!" I had no idea I could scream that loud, especially with a headache.

"You can't throw me out."

"We're not married, remember? I can throw you out. My money pays for everything in this miserable place."

The girl kept giggling under the covers, as if we were actors in a movie *she* was watching, a comedy.

"Don't make me get ugly, Cass."

"You're already ugly, for some reason I'm just now admitting it. You're toxic, Ronnie, being with you has been like wandering through a poison fog these four years. No more. Get out now or I'm calling the police."

"You wouldn't."

I picked up the phone, and then thought about Sam at the babysitter's. "I'm going to pick up Sam, right now, and if you're still here when I get back I'm calling the cops. I bet if you had to take a drug test right now, you'd fail."

I could tell by the look on his face the words struck home, so I kept going. "I'm having the locks changed this afternoon, so make no mistake, you don't live here anymore. I never want to see you again!"

"But I'm the kid's dad."

"The kid? The kid? That's how you refer to your son? And actually you aren't his dad, legally. You've never bothered to look at his birth certificate, have you? Since things have always been shaky and we aren't married, I had the hospital put 'father unknown' on the certificate. So you aren't Sam's dad, you're not anyone."

I stormed out, my head still throbbing. I stopped the car on the way to the sitter's to throw up, cursing my weak stomach. By the time I got back to the apartment with Sam, Ronnie was gone, along with his clothes and the giant TV. *How in the heck did he get that thing out of here?* He'd obviously found a way, as it was the one thing he cared about. I spent the last dollars in my bank account hiring a locksmith and taking myself to Patient First for antibiotics.

I woke up, surprised to find myself crying. Not over Ronnie or years lost, but over Chase and the good, decent thing I thought I'd finally found, the glimmer of hope he'd doused before it even became a spark. I guessed I was wrong, again. Wrong again seemed to be the story of my life.

***

"I told you, Sam, Mr. Eversoll's a busy man. He's got a lot going on this time of year."

"But I know he'd want to see me ride Belle for the first time."

I wasn't up for this. My heart wasn't in it as I saddled the filly, who stood quietly enough while I tightened the cinch. This was supposed to be a monumental occasion. Mom and Dad waited outside the round pen, waiting to watch Sam ride.

"Samuel, not one more word about Chase Eversoll." I sounded cross and they all raised their eyebrows. I wasn't about to divulge any details. As far as I was concerned, the subject was closed.

"All right Samuel - Sam - we're going to take this slow and easy, see what she knows. I want you to come put your left foot in the stirrup, bear some weight on it, and then get back down. We'll see how she reacts."

I didn't like the idea of Sam backing a possibly unbroken horse. But Belle had been an angel to work with, never giving us a moment's trouble. From her obedience on the longe line, I suspected she must be broke, and Chase had dismissed my concerns, anyway, so I decided to let Sam give her a try.

Sam placed his foot in the stirrup and stood up like he was going to mount, but then hopped back down to the ground. The filly could've cared less, so I let him mount the next time, sitting still in the saddle. Again, the filly affected complete unconcern.

Sam and I smiled at each other. "She doesn't mind at all, Mom, see?"

"I guess you're right"

Dad and Mom watched as the filly began to walk around the round pen with Sam on her back. She ambled along and he steered her around the perimeter.

"Can I trot?"

I should have said no, walking was plenty for the first try. But Sam was so eager, and the filly so cooperative, I thought, *why not?*

"Sure, just ask her nice and easy."

He kissed to the filly and her ears swiveled back, but she continued walking. I knew from longing her that she knew the cue, but Sam kissed again and this time she flattened her ears back. Her tail began twitching back and forth.

"Sam, I don't think…"

He nudged her with his heels and the filly froze, trembling. Before I could reach him, Sam kissed again, said "Come on, Belle!" and gave her a firm kick, like he would've kicked Boomer or Jack if they'd refused to move. Our sweet, quiet filly exploded, bucking three times in explosive succession.

Sam went airborne. I watched my child sail through the air in what seemed like slow motion. Completely helpless, I watched him fly, and then smash into the object destined to bring him back to earth.

He collided headfirst into the round pen fence. That sound of his head hitting the post, like a baseball bat slamming into a pumpkin, jarred me in a way that would make me shudder until the day I died. Then his body crumpled, hitting the ground like a boneless heap.

God, no!

I screamed, running to him. Mom and Dad rushed inside the pen. Belle galloped to the other side of the arena, her sides heaving.

"Sam!"

Blood streamed from his scalp. Dad crouched next to him, "Son, look at me. You okay?"

"All right," Sam replied weakly. I held his head in my lap and found an oozing, crooked six-inch gash along his hairline where he'd hit the fence.

I held up two fingers.

"Samuel," there I was, using his whole name again. Not in anger though, so far from anger that time, "how many fingers am I holding up?"

"Two," he got the words out before he craned his neck and threw up in dirt. At that angle, I could see an enormous, blackening goose egg rising beneath his cut.

Mother ran for the house, yelling over her shoulder. "I'm calling an ambulance."

I fought tears; I couldn't break down in front of Sam. "It's okay. We'll get you to the hospital and have that stitched up."

"It wasn't Belle's fault."

I seethed with anger. "For two cents I'd send that filly back to Chase Eversoll's. This whole thing is his fault."

Dad and Sam both looked at me in astonishment.

"You can't blame Chase, Cassie," Dad lectured.

But I did. I blamed him for everything.

chapter

EIGHT

The hospital didn't bother me like it would've most people. Mom used to work part-time for a doctor as a billing specialist, so the sterile smells, waxy floors and staff running around in scrubs didn't freak me out. In fact the atmosphere provided an odd sort of comfort, a sense of competence and professionalism that made me think Sam would be all right.

I held his hand as they disinfected the meaty wound on his forehead, and then applied liquid cocaine to numb the area they planned to stitch. Sam assured me he felt comfortable and seemed pleased by the nurses fussing over him. His doctor advised me he had a mild concussion and they'd keep him overnight for observation. Otherwise, no harm done.

"Be careful around those horses," Dr. Pearman shook his finger at both of us, making the sleeve of his white lab coat jiggle. "I see more than my share of horse wrecks in here, too many rodeo cowboys in this part of the country. It could have been much worse." Sam and I both rolled our eyes, although there was more than a kernel of truth in what he said.

Dr. Pearman finished noting his chart. "I'll send Kimberly, my physician's assistant, in to stitch that up."

I didn't feel queasy until the physician's assistant, or P.A., began stitching the cut. I told myself I was just hungry and thirsty. I'd skipped breakfast that morning, and with the accident, had no opportunity to eat or drink. But as the needle pricked Sam's skin and the sutures threaded through, I watched him flinch bravely and knew I was going to faint. I'd insisted that Mom and Dad wait outside, but I wondered if I ought to call them in. I tried to hold Sam's hand and smile, but his face looked fuzzy.

"Ma'am, are you all right?" The P.A. seemed concerned. At that moment the door opened and none other than Chase Eversoll walked in, carrying a stuffed horse the size of a small pony. Seeing the P.A. in mid-thread, he put the horse down and stood by Sam. Enraged, I wanted to ask him to leave, but Sam smiled at him so brightly I couldn't.

"Mr. Chase!"

"Hey buddy, heard about your spill." Chase turned toward the P.A. "Am I in the way?"

She winked at him and I felt a stab of annoyance. "No, you may have showed up in the nick of time. Ms. Roberts looks pale; she could probably use a break." I started to protest, but the room grew fuzzy again and I sat down in a nearby chair. Wordlessly, Chase took my place and held Sam's hand. *Too little, too late,* I thought.

A nurse brought me an icy cup of water, and I felt better. "Thanks, I'm just a little dehydrated." I said it loud enough for the whole room to hear. I didn't want Sam, Chase or the pretty physician's assistant to know I had a weak stomach. At last she finished the stitching and called me over to inspect.

"I tried to keep the stitches tight, so there should be minimal scarring. These will need to come out in two weeks, and they should be kept clean in the meantime." She offered Sam a mirror, and he viewed his battle scar.

"I look like Frankenstein or something."

"You do not." I said sternly.

"But scars are cool, Mom. Now Nate Wilson will have to shut up about the burn marks on his hand where he touched a tractor muffler." He fingered his sutures. "These are way better." Everyone laughed but me.

"Well, he certainly seems in good spirits." The P.A. logged some notes on her laptop. "We'll transfer him to a regular room for the night to keep an eye on the concussion, and then I don't see why he can't go home tomorrow. But no horseback riding for six weeks, until the stitches come out and the concussion's healed."

"No arguments on that one." I agreed before Sam could protest.

"Should I get his grandparents from the lobby?" She asked on her way out.

"Please."

Chase picked up the stuffed horse and showed it to Sam. "Well, it's a poor substitute, but this will have to do for now."

"Thanks, Mr. Chase, how'd you know?"

"Word travels fast in small towns."

I wanted to tell Chase to get lost, that we didn't need his sympathy or show of concern, but I was trapped in the small room, and I wasn't going to leave Sam. Mom and Dad bustled in the door, hovering over their grandchild like helicopters.

"Well, you're a true Roberts now." Dad admired Sam's stitches and pointed to his own forehead, where the butt of a rifle had kicked back when he was a kid, leaving a similar scar. Mother rolled her eyes.

"I guess I'm the only one who doesn't think this is a laughing matter. Cassie, I don't know what got into that fool head of yours, putting him on that wild mare!"

Three shouts of protest rang throughout the little room, Dad's, Chase's, and Sam's. I couldn't make out what they were saying, it all garbled together.

"I'm the one that sold the filly…"

"Can't blame Mom, I begged her…"

"You saw how quiet that mare was…"

"I should never have told her it was okay…"

I waved my hands to silence them. "Enough! She's right. As soon that filly's fit to sell, she's on the market."

"Mom, no!"

"Buying her was a mistake."

Sam's eyes welled up with tears. Mother shook a finger at me. I was tired of fingers being shaken at me.

"What's gotten into you? You're only making this worse."

"Easy there, Mrs. Roberts." Chase talked to Mom in those dulcet tones of his. "I think Sam's been through enough for one day. Why don't you two keep him company for a few minutes? I'm gonna take Cassie to the cafeteria for a bite and try to talk her into keeping Sam's horse."

He winked at Sam, and the child relaxed. I didn't want to go with Chase, but I didn't want to stay in that cramped room with my mother, either. I let him steer me out the door.

Once we escaped the confines of the hospital room, I stormed ahead of him, tears stinging my eyes. I wasn't sure which way the cafeteria was, so I headed for the nearest elevator.

"Whoa, there." Chase caught the elevator before it closed on him, slipping into the tight space with me.

"I'm not a horse, don't tell me 'Whoa.'" I snapped.

"I guess I had that coming." At least he didn't play that dumb "What are you mad at me for?" game, as if he really didn't know what he'd done to make me angry.

"Why are you here?"

"I felt terrible when I heard about what happened. I'm so sorry Sam got hurt."

"We don't need your sympathy."

He put both hands on my shoulders, turning me to face him.

"Don't." I tried to push him away, but he stood firm like a boulder.

"Let me buy you a bite to eat and hear me out, and then I'll leave if you want. Just give me a chance to plead my case."

I hated myself for giving in to the warm eyes and the firm hands on my shoulders. "Whatever."

Chase escorted me to the hospital cafeteria. "The chicken's not bad, the pizza's frozen, the salad's probably wilted, but the chocolate chip cookies are baked by the local Baptist Benevolence Club, and they're out of this world."

"How do you know so much about the food at this hospital?"

Chase looked sheepish. "This is the only major medical center for miles, and I'm a horse trainer, remember?" I tried not to laugh.

His face looked more somber as he added, "This is also where we took Dad for his heart cath, and where Grandma died."

"I'm sorry," I said.

I settled for a BLT, cookies and a tall glass of sweet tea. Chase got a plate of chicken tenders and a soda. He paid our bill and motioned to a table in the corner. The cafeteria was quiet, only a few doctors and nurses wearing stethoscopes and scrubs occupied the tables, most reading medical journals and case notes.

Chase insisted on saying grace before the humble meal. He took my reluctant hands and prayed for Sam's recovery, then blessed the food. I echoed his "Amen" and reached for my glass.

I guzzled the tea, realizing I truly was dehydrated. I drank it down to the last drop in just a few swallows. Without my asking, Chase returned to the drink counter and purchased another tea.

"Sorry, I was thirsty."

"I'm the one who's sorry. This whole thing is my fault."

Despite the fact I'd recently thought the same thing, I protested. "No, it's not. I. . ."

I couldn't finish the sentence, so we lapsed into silence as he bit into a chicken tender. I fiddled with my sandwich, managing a few nibbles. Then Chase put his half-eaten chicken back down on his plate.

"Look, I owe you a better explanation than the crud I pulled the other night on the phone. We're not teenagers playing games." He reached across the table and grabbed my hand, massaging my palm with his fingers. I had to remind myself to breathe. Inhale. . .Exhale. Inhale...Exhale.

Chase continued, "I think we're grown up enough to know we've got feelings for each other. I mean, the moment I first saw you in your dad's barn – dirty, sweaty and full of attitude, the tip of your nose all sunburned and your hair halfway falling out of that thing, what do you call those, scrunchies? Anyway - I thought you were the prettiest thing I'd ever seen."

He pulled my hand to his lips, kissing it, gentle as a whisper. His lips felt silky soft against the skin of my hand. Inhale...Exhale. Inhale. . .Exhale.

"Then you fell in love with my half-starved rescue horse, and I thought, here's someone after my own heart. If I wasn't already head over heels by then, when you showed up at the barbeque in that red dress, my heart sped up like Jeff Gordon heading for the checkered flag."

Okay, I melted. I could have swooned right into my BLT, except for the fact my feminine intuition sensed a 'but" coming. I tried to look skeptical and said, "go on."

"The signals I get from you are about as clear. I mean, we really connect." He interlaced his fingers with mine, smiling at me with bedroom eyes. "You realize you shiver when I touch you? Any man would find that irresistible."

I didn't need to answer; my body trembled slightly and proved him right.

He shook his head, like he was dizzy or something. I tried to focus as he continued, "You have no idea how bad I've wanted to call you. I've dialed your number about a hundred times and stopped just short of hitting 'send.'"

I knew I was turning into a puddle of jelly, so I retracted my hand and rubbed it, as if trying to erase the feel of him.

"So why didn't you?" This was where the 'but" had to come in.

"Here's the thing," he sighed, as if he knew I wasn't going to like what he had to say. "I agreed to do a job for your father. You know more than anyone that this colt is his life's work. I owe it to him to give everything I've got to making that dream a reality."

"So you want to do a good job for my dad, I get that. I want the same thing. What does that have to do with you and me?"

"There's no way I could concentrate on training your dad's horse if we were dating. It wouldn't be professional, or fair to your father."

Relief washed over me like a warm shower. I hadn't misjudged Chase's feelings; in fact, he seemed as interested as I was. I felt certain his silly "work ethic" thing would be easy enough to overcome. It had to be, because no man had ever made my heart flutter like Chase Eversoll. I couldn't remember anyone who'd made my temperature rise just by looking at him.

"Chase, I really don't think Dad would have a problem with us seeing each other. We can just ask him. I'm sure he wouldn't mind."

Problem solved.

Chase shook his head. "I wish it were that simple, Cassie, but believe me, I've thought this through. Best case scenario – we hit it off and fall madly in love. I'd never be able to concentrate on Splash or give his training my best. I'd be too obsessed with how you fill out your jeans and how you do that snicker thing when you laugh. Worst case, we have a big fight or part company, I'd be even more distracted, and how awkward would that be? It could jeopardize everything your dad's worked for."

I couldn't believe what I was hearing, it seemed so ridiculous. "So long and short, I'm not worth risking a business contract?" I stood up, but sat back down again when he grabbed my arm.

"It's more complicated than that." He raised a hand to his forehead and rubbed it like he had a headache. "I can't let your father down. This is his last chance. I owe him my best until that colt is trained."

"How about Cliff Kesterson?"

"What?"

"You heard me. He's more than qualified, and for some reason he wants the job. Let him take it."

"Well, I don't know, I mean, um..." I let him squirm until he stopped hemming and hawing.

"Just what I thought."

"Huh?"

"This isn't about Dad, it's this crazy one-up thing you've got going with Cliff. You want to train Dad's colt and beat the pants off Cliff, and you don't want any emotional baggage in the way. Well don't worry about it. I can assure there won't be any, at least on my end. So that's it, then?"

Chase shook his head. "You've got it all wrong. Sure I enjoy razzing Cliff, but that has nothing to do with your family or this job. I just want to honor my word, and I think my vision for Splash is unique. Cliff would run your colt through his training machine and spit him out."

He laced his fingers through mine again.

"Cassie, I don't know what the future holds, and I hope it holds something for us. But I can't start a relationship with you now. That doesn't mean forever. I hope you'll be patient and we can be friends, even work together, until I figure this thing out."

I unlaced our fingers, again withdrawing my hand. "I'm a little old for the 'let's just be friends' speech."

I pushed myself back from the table and stood up.

"Here's what I think, I think if you really wanted to take a chance on us, you'd find a way. So I'm not into being 'just friends.' As far as I'm concerned, if you want this professional, fine by me. I'll see you next spring."

I turned to leave.

"Cassie! This isn't what I want."

"Then do something about it."

"I can't right now."

"Then that's that."

"Cassie!"

"What?"

Some of the hospital staff cast amused looks in our direction.

"I don't want Sam on that filly until I've come out and worked with her. Will you at least let me do that?"

"You're a busy man, Chase. In fact, today's Saturday, don't you have a competition or something?"

"In fact I did. The Oklahoma State Fair with Stetson."

My mouth flew open. "Then why on earth are you here, what about your entry fee?"

"Forfeited. But that's not important. I'm concerned about Sam's safety, and yours."

"Fine, suit yourself. Now I've really got to get back to my son."

I left him sitting at the table with the hospital staff quietly snickering. I wasn't sure whether to feel happy or sad. Happy that at least I hadn't hallucinated Chase's interest in me, sad that I ranked below his contract with my father. I knew one thing, though. I planned to make it very hard for him to keep things strictly business.

***

Sam waited outside the round pen while I stood in the center with the longe whip. Chase, mounted on Belle, ambled around the arena. He rode her without a bridle, letting her walk slowly around the perimeter of the ring. I flicked the longe whip when she strayed too close to the center – never touching her with it, just creating enough of a cracking noise and movement to catch her attention and send her back toward the rail.

Chase lectured as he rode the filly. "Here's my best guess as to what happened, Sam." He directed the comments to Sam, but I listened intently. "I think this filly was started in western pleasure by one of the old timers."

Sam looked puzzled. "An old man, like Grandpa?"

"No. Your grandpa's training methods were gentle and revolutionary for his day. I'm talking about someone of any age who's still using outdated or abusive shortcut training methods. Like any sport involving horses, western pleasure can be athletic and beautiful or it can be ugly. Most trainers do it right, using solid training to create balance and suppleness at slow gaits. But others create artificially slow, almost crippled-looking horses. They'll do anything to force a horse into a frame and make it go slow, because an uneducated judge might place them. To create that effect some trainers use all sorts of cruelties - draw reins attached to shanked bits, sharp spurs, even withholding food and water and working the horse all night before a big show to make it dead tired."

Sam and I exchanged horrified looks. We'd never treat a horse that way no matter what the ends, nor would any trainer worth a flip.

"Fortunately, kinder methods of training pleasure horses are more popular now, but they're actually older methods, dating back to classical dressage. Today's pleasure horses are taught how to use their bodies correctly without cheap tricks or gimmicks, so that they drive from their hindquarters and collect themselves in balanced, fluid gaits that are beautiful to watch. The Stock Horse Association should be commended, they've done a lot to reward correct training and stop judges from pinning dead-looking horses."

Sam chewed a piece of straw. I started to tell him Texans didn't really do that, only cowboys in hokey Hollywood movies, but he was too focused on Chase to listen.

"So if judges aren't pinning that look anymore, why do some trainers still abuse their horses?"

"The Stock Horse Association's done a lot to improve things for pleasure horses, but it hasn't completely filtered down to the local levels yet. Small-time trainers can still make good money selling gimmick-trained horses for local shows. At most lower levels of competition, the horses just have to go slow to place. Local judges don't have to meet the same standards, and while some are well educated, others still don't know better than to place the slowest, first."

I tried not to jump into the conversation, but couldn't keep my mouth shut.

"Why not just train the right way, and sell their horses for even more money? Why not train horses that excel at both breed shows and local levels?"

"Old habits die hard. These guys learned these methods when they were apprenticed to senior trainers. They either don't want to take the time to do it the right way, or just don't know how. Now take this filly," he reached down and patted Belle's shoulder, "my guess is she flipped out with Sam because she was afraid to go faster than a walk. Chances are, some yokel tried to train a slow jog into her by yanking on her mouth, probably shanked in draw reins, every time he asked for a jog and she sped up. Or judging by the spur scars we can see now that her old coat's shed out, she might have been spurred and backed up every time she moved forward too quickly."

"So now she freezes when we ask for a jog? Makes sense."

Sam swung his leg over the top rail and sat on the fence. "But *I* would never hurt her. Doesn't she know she doesn't have to be afraid of *me*?"

"It's a gut reaction, Sam. She's so used to being hurt she doesn't know how to trust, so she freezes instead, or explodes. We've got to show her there's nothing to fear, and that'll take time."

Chase let the filly walk another fifteen minutes, and then he asked me to cue her to trot with the longe whip. "I want the cue to come from you; I'm not going to apply any pressure with my legs. I just want her to learn it's okay to move forward with a rider on top."

I flicked the longe whip and cued the filly to trot. She twitched her tail and kept walking. Chase talked to her and patted her neck. I raised my eyebrows and Chase nodded. I flicked the whip again, a little more aggressively, and urged the filly forward. She broke into a ragged trot, letting out a strong buck. Chase hardly moved in the saddle.

"It's all right!" Chase yelled. "Keep her trotting." I flicked the whip again and clicked; Belle settled into a brisk, irritated trot. Chase's legs hung limp as spaghetti noodles while he chattered to the filly in gentle tones. After five minutes or so, her pace slowed to a respectable, quiet jog. She dropped her head and licked her lips, signs of acceptance and relaxation.

Chase quit immediately, asking me to halt the filly. Sam brought the bag of carrots he had waiting. We all praised Belle and fed her the treats.

"She needs lots of repetition with this exercise. Eventually we'll put the bridle back on, and she'll have confidence we're not going to hurt her. I don't want you two doing this by yourselves, not yet. After a couple more sessions, Sam, you should be able to take the longe whip with your mom riding."

"Thanks, Mr. Chase." Sam turned to me. "See Mom, what if we'd sold her? She might have ended up back at the meat auction. She just needed some understanding."

"Maybe so, Sam."

Chase stripped the saddle off Belle's back. "My guess is she ended up on the auction block because she blew a mental fuse, refusing to submit to the spurring and yanking. Some fillies just need a gentle hand."

He winked at me but I pretended not to notice. I was one filly who wasn't falling for a bag of carrots and a few soothing words whispered in my ears.

***

We saw little of Chase after that. The fall fair circuit consumed his time, which was fine by me. At least that's what I told myself.

October blew by, and then Thanksgiving came and went, leaving me brooding over the problem of Christmas. Sam's list contained only one item, a pair of real cowboy boots, and I had no way of affording even a modest pair. Genuine boots - not the discount store knockoffs - started at around two hundred dollars, and I didn't have that kind of cash. Sam's request seemed so simple and practical, I didn't have the heart to tell him that Santa, a.k.a. Mom, couldn't deliver.

I thought about asking Chase if I could help out at his place when I wasn't tending the ranch, but quickly dismissed the idea. He'd either feel sorry for me or think it was a ploy to throw myself at him, and I couldn't stand the thought of either. I wanted to ask Dad for the money, but he'd already paid my salary in the form of Belle and her upkeep, so I didn't have much leverage there. Mom didn't even bear thinking about. I finally decided to take a gift-wrapper job at the local mall on Saturday and Sunday afternoons, working just enough hours to get the boots, and maybe something small for Mom and Dad.

The job proved humiliating to say the least. My boss dressed me in an elf costume complete with jingly shoes, candy cane stockings and a Santa hat. Which wouldn't have been too bad if I waited on total strangers, but it seemed that every old high school classmate, every forgotten cousin, every long lost relative who still frequented Summerville shopped at the meager Lil' Tex Mall for the holidays.

I lost track of the number of times I heard, "Is that you, Cassie?" And I made up some lame story about losing a bet, or taking the job for charity or some hogwash like that. I had no doubt word was spreading throughout Summerville, "Do you remember Cassie Roberts, the rodeo queen? She's really made something of herself, vice president of gift wrap at Santa's Workshop."

Only the thought of Sam opening his Tony Llamas on Christmas day kept me going. I selected a gorgeous pair at Cavender's and put them on layaway. Two more payments to go, and Cassie the elf would be just a bad memory. I couldn't wait to ditch the curly-toed shoes and green velvet dress.

I felt a small measure of relief the last Saturday before Christmas. It was my last day at the wrap booth, and I planned to collect my final check after my shift ended. Hopefully I'd have enough for the remaining payment on Sam's boots, plus the cookbook I'd picked out for Mom and a new silver hatband for Dad.

I prayed I'd escape the last day with a scrap of dignity, and that the two people I most wanted *not* to see me in an elf outfit would shop elsewhere this season. I shown have known Cassie Roberts didn't possess that sort of luck.

As the day wore on our booth became frantically busy. I wrapped packages as quickly as I could, hardly sparing time to wish the customers "Merry Christmas." I wrapped bathrobes, bottles of perfume, stuffed animals, clothes, toys, kitchen gadgets, and strangest of all, a bag of kitty litter (I didn't ask questions). All went relatively smooth until an open ring box with the largest ruby I'd ever seen was thrust in front of me, even though I was in the middle of wrapping a Disco-Beat Dancing Bear. I thrust the garish ring back at the customer, "Excuse me, Sir."

I froze when I looked up and saw Cliff Kesterson, larger than life, smiling as I pushed the ring toward him.

"What do you think, Cassie? Or should I say Mrs. Claus?" Everyone in line laughed in good-natured humor. I honestly couldn't tell if he was cracking a harmless joke or making fun of me. I still hadn't forgiven his remarks at the barbecue, although I now blamed Chase Eversoll just as much.

"I'll have you know that I'm not Mrs. Claus." I decided to play it off, jerking a thumb over my shoulder at my co-worker Belinda in her white wig, spectacles and sour expression, "she is."

Cliff roared.

"This is too rich, even for you. Seriously, you think Mandie's gonna like her Christmas present?" He looked at me with the hound dog eyes I remembered from high school. I stared at the huge red ring and had to admit it was beautiful. It shone a rich, deep, multi-faceted claret color, apparently natural and not lab created. I figured maybe I could kill Cliff with kindness.

"Any woman would be thrilled with a ring like that."

"Glad you like it. Now how about wrapping it up for me? Pick some pretty paper you think will suit Mandie."

I thought it couldn't get any worse, standing there wrapping Mandie Kesterson's Christmas gift, which probably cost more than my family's net worth. But it did get worse. As Cliff supervised my wrap job, a familiar figure stepped in line behind him.

"Well, Merry Christmas, Kesterson."

Cliff turned around to face Chase. *God, please create a giant rock for me to crawl under.*

"Well, Eversoll. I see you've kept your girlfriend in fine style over the holidays."

I waited for Chase to assure Cliff I was in no way his girlfriend. *Just get it over with. Put me out of my misery.*

"My girlfriend is the hottest thing in the North Pole, not to mention Summerville. In fact she only took this job because she gets to keep the elf costume, and I luuuuuvvvv the elf costume."

I handed Cliff his package, beautifully wrapped. He made a gagging motion and gave me a twenty-dollar bill. "Keep the change, Sweetheart. I better get out of here before I yak."

Chase stepped to the front of the line and handed me a small gold cross accented with blue aquamarines. It was lovely and simple compared to Cliff's gaudy purchase.

"Would you mind wrapping this for me?"

I turned eight shades of red and couldn't look him in the eye. "Sure, I guess I owe you one. Thanks for that crazy story you told Cliff."

"What crazy story? You're the cutest thing in candy cane tights I've ever seen."

I blushed, hotly, too embarrassed to feel angry.

"What happened to strictly professional?"

"Momentary lapse."

I wrapped the cross, figuring it was for his mother or Aunt Clara, choosing a silver snowflake wrap with a sparkling ribbon. I took extra care to make it pretty.

"Here you go."

"Merry Christmas, Cassie." He paid and left. My shift ended and I changed clothes in the mall restroom, not that it really mattered who saw me in the ridiculous costume anymore. I drove to Cavender's, picked up my purchases, and felt glad to be done with Christmas shopping, anxious to be done with Christmas itself. It certainly hadn't been my most stellar yuletide ever.

On Christmas Eve Mom, Dad, Sam and I partook of the traditional Roberts' family prime rib dinner. That, at least, was enjoyable. I couldn't remember a Christmas we hadn't feasted on the delicious rare meat seasoned with fresh garlic, baked potatoes, green beans almondine and homemade rolls. We finished our dinner, stuffed as ticks, and Dad read the Christmas story, not the Santa Claus version by Clement Clarke Moore, but the real Christmas story from the Bible, Luke Chapter Two. I looked out the window into the starry night, wondering what Mary must have thought two thousand years ago, bearing her precious cargo to Bethlehem. Even she must have found God's plan an odd way to save mankind.

Christmas morning dawned with cinnamon rolls, honey ham and mugs of steaming cocoa. I felt excited as Sam about opening presents. I watched as he tore open the box from Cavender's with the Tony Llamas inside.

"Woo-hoo! Real cowboy boots. And they're leather, I can smell it!" Sam pulled the boots on and tromped around the room a few times, then stopped and pulled me into a bear hug. Even Mom nodded approval. The elf gig seemed trivial compared to Sam's happiness. Mom and Dad liked their gifts as well. For my part, they gave me plenty of staples – socks, underwear, turtlenecks - to replace my dwindling wardrobe, and Mom presented me with an especially beautiful red chenille sweater.

"Thanks, Mom."

I embraced her, and she said, "For those times you decide to look like a girl."

Dad rooted behind the tree and pulled out two more boxes. One was enormous and had been cleverly concealed by the piles of other gifts.

"This is for Sam, from Mr. Eversoll."

"Mr. Chase!" Sam tore at the packaging. I felt surprised that Chase had gotten Sam a present, and guilty, since we hadn't bought him anything. Then again, maybe he still felt bad about Sam's accident, and the gift was thanks for not suing him.

"It's a saddle!"

"What?" I asked sharply. A saddle was way too expensive a gift, one we couldn't accept. Dad read my concern and jumped in.

"Chase showed it to me; it's a used youth saddle. It's got some wear and tear, but with a good polish, Sam'll get years of use out of it. It'll fit him better than the adult saddle he's been using."

I could hardly dampen Sam's enthusiasm since the saddle was used, after all. It was plain and worn looking, but in decent condition and just his size. "That's a thoughtful gift, Sam. Don't forget to send a thank-you note."

Dad handed me a small box and a card. "And this is for you. Chase dropped these off last Saturday."

I recognized the package I'd so carefully wrapped at the mall, knowing the pretty aquamarine cross lay nestled inside the box. I scuttled off to my room, telling the others to start cleaning up the wrapping paper, I'd come back in a moment. I wasn't about to open Chase's gift in front of them.

I slid the card out of its envelope. A nativity scene edged in gold foil decorated the outside. Inside, in Chase's neat, precise handwriting, the message read:

"The cross reminds me of our day at the church, and the aquamarines remind me of the bluest eyes in Texas. Hope you enjoy. Chase."

I became furious, tempted to chunk the card and box into the trash can. Why did Chase do these lovely, unexpected things, only to let me down again? The cross, while beautiful, changed nothing. We were still "just friends," or "strictly professional," or whatever we were calling it these days. The cross was just a reminder of what I couldn't have. I started to throw it in the trash can, but couldn't. Instead I placed it under my pillow, where I slept with it many nights.

chapter

NINE

"So this rangy yearling's going to Eversoll's next week, eh?" Guy shoved the shot in Splash's neck; I held the halter while the colt pawed in protest.

"Yes, and good riddance! He's driving all of us, not to mention poor Prissy, crazy."

"He's well past weaning, the mare looks peaked. It'll be good for both of them to get him off the property."

"We tried weaning him. Dad put him in the side pasture with the geldings, but he wouldn't stand for it. Screamed and ran up and down the fence, stressing Prissy, Boomer, Jack and everyone else. Only Belle could've cared less. We were afraid he was going to tear himself up on the fence, so we gave up."

Guy finished the injections, and then patted Splash on the rump. The colt had grown into an awkward teenager, rump high and gangly legs, scrappy and scruffy looking. "Chase gonna begin ground work?"

"We've done a little here and there, teaching him basic manners, but yes, Chase will be making the real effort. After all, that's what Dad's paying him for."

"He's not starting him this year?"

"Not til he's a full two. And then it'll probably be me backing him."

Guy surveyed the colt. "Yeah, he'll need a lighter rider than Eversoll, at least to start. I know most trainers think nothing of putting a two-hundred-pound man on a fourteen-hand horse not yet two, and I shouldn't complain, because it makes for a good profit on my end. But I hate to see nice horseflesh run into the ground like that. "

"Well, I've never ridden a reining horse before, so maybe Dad'll have to come out of retirement." I slipped the halter off Splash and turned him loose. He took off like a bullet across the field, bucking and tooting. Guy laughed.

"Now wouldn't that be somethin,' almost as crazy as me running a vet practice at my age. Speaking of which, Jeffrey's home from A&M; he graduated vet school in December. He'll probably start making rounds with me."

"That's great." I hung Splash's blue halter back on the hook and grabbed Belle's lime green. "I haven't seen Jeffrey in ages."

"I told him you were back in town. Says he wants to get together; he'll call you soon." Guy winked at me. "And this would be the perfect chance for you to give Eversoll a wake-up call."

I shot Guy a suspicious look.

"What are you talking about?"

"I know about this work ethic thing with Chase. You gotta make him see he can maintain work ethic with you in the equation."

I stormed out of the barn to get Belle and found her grazing in a clump of tall grass. Yanking her head up with my arm, I snapped her halter in place. She stared at me with a startled expression, as if to say, "What's wrong with you?" It chapped my hind end that everyone – even Guy - apparently knew about my woes with Chase Eversoll.

I brought Belle into the barn. Guy grabbed a syringe. "Coggins on this one?"

"Yeah, I guess. Sam thinks he might try to show her at the saddle club."

"Okay." Guy inserted the syringe and drew the blood to send to the lab. Then he grabbed a pencil and sketched out the mare's markings for the paperwork.

"She looks a good sight better than when she got here."

I nodded my head and smiled, despite my chagrin. Her spring coat had grown in a rich, dappled gold, much darker than the faded cream she'd worn for fall and winter. Most likely a product of vitamin and coat supplements, and

Sam's meticulous grooming. With the darker coat, her blaze and four white socks became visible, adding some flash to her appearance. Filled out and muscled from regular riding, she looked like a far cry from the scrawny, dull creature of eight months ago.

"Yeah, she's done Sam and I proud."

He injected the filly with a regimen of spring shots. "I didn't mean to set you off, you know. I'm just telling you what to do from a man's perspective if you want the Eversoll boy."

"I thought men didn't like games?"

"We may not like them, but that don't mean they're not effective. You show up on the town with Jeffrey a few times and see if that doesn't make Eversoll's blood boil."

"Jeffrey's like, a million years younger than me!"

"Have you looked in a mirror lately? And Jeff's twenty-seven, that's not so far a stretch."

I patted the old vet on the back. "You do me good, Guy. Maybe I'll try it, but I doubt Chase will care. I've hardly heard a word from him since Christmas."

"Well, he's smart to stay away. Those tight britches would blow that work ethic of his right out the window."

"Very funny." I wondered if Guy could be right about Chase, if Jeff and I going out would make him jealous, of if he'd even care.

Whatever the case, Guy was true to his word. Jeffrey called the next day. Mom answered the phone and seemed startled at first, then expressed pleasant surprise.

"Jeffrey Deavers! We haven't seen you in ages. How proud your parents must be, another vet in the family. Yes of course you can talk to Cassie, she's right here."

I sat at the kitchen table slicing strawberries, so I wiped the sticky juice off my fingers with a paper towel before making a grab for the phone.

"Long time, Jeffrey."

"Cass! It's been forever."

"You were practically in diapers, I think."

"Oh, come on, I wasn't that little. I was old enough to crush on the Tri-County Fair Rodeo Queen."

"Ugh. These days I'm more of an elf."

"What?"

"Nothing, I'll tell you about it some time."

"How about this Friday? I haven't been in town long enough to reconnect with anyone, and Dad's made me take all the after-hours and weekend calls."

"No wonder he enjoys having you home. Well, believe me, my social calendar's wide open. But Jeff - "

"Yeah?"

"You're not just asking me out because your dad put you up to it, are you? He has this stupid idea…"

"That taking you out will send Chase Eversoll into a jealous rage, I know. But seriously, I've got nothing better to do, and I'd love to catch up. I just hope Eversoll doesn't get too steamed. That guy's enormous, and I'd rather not get on his bad side."

"I don't think he'd beat anyone up on my account, except Cliff Kesterson, but I'll save that story for Friday."

"Okay then, pick you up at six?"

"A date."

I hung up the phone, feeling a pleasant sense of anticipation. No butterflies or romantic inklings - Jeffrey Deavers and I had grown up together; he was the little brother I never had. It would just be good to hang out with someone closer to my own age, not to mention have something to do on Friday night.

Back in Virginia, Friday and Saturday nights had been filled with dates and parties, dancing and clubs. Since returning to Texas, my nightlife consisted of filing my nails, doing laundry and on particularly horrendous occasions, watching Lawrence Welk reruns. (My parents owned one television and Dad controlled the remote.) Jeffrey had thrown me a lifeline, and I intended to grab it.

Mom and Dad greeted Jeff enthusiastically when he arrived at the door. Dad congratulated him on vet school, while Mom fussed over what a big strapping guy he'd grown into. Jeff had once been a skinny, tow-headed freckle-face who trailed along after his dad on vet calls, even at a tender age assisting his father with veterinary work. Our family felt pleased that he'd followed in his dad's footsteps; it seemed right that the Roberts' horses should always have a Deavers to look after them.

I hugged Jeff, thinking that the past decade or so had treated him well. He wasn't tall, but broad shouldered and muscular, and his kind farm-boy face, if not handsome, certainly possessed appeal. His freckles had faded and his hair darkened to sandy brown, but his hazel eyes were gentle as ever.

"It's great to see you!"

Sam tugged on my arm, begging introduction. I put my arm around him.

"Jeff, this is my son, Sam."

"Hey Sam, glad you came home to Texas with your mama."

Sam shook his hand like a man.

"Thanks, me too. Nice to meet you. Your dad's the best vet ever."

"I'll agree with you on that one. And by the way, he thinks a lot of that colt of yours…Splash, I think he said his name was?"

Sam beamed; Jeff had found the way to his heart and quick. I felt relieved. Sam had pushed pretty hard for Chase and I to become a couple, so I wasn't sure how he'd react to my "date" with Jeff. But being the vet's son gave Jeff no small amount of clout. *Good.*

"Well, guess we'd better be off."

Jeff drove a shiny new truck, a graduation present from his parents. It was my favorite color, a deep, dark blue.

"Nice ride, I'm jealous. Makes me wish I would've gone to college."

"Yeah, I was shocked when Mom and Dad went all out, but Dad had ulterior motives. Now I don't have any excuse for not taking his emergency calls." Jeff patted the steering wheel affectionately. "Of course Bessie here's worth it."

I laughed. Jeff was exactly the sort of guy to name his vehicle.

Jeff drove to Cattleman's, the only restaurant in town where locals went to eat steak. Most of us could top anything a restaurant dished up with help from the local butcher and our backyard grills, but Cattleman's used fresh local beef, only the finest cuts, and cooked it to perfection. The restaurant wasn't fancy, but they cranked out darn good ribeyes and t-bones.

We placed our order, two ribeye dinners with salads, baked potatoes and cowboy beans. The waitress ran the order to the kitchen, and then brought Jeff a frosty Coke and me a tall iced tea with a wedge of lemon, just the way I liked it.

"So tell me about vet school, I've heard it's harder to become a vet than it is a doctor. Speaking of which, I guess I have to call you Dr. Deavers now?" It was hard to reconcile the Doctor of Veterinary Medicine sitting across from me to the kid who'd followed me around the farm and once tried to kiss me on the lips in the hayloft.

"Has a nice ring, doesn't it? Of course treating patients who can't speak involves a different set of challenges. I loved my labs and hands-on courses, hated the lectures and bookwork, especially Organic Chemistry. Had to take that one twice."

I laughed. "I can't imagine Organic Chemistry having a tremendous impact on everyday life, even for a vet, but I might be surprised."

"Yeah, I guess that's the main thing I learned in college and vet school, that education all eventually comes together if you stick with it long enough. Like, you know how in high school you think it's ridiculous that you have to study eighteenth century English poetry?"

"Hey, I liked eighteenth century English poetry."

"You know what I mean. Pretend, just for argument's sake. Anyway, you think it's ridiculous in high school, along with Calculus and Political Science and all that other junk they make you take, but you get to a certain point where you realize it's all part of a whole, that somehow Victorian literature enhances your understanding of cellular mitosis."

I made a "whew" sound and raised my arm over my head. "Wow, that's a pretty deep thought considering we haven't even got our salads yet." As if on cue, the waitress delivered our salads, and I slathered mine with honey mustard dressing. It tasted good, loaded with tomatoes, croutons and shredded cheese.

"Sorry, I guess that's what you get for going out with a guy who just entered the real world after eight years of college." Jeff dumped a paper container of ranch dressing on his salad.

"No, I like it. Just makes me wish I'd focused more on education and less on Ronnie Baldwin."

We both laughed. Conversation felt easy with Jeffrey; he hadn't changed much from the boy I'd known, at least not on the inside. He'd grown older, wiser and deeper, but the essence of him remained the same. And I hadn't voluntarily mentioned Ronnie to anyone since coming home, but for some reason it didn't seem like a big deal with Jeff.

"Now that guy," Jeff pointed his fork at me, "was a real jerk. What a sweet girl like you ever saw in him is beyond me. But I guess it's a known fact that the nice, pretty girls always go for the bad boys, and us nice guys, well, we finish last."

Jeff grinned and I didn't think he had the slightest intentions of finishing last. I said as much.

"You've got DVM behind your name, and you've got old Bessie, or I guess new Bessie, out in the parking lot. And I expect a girl or two trailing after you, that's hardly last."

"I can't complain."

Mollie, our waitress, whisked away our empty salad plates and brought our steaks. Mine sizzled, and when I poked it with a fork, spurted juicy goodness. I caught a glimpse of its perfectly pink center and started to dig in, but then remembered Chase saying grace before our meal at the hospital. *Why on earth am I thinking about him, now?*

"I guess we should probably say grace?" I asked hesitantly, even though both Jeff and I were church kids and the notion of grace before supper was hardly likely to shock him. It's just that I didn't often say grace in public, and while it had seemed normal enough when Chase did it, it felt a little awkward now.

"Oh, sure." He appeared to feel as strange as I did, and after fumbling for words, we ended up repeating a childish "God is great, God is good, let us thank Him for our food." We laughed at each other and it seemed all right.

We lingered over dinner, and then went to the Tasty Freeze of all places for dessert. We sat at a table outside since the spring weather had warmed up enough to feel balmy, even though it was only April.

"I have to tell you," I said between bites of brownie sundae, "the last first date I had at the Tasty Freeze didn't turn out so well."

"I think that probably had more to do with your choice of date than the Tasty Freeze."

"I'm sure you're right. Seriously, tonight's been a treat. It was fun catching up, and I really don't get out much these days, unless you count eating at Catfish Heaven with Mom and Dad."

Jeff bit into his maraschino cherry. "Hey, I enjoyed tonight, too. I've been away at school eight years, and I spent summers helping Dad at the practice. I've lost track of most of my old friends. I had a girlfriend at vet school, but she went home to Colorado after graduation, and we broke up last month."

He didn't seem particularly sad, but I still said, "I'm sorry."

"Aw, just one of those things. There wasn't enough between us to handle long distance. So I haven't enjoyed much company lately, either. Would you want to go out again?"

That was Jeffrey, wearing everything on his sleeve, what you saw was what you got. Refreshing. No guesswork involved.

"I'd love to go out again. I had a great time, but..." I didn't know how to explain.

"But?"

"Well, just understand I haven't done so well in the men department, and I'm pretty skittish. I'd love to hang out; I just don't know that I'm ready for more than that. I'm tired of making a fool of myself."

Jeff flipped up both palms in mock surrender.

"No pressure here. I just like your company. So the Spring Jubilee's next weekend, would you and Sam like to go?"

That was nice, really nice to include Sam. "We'd love to."

***

Chase pulled up towing a trailer the following Tuesday morning. I'd barely seen him over the previous months, aside from a few token visits to check on Sam's progress with Belle, and once or twice to look at Splash and chat with Dad. He treated me politely, exactly the way you'd expect him to treat a client's daughter.

He still paid Sam special attention, which chapped my hindparts. Why get the boy's hopes up? But Chase wasn't a parent, so maybe he couldn't understand how desperate Sam was for a father figure.

Dad, Sam and I gathered to bid Splash goodbye. Chase wanted to do a few months of groundwork with him to teach voice commands and help the youngster learn how to use his body, driving from the hindquarters. Splash would return to the farm in fall so we could continue schooling him on our own. Then Chase would take him next spring as a two-year-old to break him to ride.

Dad led Splash out to the trailer. The colt had been given a few lessons about loading, but he still snorted at the contraption. Prissy paced up and down the fence rail, and I felt sorry for her. I'd seen her kick at Splash on multiple occasions, telling him in equine terms that his childhood was over, and it was time for him to move on. But now at the sight of the trailer and Splash snorting anxiously, I guess maternal instinct got the best of her.

Chase took the lead rope from Dad. He backed Splash a few steps, turned him in a circle, and then walked into the trailer. Splash followed without a backward glance. We all praised him with "Good boy!" and Sam fed him treats through the window. We all seemed wistful and melancholy.

"Well, then," Dad muttered.

"Well, then," Chase echoed.

Somebody needed to finish the sentence, so I chimed in. "Guess you'd better be moving along." I reached into the trailer and patted Splash on the rump, and then walked toward the house without a backward glance, Prissy's whinnies ringing in my ears.

***

My fingers turned pink and stuck together, but the fluffy cotton mouthfuls delighted my senses so I didn't mind the sticky inconvenience. The confection smelled like bubblegum and tickled my tongue, making me feel like a five-year old at the Tri-County Fair with my parents. Except I was well past five, and it was spring, not fall, the Jubilee, not the county fair, and I was there with Sam and Jeffrey, not Mom and Dad.

"You're hogging it all, Mom!"

"I am not." I sounded indignant as I shoved another bite into my mouth, feeling the fluff reduce to granules of sugar, and then melt into sweet nothingness.

Jeff laughed and handed Sam a couple bucks, pointing him toward a cart where a man in a red–and-white-striped apron expertly twirled the fresh-spun cotton candy around a stick. "Here you go, buddy. I think you'd better get your own."

"You two just keep it up." I finished the last bit and dropped my stick in a nearby garbage can, wondering what to do about my fingers. "I personally don't see what's so bloomin' funny."

"I don't have a problem with a woman enjoying her food."

"Good. I forgot how yummy cotton candy tastes."

Sam returned with what looked like a pink tree; the candy man must have felt generous. Maybe Sam explained that his mother had eaten his first helping. We found a water fountain where I got the worst off my fingers, enough that if we went to the petting barn I wouldn't stick to the goats and sheep.

"So where next?" I asked the boys.

We wandered into the livestock tents. A small child maybe three or four years old lay asleep on the shoulder of a reclining Brahma bull. The bull must have weighed two thousand pounds, and looked fierce from the ring in his nose to his enormous cloven hooves, but the little girl slept peacefully while the bovine kept watch. We all smiled and shuffled along.

"Is that really a chicken?" Sam pointed to a clucking, blue-gray poof of feathers.

Jeff nodded. "Yeah, those are called silkies. You'd be amazed at the variety of poultry." He was right, not just about chickens but all the livestock on exhibit. The assortment of colors, shapes and sizes among the sheep, pigs, goats and fowl boggled the mind.

We passed the rabbit section and gawked at a gargantuan bunny. The thing must have weighed fifty pounds and hardly fit in its oversized cage.

"Now that's a lot of stew," said Jeff.

"No joke."

Sam wandered ahead and stopped to admire some lops. A pretty strawberry-blonde girl in twin French braids called his name.

"Hey, Sam!"

"Leila. Is that your rabbit?"

She cuddled a gray bunny in her lap.

"Yeah, he's one of the litter I raised. I got third prize in the lops. You wanna hold him?" Sam nodded and she passed the rabbit.

"He won't scratch or bite, will he?" I asked. I let Sam ride thousand-pound equines despite his disastrous spill on Belle, but I wasn't familiar with large rodents, and I didn't like the look of those big buckteeth peeking out from under the pink, twitching nose.

"He's tame, Ms. Roberts. All of them are. I wouldn't sell a rabbit that bites or scratches."

So the bunnies were for *sale*.

I realized we were dealing with a clever little livestock trader. Judging by the look on Sam's face as he cradled the ball of fur, Leila had him wrapped around the rabbit's foot.

"You two know each other from school?" Sam flushed a little, but Leila seemed quite comfortable.

"We've got Earth Science and English together. Sam's my lab partner."

"How nice."

I wasn't sure if I meant it or not. I supposed it was nice that the opposite sex found Sam appealing enough to partner in science; at the same time I wasn't sure I was ready for girls to notice him, especially cute girls with turquoise eyes and titian hair.

Jeffrey asked the kids about their science experiments while Sam stroked the animal's coat. Inevitably, Sam's blue eyes rose to mine and locked.

"Mom, can I have a rabbit?"

I stroked the bunny's droopy ears, which felt like silk.

"He's cute, Sam, but what on earth do we need with a rabbit? We own more than our share of critters."

Sam and I shared the same weakness for animals, so he knew I was a sucker for anything with fluff and whiskers. He also knew how to play on my single-mom guilt complex. I fumbled for a good argument.

"We don't have a cage."

Jeff looked at me apologetically. "You'll probably shoot me for this, but Dad and I've got some old small animal cages at his office. I'm sure you could have one."

Sam brightened and I scowled.

"You're right. I am going to shoot you."

"I'll buy his food out of my allowance. Please, Mom."

I turned from Sam toward the young temptress.

"Leila, you wouldn't know if that rabbit's male or female, would you? I absolutely do not want baby bunnies."

"Oh, he's a boy, Ms. Roberts."

I turned to Jeff, raising my eyebrows.

He shrugged his shoulders. "Hard to tell when they're babies." He took the rabbit from Sam and poked at the poor animal's private parts. The rabbit endured the rude exam placidly. "I think she may be right."

We ended up the proud owners of a lop-eared rabbit. What I lacked in liquid cash I made up for in pets. Fortunately Leila gave us the "friend" discount and only took us for fifteen dollars. Sam droned on and on about the bargain.

We left the rabbit with Leila to avoid carting him around the fairgrounds. Jeff opened up a map with the day's schedule posted.

"Now that you've bought yourselves some livestock," - *if looks could kill* - "anyone interested in watching the quarter horse show in ring B?"

"Me." Sam waved his hand. "If I'm going to compete this year, I need to watch for experience. Although I wish Mom would let me try speed events instead of boring old western horsemanship."

"You *might* be showing Belle this year," I cautioned, "I still haven't made up my mind on that one. And it'll be a definite 'no' if you mention speed events again."

Sam started to protest, but in the wake of his rabbit victory, wisely shut up before trying my patience. We made our way through the midway section of dizzying, poorly-constructed carnival rides to the other side of the grounds, which housed a large indoor equestrian arena. During the Jubilee, the complex hosted horse show classes during the day and rodeo events by night.

We caught the horse show during a lull, as riders in both western and hunter tack schooled in the arena, careening in both directions, trotting and cantering in an apparent free-for-all. One of the riders on a seal brown horse caught our attention. Sam flew towards the arena rail.

"Mr. Chase!"

"Sam…" I called him back but it was useless, Chase had spotted Sam and rode toward the fence. Jeff elbowed me and for about the hundredth time that day, I wanted to kill him. There was nothing to do but follow Sam toward the arena. Sam stood petting Chase's horse through the rails.

"You showing today?" Sam asked.

"Yeah, this is Grizzly." Chase nodded to Jeff and I, and if he experienced any displeasure at seeing us together, he didn't let on. "Hey Cassie, hey Jeff. Nice day for a Jubilee."

"Beautiful day," Jeffrey looked at me pointedly, and then gestured toward the hind leg of Chase's mount. "That the gelding I injected last week?"

"He is," Chase nodded. "And his stifle hasn't slipped once since the injection. I owe you."

"Nah." Jeff shook his head. "If I remember right, I charged you a pretty penny for that shot."

The men laughed good-naturedly, without any trace of the cynicism exchanged between Chase and Cliff.

"Sam was hoping to catch the western horsemanship class," I said.

Chase pulled his hat off and used it to fan himself. "Finished over an hour ago, sorry. Everything's wrapped up except the show jumping and reining championships."

"Aw." Sam said.

"That's what you get for tying us up for an hour in the flipping rabbit tent," I folded my arms.

Chase raised his eyebrows as Jeff muttered "There she goes again."

"It's a long story." I added.

Sam wisely changed the subject. "How's Splash?"

"He's settled in with the younger bachelors. That horse is a real scrapper."

"I hope they haven't tried to clean his clock, even though he probably deserves it." I worried about Splash in the field with those young stallions.

"He's got a few nicks from pecking order scuffles, nothing more. I promise you, he's fine."

Sam asked if Chase was competing in the reining championship.

"I am. We made the finals. Jumping's next, reining starts in a couple hours if you want to stick around." Chase looked hopeful, and I wondered if he wanted the chance to show off.

Sam asked if we could stay. I shook my head "no."

"We've already been here a long time, Sam, and we better get that rabbit of yours home. Plus we have to stop by Jeff's for a cage."

Sam and Chase's faces both fell. Jeff put one hand on my shoulder, and his other hand on Sam's.

"Good luck, Chase, but I reckon the lady's right. I better run them by the feed and seed for some rabbit pellets before they close."

We said goodbye, leaving Chase slumped on the gelding with a befuddled look on his face. I wondered if it bothered him, seeing Jeff and I together. Chase certainly hadn't seemed flustered, but he hadn't looked real thrilled, either.

Fact is, I wanted to stay and watch him compete. But I'd rather go buy bunny pellets than let him know it.

chapter

TEN

Dad came down with a summer cold, complete with fever, sore throat, and runny nose. He suffered for two days, and on the third day Mom carted him to the doctor, who prescribed antibiotics, excessive fluids and rest. Mom warned Sam and I to keep the house quiet and "not raise any ruckus," which was plain silly because we stayed outside most of the time anyway, and neither Sam nor I ever made much in the way of ruckus. But Dad did feel miserable, so we didn't argue.

On the morning of day-four Dad summoned me to his bedside. His forehead beaded with sweat, and his nose glowed red from all the blowing. I felt bad for him.

"Sorry you're feeling so crummy. Anything I can do?"

Dad reached for a Puff's and honked into it.

"Actually, yes," he said between sneezes. "I promised Chase I'd come out this week and see what he's done with Splash. Obviously I'm not going to make it out there. Would you go check on him?"

"Sure it can't wait 'til next week? You'll be better by then."

"Chase is going out of town to look at a horse for a client, and I don't want to wait that long."

I didn't have the heart to fuss with him. "Oh, all right."

Dad rehashed directions for me because I couldn't remember how we finally found Chase's place the last time. Mapquest didn't recognize his address. Dad said he'd call and give Chase a heads-up, so I set off with my scribblings in hand.

The drive felt a lot different than the one I'd taken a year or so ago, filled with curiosity about the cute horse trainer. Now I knew he was just another jerk caught up in cowboy pursuits and getting the best of Cliff. *Who needs that?*

Unfortunately needing and wanting were two different things.

When I pulled up in front of the trailer, I saw Splash trotting lazy circles in a round pen near the pasture. Chase stood in the center with an old longe whip. He raised a hand in greeting, and I ambled over to the fence.

"Hi." I didn't sound very enthusiastic, although I had to admit Splash looked great. I could tell he'd firmed up, and his coat gleamed like red flame. "Splash looks nice."

"He's coming along." Chase nodded as Splash continued jogging. "Come on in here and I'll show you some of what I've been working on. Sorry to hear your dad's under the weather."

"Not any weather to be under," I pointed to the bright sun, "but he's got a pretty bad bug."

"I could tell by his voice. Hope he feels better soon."

"Thanks."

I entered the pen and walked to the center where Chase stood. Wet spots on his tee shirt testified to the heat of the day, and I felt smug, cool, and comfortable in my shorts and halter top.

"Where's Sam?" He didn't look at me when he spoke.

"At the lake with friends. If Dad had sprung this on me sooner, I'd have brought him with me."

Chase shrugged. "Well, tell him I missed him."

So this was how we were going to play it - cordial, polite, and stone cold. Well, I could hang. He wouldn't find a warm spot on my ice wall.

Splash stopped his trotting and stared at us, as if to say "Remember me?"

"Okay, fella, time to do some work." Chase slapped the whip against his jeans, and Splash snapped to attention. His pace picked up to a businesslike, working trot.

"I didn't think reining patterns included trotting?"

"They don't, but it's good conditioning, and any ranch horse ought to have a decent trot." He sounded defensive.

"Okay, whatever, looks good."

Chase snapped the whip against his thigh again and Splash picked up a lope. The lope seemed smooth and collected. After a few laps at that pace, Chase made kissing sounds with his voice, and Splash turned up the speed, moving into something between a lope and gallop. I noticed that once he transitioned into a gait, Splash maintained the pace until Chase gave him another cue. I filed that tidbit away to tell Dad.

Chase stepped in front of me and twirled the longe whip over his head. Splash sat on his haunches and pivoted, and then stepped out in another ground covering lope in the opposite direction. I noticed Chase didn't do a whole lot with the whip, other than an occasional gesture or slap against his thigh. Many so-called "horse whisperers" drove horses relentlessly with flags or whips. Chase didn't seem that invasive, he simply asked nicely, and Splash seemed content to do what the trainer wanted.

After ten minutes or so, he dropped the whip to the ground and said, "Easy, boy." Splash came to the center of the pen, approaching me first, nuzzling me with his whiskered muzzle.

"Hey, fella. How's my boy?" I caressed the colt with affection, hugging his neck and scratching the itchy spots behind his ears. I'd missed the little scamp, although he wasn't that little anymore, almost fifteen hands.

"Well, I know that wasn't much, but I told your dad I'm taking it slow."

"He's learned a lot in a few months. I'm sure Dad'll be pleased, and he'll be here himself soon enough."

Chase snapped a lead rope on Splash's halter, leading him out of the pen.

"Let me put this guy up and run into the trailer for a fresh shirt, then I'll take you to that Mexican place down the road. I'd like to flesh out my training plan for you."

I couldn't believe he expected to take me out, as if nothing had ever happened between us. I tried to sound as casual as he did.

"I probably ought to be getting back. Dad will want a report and I need to pick Sam up at the lake."

Chase looked at his watch. "It's only noon. I can't imagine Sam's finished swimming yet, and you haven't been here a half-hour. Besides, it's lunchtime."

I couldn't think of a logical reason not to go, and making a stink about it would just give me away.

"Okay."

I did insist on driving separate cars. Silly I guess, but it would save a few moments of awkward conversation, and if Chase annoyed me in the Mexican joint, I could get up and leave. I pulled in behind him at the parking lot of a small, brick dive with a red, white and green awning out front. He got out of his truck and held the door for me.

"It's a hole in the wall, I know, but I promise you'll like the food."

The restaurant appeared clean inside, and it wasn't cluttered with junky-looking sombreros, plastic donkeys or cheap woven ponchos. The décor consisted of terra cotta pots filled with red flowers and ferns, and some blue mosaic tile in the entryway. The honey-skinned hostess obviously knew Chase well and directed us to a nice corner table.

"Sophia will be right with you." She batted her dark eyelashes, apparently happier with Chase's company than I was.

I flipped open my menu and buried myself in it. Sophia, an attractive dark-haired girl, brought Chase a Coke and took my drink order. I started to comment about how well the wait staff knew him, but kept silent.

My drink came and we ordered our lunch. Chase launched into a discussion about some "five-year plan" he had for Splash, and I paid attention to maybe half of what he said. Mostly my brain focused on reminding me that the handsome man who sat across the table had passed me over for a training gig.

"Cassie, do you hear what I'm saying?"

"Huh? Sorry…"

"I just told you that it's official. I wanted to tell your dad in person, but since he couldn't make it, you'll have to tell him for me. Reining's officially gone global; it's made the roster of the London International Equestrian Games."

I felt complete shock. "You're kidding me."

"Not at all. Do you realize that's only six years away?"

The thought took a moment to digest. I momentarily forgot my disgruntled feelings for my lunch companion and allowed the implications to sink in. "Splash will be seven by then, and eligible to compete. Do you think he's got a shot?"

"It's hard to tell. He's still got a lot of maturing to do, but he's a mover, and a quick study." Chase drummed his fingers on the table in excitement, rambling on about Splash's odds and the wealth of opportunities now available for reining trainers. He probably wished Dad were there instead of me, so they could discuss the subject ad nauseum.

Sophia brought our plates, and the sour cream chicken enchilada I'd ordered smelled mouth-watering. I dumped an entire dish of salsa on top and glanced at Chase before digging in. He bowed his head and offered a quick grace. The spicy enchilada tasted delicious, and I dipped my fork in a bit of guacamole to cool the heat.

"You like it?"

"You were right," I admitted. "This place is great."

"As you know, I'm not great at feeding myself, so I'm a regular. I've eaten everything on the menu, except the cabrito. I draw the line at goat."

"Probably wise."

I wondered why he had to be so charming. I wanted to scream, "I'd cook for you, you big dope, if you'd just ask me out," but of course I just shoveled more guacamole in my mouth instead.

"By the way, I know this is a little awkward to bring up, but Summerville grapevine has it you've been seeing a lot of Jeff Deavers."

My fork froze midway between my mouth and my plate.

I shrugged my shoulders."The joys of small-town life."

I wasn't about to explain that Jeff didn't count as seeing someone.

Chase continued, "I mean, I kind of figured it out for myself after the Jubilee. I have to admit I'm disappointed, but he's a nice guy, and I want you to know I wish you the best."

I fumed. How chivalrous to grant his blessing, as if he had any say-so about my social life. He was probably just relieved to have me spoken for and out of his hair.

"I don't recall asking your opinion." I pushed my chair back from the table and folded my arms.

"You didn't. I just wanted to make peace, and tell you I was happy for you."

The last thing I wanted was for Chase to be happy for me. I wanted him to rant, rave and tell me that training gig or no training gig, he intended to fight for me. Things weren't going according to plan.

"If you ask me, the situation worked out well for you. You've got me off your hands, so now you and Dad can share your delusions of grandeur. Hope you two make a great couple. Or I guess you, Dad and Splash actually form a ménage a trois."

I sounded snotty and horrible and I knew it, but it hurt – deep - the way he talked about our relationship, or lack of one, so casually.

He slammed his glass on the table. "Are you determined to be hostile? I was trying to take the high road. In fact I've tried to take the high road about this whole thing, and you keep kicking me in the butt for it."

"Poor Chase!" I got up and shoved my chair back under the table. "You haven't seen kicked in the butt yet." I started to storm out of the restaurant, and it dawned on me this was twice I'd walked out on Chase in the middle of a meal. I only hesitated a second, fumbling in my purse for a ten dollar bill. "Here, keep the change." I dropped the ten on the table and stormed to the parking lot with my head held high.

Thank goodness I'd driven my own car.

***

"You're right, he probably hates you."

Jeff twirled spaghetti around his fork and plunged a bite of the pasta into his mouth. I sat across the table from him playing with my food. Gus' Steak House was famous for its spaghetti (not its steak), but I didn't have much of an appetite.

"Well, I don't care. I don't see what difference it makes if he does."

Jeff grabbed some garlic Texas Toast from the breadbasket, and it crunched as he bit into it. His preoccupation with the meal was starting to annoy me. Finally he stopped chewing long enough to comment.

"Isn't this getting a little teenaged? Walking out on him in restaurants?"

"The first time was at a hospital cafeteria, which doesn't count, and he really ticked me off at the Mexican place."

He slugged down half of his soda in one swallow, and then placed his glass back on the table. "You two just need to get a room at Crossways Inn and get it over with."

I threw my napkin down and rose to leave, only half in jest. Jeff stood up as well.

"Oh no, you don't. I'll beat you to the door. You're not leaving my hiney high and dry." We both laughed and sat down.

"Maybe you have a point. I don't know why I'm acting like such a lovesick kid."

"I do."

I wanted to wipe the smug, knowing look from his face, but I couldn't deny it.

"You think I'm in love with him."

He didn't respond, just gave me a "no, duh" expression and started twirling another mouthful of pasta. Our waitress came by and topped off my sweet tea. I grabbed a sweetener and mindlessly stirred it into the glass, and then nearly spewed overly-sweet Luzianne on Jeff when I realized what I'd done. He raised his eyebrows and I crumbled.

"Fine, I'll admit it. I'm nuts about him, okay?"

Everyone – Dad, Sam, Guy and Jeff - all seemed to know exactly how I felt about Chase Eversoll. There didn't seem much point in token denial.

Jeff didn't say anything so I rambled on. "He looks hot in blue jeans, he's a heck of a horseman and not to mention the nicest guy I've ever met. And he makes me hum sappy old Air Supply songs and dream about stupid stuff like Mabel Williams' version of 'Here Comes the Bride' on the Pleasant Oaks piano."

Jeff grinned. "Tell me how you really feel."

"But this 'no dating clients' daughters' thing of his. Doesn't that make him kind of a jerk?" Our waitress replaced my ruined glass of tea.

"Have you tried telling Chase all this?"

"That I love him? Don't be ridiculous. He knows I'm into him, and still rates my dad's horse higher than me."

"He's trying to do the professional thing. He takes this dream of your dad's seriously and doesn't want to let him down. Maybe he thought you'd wait for him? I don't think you should make any more snap judgments."

"So what should I do, since you're all about giving me personal advice tonight?"

"Hey, you asked for it."

"I guess."

"Tell him how you feel, and give him a chance. I expect our friendship digs deeper than he lets on. Just shoot straight and see how it turns out."

Maybe it wasn't such a bad idea. All the speculation was driving me crazy. If he knew how I really felt, maybe it would change things.

"Fine, I will. I'm going to talk to him. But if he stomps all over my heart with those worn-out boots of his…"

Speak of the devil.

Jeff turned his head to see what caught my attention.

I couldn't believe my eyes as the hostess seated a stunning couple two tables down. The woman stood much taller than I, a statuesque, chestnut-haired beauty. I recognized her as one of my rodeo princesses from the year I'd reigned as queen. Her escort was none other than the man who made a secondary career of toying with my emotions. His eyes widened in shock and registered "uh-oh" as I stalked to their table. Jeff turned around to see what I was up to, and then tried to hold me back.

"I won't make a scene," I whispered.

By the time I reached the table I was all smiles. "Shawna, can it really be you?"

"Cassie!" Her voice expressed genuine pleasure and she stood up to hug me. "Chase told me you were a client of his. When I heard you were back in town, I hoped I'd run into you."

She looked me up and down. "You haven't changed a bit. So now you're into reining horses?"

"Not really. I leave most of that to Dad and Chase. What about you, do you still ride?"

She smiled, revealing perfect white teeth framed by prissy-pink lips. "No, at least not often. I'm an accountant these days; most of my time's spent in a cubicle."

I nodded. "Same here. Until this past year I hadn't been on a horse in ages. And I doubt I'll have time to ride once I head back east."

She gave me a puzzled look. I thought I sensed surprise from Chase as well, but it might have been wishful thinking.

"I thought you were home for good? I mean, that's what I heard." She looked at Chase for a split second, and then back to me. "I've been meaning to call you."

I made a dismissing motion with my hand. "Oh no, my deal with Dad is temporary. I said I'd give him two years, which is up next summer. After that I'm heading back to the ocean where I belong."

The words flew out without much thought, my only intention to hurt and shock the cowboy sitting at the table with my former best friend. Chase didn't speak a word.

"I'm sorry to hear that. I'd still like to call you sometime." Shawna offered.

I patted her hand affectionately. "I'd like that. I haven't hit on much in the girlfriend department since coming home, so it's great running into you. Call me at the ranch, same old number believe it or not, in the phone book under Dad's name. Now I'd better get back to my table, before Jeff eats all my spaghetti."

I pointed to Jeff, who smiled and waved. I knew he wouldn't approach the table even if buzzed with a cattle prod.

I turned to go, but not without a parting shot at Chase. "Take good care of her, Chase. She's a great girl, I'm happy for you." I tried to echo the remarks he'd made about Jeff, and my words were sweet, sweet as a glass of tea laced with arsenic.

***

I rehashed the scene over and over in bed that night, unable to sleep. Unwanted tears filled my eyes. I liked Shawna, always had, but if she sprouted a batch of unsightly moles overnight, or a nasty case of adult acne, I'd only feel mildly sorry.

It hurt to think about Chase's arm on her back as he led her into Gus' restaurant. I remembered Ronnie telling me once that one of Texas' few endearing traits was its abundance of pretty girls, *a dime a dozen*, he'd said. I suppose he was right.

I grabbed my spare pillow and held it tight, but its lumpy comfort did little to soothe me. I thought of what I'd told Shawna about going back to Virginia. I didn't want to go back, not anymore. There was nothing for me there, but there was nothing for me here, either. At least in Virginia I could escape hometown humiliation.

Even Jeff, once amused by my plight, seemed finished with me. We hadn't talked much on the way home; I figured my antics with Chase had finally turned him completely off. Leave it to me to alienate my one friend.

Unbearable loneliness suffocated me like the hot evening air. I'd once thought of myself as a fighter with a resilient spirit. Now I wondered just how much emotional turmoil a person could take before they imploded.

I sat up and looked at the hateful, luminous red digital display on my alarm clock. Only two a.m. Rest didn't seem to be on the evening's agenda. I wondered how many sleepless nights I'd spent longing for a soulmate, or more specifically, a husband. Didn't seem like such a complicated request. I had a hard time believing that if there was a God in heaven, he couldn't handle something so basic.

I'm here for you.

I didn't hear the words audibly, but I felt them, like a tiny pinprick, in my heart.

No, I thought back. *You've never been here for me.*

The thought occurred to me that maybe God had been there, but I'd been too wrapped up in my own mess to sense Him.

I sobbed into my pillow. The cries were empty and useless, not cleansing and healing. I needed God, but I'd turned my back on Him long ago, and if there was such a thing as too late, I was way past it.

You're not too late.

I took the pillow and pulled it over my head, trying to shut out the voice. Nothing more than my lovesick mind playing tricks. And even if God was speaking to me, I'd never let Him see all the garbage I kept bottled up inside.

Don't you think I know? And I love you anyway.

But it wasn't true, and I didn't trust Him. No one in this life loved anyone for free. You had to buy their love with money or a hot body or an over-achieving list of accomplishments. Or by pumping their ego until they felt better about their sorry selves.

"I can't," I whispered brokenly, clutching my pillow again for dear life, cuddling it to fill the ache inside.

***

Belle shuffled along the white fence rail. Sam sat on her back, only slight twitches at the corners of his mouth betrayed his nervousness as he guided the filly around the show arena. The announcer's voice boomed over the loudspeaker.

"Lope please, lope your horses."

I held my breath each time he asked the filly for anything beyond a walk. Not that she'd ever again bucked with him, or shown any signs of regressing, but I'd never forgotten the moment he'd crashed into the round pen at home. The queasiness ebbed as he cued the filly and she responded, falling into a gentle, rocking canter in the show pen. The judge followed the pair with his eyes and scratched some notes on his judging pad. I knew what that meant and felt excited for Sam, in all likelihood they were going to win a ribbon.

"He's a chip!" Shawna patted me on the back. It grated my last nerve that Chase had not only appeared at the horse show, but brought Shawna as well. He talked quietly with Dad a few bleachers back while Shawna and I watched the youth western horsemanship class. She continued her kind chatter.

"That horse reminds me so much of Trixie."

I softened at the mention of my old horse's name. "Yeah, that definitely played into my buying her. Funny what nostalgia does to us when we get old."

Shawna laughed in a pretty, musical way, so unlike my own dopey snickers. "You're silly," she said, "like you're that old."

The announcer called the class to line up in the center of the ring. I caught Sam's eye and gave him the "thumbs up."

"And first place goes to Hunter Carmichael on Strawberry Sensation." A pretty girl on a red roan rode forward to receive her flowing blue ribbon.

"Second place goes to Sam Roberts on Doc's Crystal Feature." Sam patted Belle on the neck and rode forward to collect his prize. Dad whooped and hollered loud enough to embarrass all of us. I walked to the arena exit, where Sam emerged.

"Sam, that's fantastic! Second place your first time out." I admired his red ribbon.

"We did pretty good, but how come we didn't get first?"

He'd caught the show bug, all right.

"Think about the kids who didn't place at all," I nodded towards the arena where the announcer finished naming the remaining placements, leaving several broken-hearted kids riding out of the ring without an award. Sam changed his tune.

"You're right, Mom. Wasn't Belle great?"

"Yeah, she was pretty great."

A host descended upon us, including Dad, Chase, Shawna, and out of nowhere, the pretty rabbit peddler, Leila. Sam's smile widened about a mile at the sight of her. *Even my own kid is luckier in love than I am.*

All of a sudden I felt out of place, as if I was the one who didn't belong there. I slipped away and snuck back to the trailer, straightening up the tack compartment for the ride home. I was organizing bottles of fly spray alphabetically by brand when I heard someone say, "Cassie?"

I knew the voice, and I stepped down out of the trailer.

"What is it, Chase?"

"Congratulations on Sam's second place. That's great for a first show. Better than I did my first time in a show pen…"

I cut him off. "Thanks. Now if that's all…"

He wasn't dismissed that easily.

"Does it have to be like this?" His face looked grave, striking a chord within me, but I remained frigid.

"Like what?"

"Confrontational. I'm still trying to figure out how I handled things so badly you can't stand the sight of me, but we're business associates if nothing else. Surely we can at least act cordial?"

"Business associates? Your dealings with my dad have nothing to do with me, so don't be nice to me on his account. And yes, I can be cordial during those occasions we see one another. But I don't understand why you're stalking my family, bringing your girlfriend to Sam's horse show?"

"Stalking?" He put one hand on his hip, wiping sweat from his brow with the other. "After Sam landed in the hospital last fall, I wanted to be sure he didn't come to any harm today on that filly. And I don't know why you have a problem with Shawna coming. After all, you gave us your blessing." His voice escalated to a yell.

"Mom?" Neither of us heard Sam ride up. We both turned towards him.

"Yeah, Sam?" I didn't feel like pretending Chase and I hadn't been fighting.

"Can I go get an ice cream with Leila? Her Mom will drive us." Chase and I just stood there, saying nothing, and Sam added, hesitantly, "I mean after I untack Belle and all?"

Given my current take on love and romance, I wanted to snap "no," but I reasoned the sweet girl in pigtails posed no real threat.

"Sure."

"Okay. I'll, uh, go tell her." Sam spun the filly around and trotted off. I didn't blame him for fleeing the scene. I turned my back on Chase and continued "straightening" the immaculate tack area, but he caught me by the arm and turned me to face him. I hated myself for tingling at his closeness in the middle of the unpleasant encounter.

"I don't want things to be like this."

"Why do you care?"

"I'm not the bad guy here."

"You're all bad, every last one of you. You're all the same."

Chase's expression changed. "Where's Jeff?"

"What?"

"Where's Jeff?"

"Not that it's any of your business, but I haven't the foggiest where he is. I'm not his keeper. Now if you'll excuse me, I have work to do."

He took a step toward me, pointing his finger. "You know, I don't know where you get off. You walked out on me not once but twice, and treat me worse than hired help. This is ridiculous."

"I guess you just can't take a hint, and as you constantly remind me, you are the 'hired help.' Now your girlfriend is probably waiting for you, and I don't have anything more to say. So just go already."

He did. Out of the corner of eye I watched him return to the bleachers and collect Shawna, leaving the show grounds with his arm around her shoulders. I bit my lip until it bled to keep from crying yet again.

chapter

ELEVEN

I broke down and phoned Jeff. Ever the patient, long-suffering soul, he showed up at the ranch in his fancy pickup and took me out to the lake for an evening walk. Mosquitoes feasted on my flesh, but I didn't care. We sat down on a picnic table, and without preamble I burrowed my head in his shoulder and sobbed.

"Come on now." He rubbed my head in a steady rhythm with his sturdy fingers. "You're too pretty to break over a guy. Trust me, we're not any of us worth it."

"You're so nice," I said between sniffles. "I thought you'd had it with me after that night at Gus'."

He tilted my chin up so that I looked him in the eyes. The moon shone full over the blue lake water, casting a smurf-like glow over both of us.

"We're friends, aren't we? I couldn't get tired of you."

He kissed me and I wasn't expecting it. I figured he thought of me as a childhood friend a few years his senior, someone to pal around and amuse himself with. So his tender lips on mine caught me by surprise. I tried to muster a response, tried to feel something besides platonic affection. If only I could transfer my emotions for the arrogant horse trainer to the salt-of-the-earth veterinarian.

I didn't pull away, but I didn't reciprocate, either. Jeff pulled back and smiled.

"You can't blame a guy for trying."

"You're not mad?"

"Mad? I'm the one trying to take advantage of your broken heart. Like I said, we're not worth it. We're all pond scum."

I laughed through my tears. "Yeah, you are. But you're one of the nicer varieties of pond scum."

He held me as we listened to the night frogs and crickets, and I felt comforted, yet still sad.

"Sorry I can't help you," he apologized.

"You've helped more than you know, just having someone to talk to and get me out of the house. That's one of the hardest parts, living at the ranch with Mom and Dad. I've never been big on discussing my personal life with them, and it's hard pretending everything's okay, when I just want to scream, throw things or sob buckets of tears."

"Why don't you talk to your dad? I mean, a lot of this has to do with him and Splash. Maybe he could do something."

"My dad just happens to employ Chase; it's *Chase's* decision not to see me. Besides, it's a moot point. I don't stand a chance against Shawna, now."

"I don't know about that, he could be using Shawna the way you're using me."

"Jeff! Is that what you really think?"

"I didn't mean anything by it. I mean, I volunteered, didn't I? I'm just saying, his friendship with Shawna might not be all it's cracked up to be."

"Why not? She's prettier, gainfully employed and doesn't have a kid."

"She's not, so are you – kind of, and so what? Sam's great."

I grabbed my purse and fumbled for my wallet. "How much do I owe you?"

"For the therapy?"

"Yeah."

"I'll add it to your next vet bill."

"Well then, here's another problem. Shawna called me and wants to have lunch next week."

"That's weird."

"Not really. We used to be best friends, and the funny thing is, I still like her. I wouldn't mind having someone to do girl stuff with." Jeff sniffed, pretending to be hurt.

"Seriously," I continued, "I'd like a girlfriend, but with her dating Chase, I'd freak out if she started talking about how wonderful he is, or heaven forbid, telling me he's a great lover."

"She's not likely to do that; she's a member at Tabernacle Trinity Church. They're old-school; she's probably a thirty-year-old virgin."

My mouth dropped open.

"Wow, what a concept. Score another point for her. But if she did?"

"Then you just tell her what an amazing lover Jeff Deavers is, that he's got the most stamina in four counties, more passionate than Don Juan..."

I laughed so hard I erupted into a coughing fit, and Jeff had to thump me hard on the back several times. I wiped tears from my eyes and he put his hand back on my head and fluffed my hair.

"This too shall pass, sweet Cassie. This too shall pass."

I smiled at him, but I wasn't so sure. Jeff's friendship was a soothing balm, but the ache inside felt like it was there to stay.

***

Dad found me in the barn cleaning tack. I'd mixed peanut oil with lard, heating the mixture slightly until it turned clear, and doused my vintage Tex Tan liberally with the concoction. It made the leather softer and more pliable than any commercial leather conditioner.

"Where'd you dig that up?" he asked, pointing to my old Barrel Racing saddle.

"Found it buried under an old Billy Cook. You know some of these are probably antiques by now."

He grabbed a cloth from a nearby rag pile and soaked it in the mixture, and then began working the opposite side of the saddle as we talked.

"You haven't seen antique. I'll have to dig my McClellan out of the attic sometime."

"I guess if the ranch goes broke we can host an antique tack auction."

"Very funny."

My voice took on a sarcastic note. "Oh yeah, I forgot. Splash is going to win the Games and secure your retirement." The words came out more bitter than I intended.

"That's actually what I came out here to talk to you about."

What does he want from me now? I'd already given up my life and potential love interest. But all I said was "really?"

He hedged a moment, wringing the moist cloth. "I've tried to stay out of this thing with you and Eversoll. I know you two had something going on, and whatever it is came to a halt. I understand that has something to do with him being Splash's trainer."

I paused from rubbing the leather. "That about sums it up. Not much more to say." I resumed work on the saddle, working the oil and lard in with circular motions.

"I'm worried about you. If there's something I can do to fix the thing with you and Chase, let me know."

"It's not your fault."

Dad sat down on a bale of hay.

"In a way it is. You wouldn't even be here if it weren't for your ol' dad and his half-cocked dreams. I wanted you to share this with me; this may be the last dream I get to chase. But if I had to trade it for your happiness, I would."

I sat down next to him and he took my hand, just like he used to when I was a girl. Funny, I felt surrounded by masculine comfort, first Jeff, now Dad. While I appreciated it, it wasn't their comfort I wanted.

"I know you would, Dad, and I want to share this dream with you. I don't guess any of us predicted the mess Chase and I made of things, but it's over now. I'm sure by spring we'll be civil enough to work with Splash together."

Dad scratched the gray stubble on his chin.

"Would you rather I call Cliff?"

That, at least, made me laugh.

"Talk about the lesser of two evils." The thought did intrigue me. I wondered how Chase would like losing the training job to his arch rival, if even his new girlfriend would provide enough consolation. But remembering his gentle way with Splash in the round pen, as much as I wanted to stick it to him, I couldn't do it. "I guess not, although your offer's tempting. Keep your commitment with Eversoll. I'll deal."

He squeezed my hand. "Life hasn't been easy for you, has it, Baby Girl?"

"I'm used to it being hard."

"Well, you know in the Bible, suffering always made the heroes better people. It's a character builder."

A character builder? Character's over-rated.

Dad stood up and nodded toward the saddle. "Keep working at that, it's starting to look right pretty."

I held my rag limply as I watched his retreating form. I looked at the saddle, noting how the leather had returned to its original rich hue, shining with luster. I eyed the lard and peanut oil, wishing the solution worked on humans as well.

***

I threw the longe whip down and cursed.

"Splash, you fool horse!"

The red stallion zoomed around the pen, oblivious to my verbal or visual instructions. Chase had made it look so easy at his place, a twitch of the whip here, a soft word there. I think Splash would have danced the Pas Des Deux from the Nutcracker with him if he'd asked. Meanwhile, I couldn't get the horse to execute a simple "Whoa." He stopped galloping in circles and slowed to a fast trot, his long red tail held high like an Arabian.

"Just act like an idiot, see if I care! Is this what that sorry trainer taught you?"

A shout from behind made me jump.

"I expect you're right about that!" I turned around to see Cliff Kesterson standing outside the round pen fence. He smiled and nodded toward Splash. "About the colt's trainer, that is."

I felt a shiver run down my spine. I wondered if Cliff had mental telepathy or something. Could Dad have called him, despite my advice to keep Chase? Not that Dad ever listened to me anyway.

I walked over to the fence rail.

"Hi Cliff. What are you doing here?" I looked back at the house toward the driveway and saw his fancy pickup.

"I guess you wouldn't believe I was in the neighborhood and happened to stop by?"

I shook my head. "Uh, no."

Cliff shrugged his shoulders. I squeezed myself into the fence rail as Splash trotted by, feeling acute embarrassment over my obvious lack of control. Chase had dropped the colt off last week and given Dad instructions on continuing his training during the fall and winter months. Dad had relayed said instructions to me; something must have gotten lost in translation.

Cliff shoved his hands in his pockets. "I wanted to check up on you, see how things are going."

I couldn't figure why Cliff of all people would want to check up on me. I put my hands on my hips.

"Why are you *really* here?"

Splash finally stopped trotting and ambled over to say hello. I pushed his long forelock out of his eyes and rubbed his white blaze. Cliff looked at the ground and seemed hesitant.

"Okay, here's the thing. I saw your boy Chase at the movies with Shawna Jarvis the other night, and I figured you might be down in the dumps about it. I felt bad about the way I hassled you two."

I held up my hand in a "stop" motion. "Enough. I appreciate you coming all the way over here to tell me that, but it's not necessary. I could care less who Chase Eversoll dates, and as a matter of fact is I like Shawna very much."

"Well that's very civilized. Guess you learned that on the East Coast."

I arched an eyebrow. "Learned how to spot a line of bull, too. What are you here for?"

Cliff didn't answer, but reached over the fence rail and patted Splash on the neck.

"Not a bad little horse."

I tried to see Splash through Cliff's eyes. After his season at Chase's he looked muscular and fit, and his coat gleamed. His delicately shaped head rested on a graceful neck, supported by a sturdy body and clean legs. He still appeared half-grown and gangly, but he was, after all, only a year and a half old.

"Let's just hope he grows into that rump and chest." Cliff gave me a knowing wink and it irritated me. I couldn't argue the fact Splash was butt high, or that his growing chest turned his front legs slightly pigeon-toe.

"Then I guess it's just as well he didn't go to Star Maker Ranch. He would have looked out of place with your perfect horses."

"Funny you say that."

Okay, now we're getting down to it.

Cliff ran his fingers through his hair. "I actually wanted to make you and your dad a last-ditch offer, in case the thing with Chase is too awkward now that he's moved on down the trail, dating-wise, that is."

"Oh really?"

"Well, obviously Eversoll hasn't done much with the colt so far. It's not too late, Cassie. I can send a man out with a trailer this afternoon." He patted Splash's ample rump. "This colt's almost a long yearling. Does Eversoll intend to let him sit all winter?"

"Actually *I'm* working with him."

Cliff laughed loud enough for the entire Tri-County area to hear. "This colt needs to be started under saddle. Futurities are coming up."

"We're not working toward the futurities."

Cliff's eyes bulged. "You can't be serious."

"Chase wants to bring him along slow."

Cliff eyed Splash up and down. "What a waste." He shook his head again, and then turned back to me. "You're sure? Won't you at least talk to your dad? This thing with Chase has to be awkward for you."

"That doesn't matter. This is about Dad and what he wants, and he wants Eversoll."

"Well then I'm very sorry, Cassie."

I snapped a lead rope onto Splash's halter. "About what?"

"I'll be showing against Chase and your colt at every competition. Your dad's dream horse is going to get crushed."

"Maybe."

"No maybe to it. I thought your dad had more class than to go out like this."

That ticked me off. "Dad has more class than what's found at Star Maker Ranch."

"Taking pot shots at me doesn't change the situation. Eversoll's not world class. You think I don't know your dad's aiming for the International Equestrian Games? He won't get there without me."

Splash turned toward Cliff and glared at him, almost as if he understood. The red stallion let out a bugle and pawed the ground.

"I guess we'll see."

"I guess we will."

Cliff lumbered toward his vehicle, leaving Splash and I to our righteous indignation. I'd talked a good game, but I couldn't help wondering if Cliff was right.

chapter

TWELVE

I twirled at the end of Jeff's arm as the orchestra played. I couldn't get over how dashing and unlike his normal self he looked in the rented tuxedo. I also couldn't get over his prowess on the dance floor. My farm-boy best friend had somehow transformed into 007 for the evening. He looked so suave and debonair that just being with him made *me* feel glamorous, and I needed to feel glamorous that night.

Chase and Shawna danced just a few couples over on the ballroom floor, without much in the way of style. It was bad enough that we all had to socialize at the Tri-County Cattleman's Christmas Ball together, but had they turned out to be Fred and Ginger, I would have gone home. Fortunately Chase looked robotic and Shawna like a leggy filly as the orchestra played a gorgeous version of "My Favorite Things."

Jeff and I, on the other hand, cut quite a rug and drew a round of applause as the song concluded. I remembered Dana and could have kissed her right then for all the coaching she'd given me on society dancing. I hadn't put the training to good use since leaving Virginia, but it paid off now.

Jeff gave me a little squeeze and I smiled at him. I wanted to know where he'd gotten his moves.

"Where on earth did you learn to dance like that?"

"I prefer to remain a man of mystery."

I jabbed him in the side with my elbow. "Fess up."

He leaned close to my ear and whispered.

"Don't you dare tell. My freshman year I needed a cheesy, easy A, and I waited until the last minute to register, so I ended up taking Ballroom Dancing 101."

I laughed hysterically, hoping that Chase noted every second of our exchange. By all appearances Jeff and I were having a marvelous time.

Jeff guided me from the ballroom to the punch and h'ors deuvres area nearby. The linen-topped tables were laden with expensive delicacies; the Cattleman's Association spared no expense. I felt hot from the dancing and only took a bit of sparkling white grape punch. It tingled, cool and delicious on my tongue.

Jeff filled a small plate and nibbled. "Don't look now," he hissed at me.

Of course I did look. Sure enough, Chase and Shawna made their way to the buffet tables, heading straight for us.

I searched for a graceful exit and found none.

"Hey you two," Shawna waved. "Who knew we'd be 'Dancing with the Stars' tonight?"

Chase looked annoyed. "Yeah, not bad for a vet and a rancher's daughter, but I wouldn't quit your day jobs."

I wanted to slap the smug look off his face, although the way he looked in his simple tux stirred something in the pit of my stomach. If Jeff looked debonair, then Chase looked steamy, completely masculine in the sleek clothes. I had to think of a pot shot, quick.

"We scored a round of applause, Chase. Your lame attempt on the floor left Mrs. Truman in tears."

Mrs. Truman was our hostess, the wife of the Cattleman's Association's president, Stanley Truman. Their mansion provided the locale for the fete, and the couple took great pleasure in mingling with their guests. Earlier in the evening Chase had spun the first lady around the dance floor at her coaxing, and in the process stomped rather soundly on her foot.

"I wouldn't want Mrs. Truman to have all the fun. If Jeff and Shawna don't object?" He turned to Jeff, who shrugged his shoulders, and Shawna, who said "of course," and then he extended his hand to me.

I couldn't tactfully refuse and didn't really want to. To keep things light I nodded to Shawna. "This doesn't mean we're switching dance partners, you know. Don't get any ideas about trading up."

Shawna snapped her fingers as if to say "aw, shucks." She and Jeff moved closer together and began chatting as we walked away. Shawna, draped in floor-length red velvet, looked like Julia Roberts in the opera scene of *Pretty Woman.* No man in the place could keep his eyes off of her, my date included. Yet Chase looked only at me as he led me to the floor.

The midnight blue satin of my dress floated around me as I walked. I wore a simple A-line evening gown and a string of pearls at my neck. I'd swept my hair up in a twist and mom's diamonds hung from my ears. I hoped I presented half the appealing picture Shawna did.

When we reached the floor, the orchestra announced a break and a deejay took over for a set. Mr. Truman, our host, grabbed a microphone and addressed the ball-goers.

"Ladies and gentlemen, let's give our delightful orchestra a round of applause."

We all clapped and he continued. "As they take a break, we'll turn to local deejay Jimmy Jay of Country Rocks Radio to keep us on our toes. He'll begin with a personal favorite of mine, and I hope yours as well."

A man in a tuxedo and cowboy hat punched some buttons on a sound system, and a moment later Rascal Flatts played over the speaker. Neither Chase nor I had expected a slow song. He held one hand against my back, and I laid a hand on his shoulder as we clasped our free hands.

"*Broken Road,*" I whispered.

"Good song." His brown eyes looked straight through me. "It have any special meaning for you?"

"No. It's just..." I could feel his breath on my face, and his hand on my back pulled me closer. I suffered a momentary brain lapse.

"Just what?" he asked.

I tried again. "It's just...that my road's so broken, if I ever did find someone, the song would fit."

Chase looked confused.

"If you ever found someone? What about Jeff?" He nodded to Jeff and Shawna, who had taken our lead and stepped out on the floor. They looked good together, I thought. In spite of what I'd said to Shawna, I wished we could trade partners, permanently. I wasn't sure what to say.

"Jeff's great." That's all I was willing to elaborate.

We shuffled awkwardly. As another couple two-stepped our way, Chase pressed me even closer to avoid bumping into them. I'd never been more aware of a man's hands on my body, and I was shivering so much that if he let me go, I'd collapse.

"You cold?" he asked, tracing the skin of my shoulder with his finger. "You've got goosebumps."

"Don't flatter yourself, it's just a chill." I didn't want him to have the satisfaction of knowing he still got to me. "Anyway, what about you?"

"What do you mean?"

"*The Broken Road*, do you like it?"

"I can appreciate it, same as you. My road hasn't been all that smooth, either."

"Really?"

"I've had my share of busted relationships."

"Any one in particular?"

He leaned in close to me as we talked, like he had at the barbecue over a year ago, when I'd first started falling in love with him. I forgot that Jeff and Shawna danced just a few couples over. I leaned towards him, listening to each word.

"I was engaged to a girl out of college, a teacher from Dallas. Sweet girl, but clingy and no grit."

"You like grit?"

"Only when it comes in the form of a woman caked in dirt and blood from wrestling a barbed wire fence." My heart caught in my throat, but he seemed to think better of the comment and quickly moved on. "Anyway, I figured out it wasn't going to work before things got too complicated."

"I guess that makes you smarter than me."

"Or just more gun shy."

I wanted to lay my head on his shoulder, but I didn't dare. I couldn't meet his gaze, either. The emotion between us was too intense, and too public. I changed the subject.

"I guess you're looking forward to starting Splash in the spring."

"I hope you are as well, since you'll be on his back."

"I don't know why you need me? I've never ridden a reining horse in my life. I'm a barrel racer."

"I'm too big, your dad's too old, and Sam's too young, so that leaves you." His face was so close to mine I could feel his breath again. "Is it going to be all right between us? We'll be seeing a lot of one another."

"I'm fine with it if you are."

"I don't know if I am or not."

"What's that supposed to mean?"

"Every time I'm near you, you make me half crazy. This is exactly the kind of distraction I tried to avoid."

"Sounds like a personal problem to me, one with an easy solution if you weren't too stupid to see it."

If anything he held me tighter.

"There you go again. A second ago I was melting, now I'm mad." He clenched my hand more tightly and I thought I'd faint if the fluttering in my stomach didn't settle down. I squirmed a little.

"Don't even think about leaving me on the dance floor. You already made me look like a chump in two restaurants."

"Your own fault!"

"Hardly!"

"Is this just a game to you?"

"I could ask you the same."

"You arrogant son of a ..."

Out of nowhere Jeff and Shawna appeared to claim us. Jeff took my arm and pried me away from Chase.

"Enough! You two are so busy with your petty bickering you didn't even notice the song ended. You're neglecting your significant others." He laughed in an exaggerated way to indicate it was all some big joke.

I allowed Jeff to whisk me away as Chase pulled Shawna towards him. I fought the urge to claw and scratch. Jeff whispered in my ear.

"You owe me. A few minutes more and the heat coming off you and Eversoll would have lit this place up in flames. I entertained poor Shawna to keep her from noticing."

"A job you didn't mind in the least."

Jeff actually blushed and made a lame attempt at humor, "And here I thought I was suffering for friendship."

We didn't see them the rest of the ball. I think they left early, which worried me. Did he take her home? What were they doing? The ball seemed colorless and flat without him. In that moment on the dance floor, I'd been so sure that the walls had come down, but in the end he'd still left holding another woman.

***

Splash snorted trumpet blasts of frosty air as he cantered around the round pen. I shivered inside my jacket, shuffling weight from one foot to the other to keep my numb feet from stinging. Blast my rotten luck, I'd drawn Splash duty on the coldest day of the year. Dad, Sam and I took turns longing him per Chase's instructions, but Sam was at school and it was my turn in the rotation. I shoved my barn jacket sleeve above my wrist to glance at my watch. *Eleven a.m.* Another frozen fifteen minutes or so and I could wrap up the longing session, change into presentable clothes and keep my lunch date with Shawna.

Dad's wonder colt looked like a red teddy bear, his winter coat thick and fuzzy. I laughed at the notion that a future world-class champion cantered before me in our rusty round pen, his trainer none other than yours-truly, attired in shabby long Johns and sweat pants. *How's this for a top notch training facility?*

I imagined Cliff and his staff at Star Maker Ranch, no doubt cozy in their indoor arena, preparing their spring hopefuls. Somehow the ramshackle round pen, unkempt horse and frumpy barn chic better suited me. So did the gray February day, which fitted my mood better than the red and green splendor of Christmas or the shiny sparkle of New Year's.

The holidays had flown by for everyone else engaged in happy activities, but for me they'd felt like endless drudgery, especially after the night at the Cattleman's Ball. All the yuletide cheer and well wishing had made me want to vomit. If I had to watch one more jewelry store commercial featuring beautiful couples kissing under mistletoe...but praise God, it was done with for another year. Of course there'd been no present from Chase this Christmas. I could hardly expect one under the circumstances, but he'd sent Sam a small gift certificate to a western store.

With spring drawing near despite the day's chill, I expected Chase would call soon for Splash, and indirectly me, since I had to back the colt. I'd fantasized about trying to get Splash used to a saddle over the winter, showing Chase up by riding the colt to greet him, pretty as you please, when he arrived with his trailer. Unfortunately it was pure fantasy. I didn't dare try because if I somehow bungled the job and scarred Splash for life, I'd never hear the end of it.

I spoke to the colt in gentle tones. "Easy, boy, trot." He'd cantered long enough in the cold, and I was frozen. Splash had other ideas. Apparently invigorated by the chill, instead of slowing down he bucked, rabbit-hopped, and plunged ahead in an all-out gallop.

"Splash, easy!" I knew yelling at him wouldn't help, but I didn't know what else to do. The red blur galloped way too fast for the small round pen, tilting more to the inside with every lap. Inevitably, he fell sideways and flipped over. Before I could scream in alarm, he jumped up and took off again in the opposite direction.

I stood in the center of the ring another twenty minutes, letting the idiot stallion finish his romp. By the time he at last slowed to a ragged trot, and then a walk, his sides were heaving, his nostrils blowing enormous puffs of air. I made him walk for another twenty minutes as a sleety mist began to fall, turning the round pen footing into icy puddles. I scanned him for any sign of lameness or other injury resulting from his folly, but he appeared to be okay. Finally, I threw a blanket on him, turning him out to pasture while consulting my watch.

I had no time to change. I knew Shawna was on her lunch break, probably waiting for me already at the Cobbler's Nook. I could have called and canceled, but she'd sounded like she really wanted to talk to me and I was curious. We met up every once in awhile, sometimes for lunch, sometimes for a mall date or chick flick. Despite my issues with Chase, I enjoyed her company. She tactfully spoke little of Chase but I gathered they were still going out, and it still hurt. Not that I held that against Shawna.

She waited for me at a corner table in the little Parisian style café, looking adorable in a fluffy sweater and gray skirt. I felt ridiculous in my barn boots, sweats and horse-smelling jacket. She smiled and waved when she saw me, motioning for me to come and sit.

I pulled my baseball cap off my head. I looked bad and felt worse. I'd felt lethargic all day; now my throat began burning with a scratchy sensation and my body started to ache.

"Hey Shawna, sorry I'm late. You won't believe the morning I had with that crazy horse."

"Oh, you're fine. I don't have a client meeting for another hour. Tell me about your morning."

We launched into a trivial discussion about my trials with Splash as our waitress brought soup and hot tea, which comforted my rapidly swelling throat.

"You know, this is nice, getting to know you again. Remember how tight we were in our rodeo youth?" Shawna spooned delicate slurps of French onion into her perfectly made-up mouth.

"Weren't we, though? You, me, Trixie and Bandit, and those hot leather outfits." We both cracked up at that one. "It's been good for me, too. I've seriously lacked girlfriends since coming home. It's nice having someone to share frilly lunches and mall walking."

"Yeah, running into you again and meeting Chase changed my life over these past months. Things got lonely here after high school. You weren't the only one who left, you know. Nobody stayed around here except me. I mean, how many single girls our age do you see in Summerville?"

"Not many."

"A handful of kids hung around after high school, but they weren't my crowd, and no one at Summerville Junior College seemed worth getting to know. So I got my degree and began working with Decker & Bright. My life's included no excitement whatsoever."

"And mine's been too exciting, except for the past two years. Funny how that works out."

I gulped my tortilla soup, seeking comfort in the familiar, spicy broth.

"Are you still leaving this summer, now that your two years are up on that deal with your dad?"

I had no idea and told her as much.

We finished the soups and split a cheesecake for dessert. Shawna picked up the tab. My throat felt better, but my body still ached, and my forehead felt clammy. All of a sudden the tortilla soup wasn't sitting so well. I reached for my keys.

"Just a minute Cassie, if you have a second. There's something I need to tell you."

My intuition radar went up, and I felt tingly and apprehensive. "Shoot."

"I know you and Chase have issues, although he's tight-lipped about it, and I haven't pressed. So I wanted you to hear this from me - I haven't answered or anything yet - but Chase proposed this weekend."

I felt nothing, not outrage, not hurt, not pain. The announcement fit right in with the rest of the lousy day. I felt as numb as I had in the round pen with sleet falling all around me.

"Cassie?"

"Well, congratulations, I guess."

"You're angry."

"Not at all." I picked up my baseball cap and pulled the bill over my face. I called on every acting skill I'd learned in Janna Storey's twelfth grade Theater Arts class. "Chase and I've had some minor run-ins, but if he's your taste, I truly wish you the best, Shawna. I'm happy for you."

Maybe she took the words at face value because she wanted to. She broke into a warm smile and began talking excitedly, making plans.

"Oh, I'm so glad. I wasn't sure what had gone on with you two, and I didn't want you upset. I should have known there'd be no problem, you're so laid back. Maybe you can help me pick colors and a theme, and you've got to be a bridesmaid."

It was too much. I felt clammier than ever and Shawna became a blurry image across from me. I pushed my hat back and put my hand to my forehead. It came back damp with sweat.

"I'd love to be a bridesmaid, Shawna," I lied, "but I'd better get home now. I think I caught a chill this morning and it seems to have turned into a fever."

Shawna reached over and felt my forehead with her cool hand, which smelled of perfume. Her expression became instantly concerned.

"You're burning up! I thought you looked flushed. I don't think you ought to drive."

I protested but gave in when I realized she was right, I couldn't drive. She escorted me into her coupe, and I remembered little of the ride back to the ranch, just that I wanted a soft blanket and bed. When we pulled into the drive I left the car without a word and went straight to my room, collapsing face first into the quilt. I heard voices in the kitchen, Shawna making explanations to my parents, but they seemed far off, like part of a dream. My head spun, and then the world melted into nothingness.

***

The doctor labeled it "Bangkok flu." After I spent two days struggling between the bed and the bathroom, unable to eat or drink, feverish and heaving, Mom made me an appointment with her physician. She wouldn't let Dad or Sam near me for fear of exposing them to whatever heinous ailment I'd acquired.

The nurse took my vitals and froze when she recorded my pulse. She asked me to lie down on the exam table covered in white sanitary paper, and then took my pulse again. She forced a smile and patted my hand.

"Wait here a minute, Sugar. I want Dr. Gray to look at you."

Mom's face registered alarm, but she kept silent. Within minutes the nurse came back with Dr. Gray in tow. The doctor, a kindly black physician with gray, wooly hair to match his name, introduced himself and held my wrist in one hand, his stethoscope against my chest in the other. His nurse consulted a stopwatch.

They took my pulse three times before he took the stethoscope out of his ears.

"Your pulse is rapid, probably brought on by dehydration. There's a bad flu going around this year, and I expect you've contracted it. I'd like to send you to the emergency room for some fluids to be safe." He turned towards Mother. "You can drive her? Be better than sending for an ambulance."

Mom said "Of course," but seemed shaken. Dr. Gray advised he'd phone ahead at the ER so we wouldn't have to wait. His word must have carried some clout at the hospital, because as soon as we arrived and registered, I was ushered into a wheelchair and taken to a bed in the ER. Some of the people in the waiting room who had obviously been there a long time glared at us, but I felt too miserable to care.

Nurses began swarming over me, taking blood samples, urine samples, samples of other things I didn't care to mention. They also hooked me up to a variety of monitors; I was plugged into more apparatus than Ronnie's old big screen TV. I threw up a few times during the process, a nasty greenish mess since I had nothing on my stomach, and to give her credit, Mother held the little plastic pan and wiped my face after every hurl.

At last a clean looking doctor in horn-rimmed glasses and a white lab coat entered the curtained treatment area. He stared at me as he read his clipboard.

"Ms. Roberts?" I nodded. "I'm Dr. Drake." My mother shook his hand for me, and then he continued. "You've got a nasty case of the flu, which I probably don't have to have to tell you. My main concern is your level of dehydration, which has elevated your heart rate. I'm going to start you on an IV and give you a shot of phenergan, an anti-nausea med. We'll continue monitoring your heart as well. I think you'd best plan on an overnight stay. I'll have you checked into a regular room shortly. Do you have any questions for me?"

I didn't, but Mom did, so they talked while I faded into a sort of oblivion. I remembered another nurse coming in to insert the IV (to my relief she found the vein without much trouble), and I was hooked to yet another piece of equipment. I felt an injection burn in my hip, and then they loaded me into another wheelchair and moved me to a quiet room on the second floor.

I stayed in the hospital two days instead of overnight. Mother hovered, and yet I felt too sick to find her presence intrusive. I drifted in and out of consciousness, my dreams haunted by strange images, hallucinations.

Of course Chase dominated my mind. He appeared in a vision and I asked him over and over, "Why? Why? How can you marry Shawna when you love me?"

I felt his fingers in my limp hair; it seemed so real. I cried for the sweetness of it. "Don't leave me," I pleaded. I heard his voice utter soothing words, felt his lips against my burning forehead. I didn't want to wake up.

Then I heard Mom's voice. "She's getting upset, maybe you'd better go."

"She asked me not to leave, so I'm not leaving." I felt his firm hand clasp mine, and I slept.

By day two in the hospital I still felt weak, but coherent, and my heart rate returned to normal, so the doctor discharged me. Mom helped me shower and wash my hair before leaving the hospital. Since the day I'd met Shawna for lunch in mucky barn clothes, the condition of my personal hygiene had only deteriorated. I didn't know how the doctor and nurses stood the stench.

As Mom combed out my fresh-washed hair, I asked her as casually as I could, "Did I have any visitors since we've been here? I was out of it most of the time."

"Yes, your father and Sam came despite strict instructions to stay away. I kept them at a distance best I could."

I noticed dark circles under Mom's eyes, and her wrinkles seemed deeper.

"You haven't left the hospital, have you?"

Mom leaned close to me. "Of course I wouldn't leave you alone in here. You can't trust your family to hospital staff, you know." I wanted to laugh at her but it made my stomach hurt too badly.

"Thanks for taking care of me, Mom."

She dismissed me with a wave of her hand. "Anyway, Sam and your father weren't your only visitors." She pointed to several bouquets of flowers and stuffed animals. "Guy and Jeff came by, so did your friend Shawna, and Chase."

"Chase was here?" I could tell by the look on Mom's face she didn't want to talk about his visit.

"He was very concerned about you."

I wondered if any of my hallucinations had been real, but Mom wasn't talking. At any rate, Chase probably just wanted to make sure Splash's rider would be recovered by spring to fit into his training scheme.

The doctor released me to go home, where I stayed in bed another two weeks, and after that only emerged for short bits at a time. I found out from Dad that Chase had already come for Splash, and would work me into his plans when I felt better.

I didn't want to help train Splash, and I didn't want to be a bridesmaid in Shawna's wedding. The Bangkok flu had sapped whatever resilience I'd once had, and I didn't want to face anyone. Concerned phone calls came in and Mom, suddenly my greatest ally, fielded them all for me, telling everyone I wasn't myself and she'd relay their get-well wishes.

In a way I felt grateful to the Bangkok flu, which gave me an excuse to opt out of life. No one could blame me for taking interest in nothing and hiding within the confines of my room. I indulged in pure self absorbtion, alternating between feeling sorry for myself and self loathing, *self* being the prevailing theme.

When I finally ventured out of the house, the seasonal transformation caught me off guard. The last I remembered of the outdoors was the frigid day in February, gray skies and brown grass. During my convalescence, the fields had turned green, jonquils popped up and leaf buds adorned the trees. Robins sang; the sun shone bright and cheerful.

Inside my heart, though, it was still winter, frigid, cold and endless.

chapter

THIRTEEN

I made my first public appearance on Easter Sunday.

I figured it was past time; I'd seen the worried looks on my parents' and Sam's faces. As much as I wanted to remain in my personal cocoon, I had to regain some degree of functionality. Guilt about how out of touch I'd become gnawed at me. For Sam's sake, I needed to resume a degree of normalcy, whatever normal was.

I dug up an old pink suit and pulled my hair back in a chignon, then added stockings and white pumps to complete the look. I found the suit in the closet reserved for ancient castoffs deemed too good to throw away, and I recognized it as mine from maybe junior high. The cut was classic, though, and I was tiny enough to fit into it. If there was a plus in suffering an extended bout with flu, it was that I'd dropped another ten pounds and was thinner than I'd been in high school. Dad said I looked bony and needed to gain weight, but I felt pleased and wished I had somewhere to wear a bikini.

Sam stood in the kitchen popping a chocolate egg from his Easter basket into his mouth. I hugged him, amazed at how handsome and grown-up he looked. Mom and Dad had taken him shopping for an Easter suit, and he wore a classic Navy blazer with khaki pants. He looked so much like a young man and so little like a boy I felt like crying, but I'd done too much of that lately.

Mom and Dad had taken over my parenting job during my illness, seeing to Sam's homework, hygiene, sports and social appointments. I don't know how I would have managed on my own, too sick to leave bed for weeks on end. Of course, had I been on my own in Virginia, I probably wouldn't have caught the blasted flu in the first place.

My parents emerged from their room in their finery, dressed for church, quite the attractive old couple. Mom stopped in her tracks when she saw me.

"That can't be that suit we bought you at Chez Madison's in Dallas when you were thirteen?"

"One and the same. I can't believe you remember it."

"I remember it," Dad said, "because we paid two hundred dollars for that suit. I thought the price was ridiculous, but here you are wearing it twenty years later, so maybe not."

We piled in the family sedan and headed for Pleasant Oaks, listening to Mom and Dad's oldies radio station on the way. We arrived at church early, but found the parking lot filled to capacity. Directed by ushers in suits doubling as parking lot attendants, Dad parked in a nearby field. We all got out of the car, and Mom and I toddled in our heels until we hit the sidewalk.

Inside the pews were packed. I felt lost among a sea of organza, silk, tulle and flowers, ladies young and old trying to outdo one another in their Resurrection fashions. We started the service by singing "Christ the Lord is Risen Today," which felt traditional and right. Then Pastor Barry launched into his sermon, which he preached passionately, sweat glistening on his forehead as he thumped the podium.

I admit I didn't pay a whole lot of attention at first, sort of drifted in and out, until he started talking about a passage in John where an adulterous woman was apprehended by some pious hypocrites who wanted to stone her. He talked about how the religious leaders tried to trap Jesus into breaking Mosaic Law, but He outsmarted them by saying "Let him who is without sin cast the first stone." They all dropped their stones and left, and Jesus asked the woman where her accusers were.

Then He said, "Neither do I condemn you."

At that point I snapped to attention, feeling like Pastor Barry directed every word of the rest of the sermon toward me.

Neither do I condemn you.

I wondered how I compared to the adulterous woman. I tried to make a mental list of my life's mistakes but quickly ran out of "paper." I couldn't possibly cite all of them. Now the preacher's words, Jesus' words, rang in my head.

Neither do I condemn you.

Must have sounded too-good-to-be-true for that woman, saved not just from stones but from humiliation and rejection. I could relate.

Pastor finished his sermon, and I expected the usual "Just as I Am," as a closing hymn. Instead a soloist, Flo Giles, stepped up to the microphone. Flo always sang beautifully and I looked forward to the special music. She began singing, and the pastor invited anyone who felt led to come forward to kneel and pray.

She sang a song called "Come to Me," and the lyrics beckoned. The invitation to lay down my burdens, to rest from my soul-deep weariness, sounded almost irresistible as Flo's gentle voice crooned. I clutched the pew in front of me for dear life until my knuckles turned white.

I can't go forward, I can't.

Why not?

Because... I'm used goods. What could You possibly make of my screwed-up life?

Despite the pull I felt, I clung to my bitterness and bleak outlook. I'd held onto it so long it had become part of me – anger, guilt and cynicism. I couldn't wrap my brain around the idea that I could let it all go and start with a clean slate.

I'd lived foolishly, making dumb decisions that caused my family pain. I'd gone through men like potato chips, trying to find one who would give me a sense of self worth, always blaming the guy when things didn't work out and he couldn't fill the emptiness inside me.

Let Me fill that emptiness.

Flo kept singing, and a few people walked the aisle toward the front of the church, kneeling to pray. The words of the song pelted me like rain, describing mercy and renewed joy. How long since I'd felt joy? Not temporary happiness, dependent on circumstances, but lasting joy.

I don't deserve joy.

Why not?

Neither do I condemn you.

Petrified, I let go of the pew. Sam looked at me as I took a trembling step over him to reach the aisle. Tears flowed as I began the long march toward the front. I couldn't feel my feet; they seemed numb, as if they moved of their own accord. I found an open spot on the stairs leading to the choir loft and knelt, pouring my tears out on the altar. Every mistake I'd ever made, and every wrong done to me, spilled on the floor of that church.

Flo kept singing but I no longer heard the words. I prayed and told God how sorry I was about everything, knowing I'd been forgiven the moment my heart had broken. I could feel all the nasty stuff locked inside released, washed away in the flood of tears. I felt relief and a tremendous sense of freedom.

Someone huddled next to me, and a feminine arm wrapped around my shoulder.

Mom.

If anyone, I would have expected Dad to join me there, but then again, Mom seemed to be the one who shared my ugliest moments, bearing the pain alongside me. I sensed a presence on my other side and Sam's hand grabbed mine as he, too, knelt in prayer. I suppose I should have felt embarrassed, so raw and vulnerable, but I only felt cleansed.

My wounds now lay exposed, lanced and bleeding, but on their way to true and ultimate healing.

***

My heart leapt to my throat as I found the brake pedal and pulled to a halt in front of Chase's trailer. I'd rehearsed my speech a thousand times, but still wasn't sure what was going to come out of my mouth. Something about being sorry for acting like a teenager and genuinely wishing him and Shawna the best. It still hurt to think of the two of them, but I felt determined to act like a good loser. Maybe if I managed to spew all that out, we could move on to the business of Splash's training, and I could get on with my life.

Chase waited for me in the round pen. Splash stood next to him, tacked up in a working saddle. Chase looked hesitant himself, as if he wasn't sure what to expect from me. I smiled and raised a hand as I hopped out of the pickup. He left Splash in the pen and ran towards me, wrapping me in a hug. I felt too surprised to speak.

"Good to see you, girl." He released me and held me at arm's length. "You gave us all a scare. Look at you, you're just a twig."

"Yeah, I know. Who expects to catch Bangkok flu in Summerville, TX?"

He looked gorgeous as ever in a tee shirt, western belt and worn jeans. Although it was early in the season, he sported a farmer's tan, which contrasted nicely with the bright, white teeth exposed by his smile. I reminded myself that he was my friend's fiancé; I had no right to notice such things.

"I called your house and asked for you a couple times, but your parents always made an excuse. Shawna tried calling as well, but I guess your folks were running interference."

"Sorry. I didn't venture out of bed much, turned into a bit of a recluse."

We stood in awkward silence for a moment, neither of us knowing what to say. I tried to muster the courage to deliver my speech, but the timing didn't feel right. Maybe after we'd worked with Splash. I pointed toward the red colt waiting patiently in the pen.

"He doesn't seem to mind the saddle."

Chase looked relieved I'd broken the quiet. "No, he's taken to it well. I've done everything I can to prepare him for his rider, a.k.a. you." He winked and grinned in that big-as-Texas, cowboy way of his.

"Let's hope so. I've seen enough of the emergency room to last me quite awhile, thank you."

He placed his hand on the small of my back and ushered me to the round pen.

"Escorting me to my doom?"

"That wouldn't do much for my reputation as a trainer, would it?"

I entered the pen and greeted Splash. He nickered and lowered his head for scratching. I rubbed his favorite spots, the underside of his neck and his forehead at the widest part of his blaze. "You always remember me, don't you, boy?"

Chase clipped a longe rope to his bridle and held the end.

"Okay, here's the thing. If we do this right, slow and easy, there won't be any trauma to you or Splash. We just move one step at a time."

We started with the mounting exercise Sam had practiced with Belle. I placed my left foot in the stirrup, like I was going to mount, but instead of mounting, I simply bore some weight in the stirrup, then stepped down.

Splash paid little attention; in fact he looked half-asleep.

"So far, so good."

We progressed to throwing my other leg over the saddle and sitting lightly astride. It gave me a little thrill, knowing that no one had ever ridden the colt; I was the first human on his back. I reached forward and stroked his long mane, praising him in the high-pitched tones I'd used since he was a foal.

"Great!" Chase nodded. "This is going to be a cake-walk. Let's longe him with you on board to see what he thinks of moving with a rider."

Chase ordered Splash to "walk" and moved to the center of the ring, still holding the end of the line. Splash stepped out hesitantly at first, turning to look at me with a quizzical expression. He tried to nibble my foot, and I pushed his muzzle away with the tip of my boot.

"He's looking at me like I'm a parasite. I think he'd rather I move my own carcass."

"Come on, he's doing great. Walk, boy."

Splash eventually got used to his human attachment. Chase felt confident and cued for a trot, which felt bumpy and unbalanced, but Splash tolerated my graceless bouncing. Chase asked me to pick up the reins and play with them a little bit, not applying pressure, just making a sponging motion with my hands. Splash's jaw softened and the trot felt a little smoother.

"Your dad should be here to see this."

"He was afraid he'd make me nervous, and he was right."

We trotted for another ten minutes, and then Chase brought Splash back to a walk.

"That's enough for today. We need to praise the fool out of him. That couldn't have gone better."

I basked in his approval, at the same time irritated with myself that Chase's opinion still mattered so much to me. He replaced Splash's snaffle bridle with a halter while I sat in the saddle, and then fed him some treats.

"Positive reinforcement."

I rubbed Splash's glossy red neck. Chase motioned for me to go ahead and hop off, so I slid my feet out of the stirrups. I could have easily dismounted without assistance, but Chase caught me as I landed.

I was about to mumble "thanks" when he turned me around to face him, still held in his arms. Our eyes locked and my breath grew shallow, electrified by his touch. *Why are you holding me like this?* He had to know how much it hurt me to be so close to him.

"Cassie." He traced the side of my face with the lightest butterfly stroke of his finger. I felt dizzy. "I can't go on playing games, pretending..."

He pulled me closer to him, and his lips came down on mine. Hard. With an explosion of emotion held in check long past its time. It was like a dam breaking, water tumbling beyond its barrier with passion, purpose, and beauty.

He twined my hair in his fingers and pulled me tighter, which was completely unnecessary since already a stalk of hay wouldn't fit between us. The skin of his face, textured with invisible stubble, brushed against my cheeks, my chin, my neck. I thought I'd die if he let me go. My pulse accelerated to light speed.

The more he kissed me, the weaker my legs became, until they buckled altogether. Without disengaging his lips, Chase picked me up and carried me out of the round pen, somehow remembering to close the gate. He carried me up the steps to the trailer, crossing the threshold and depositing me on his sofa, still tangled up in his arms. The soft, cushy piece of furniture cradled me as Chase continued his loving assault.

I wanted to lose myself in him, but a nagging thought intruded. I tried to push it to the fringes of my love-drugged mind, but the question begged answering.

"Chase?" My voice came out in a husky whisper.

"Hmmm?" His eyes were half-closed, and he moved my hair out of the way so he could nuzzle my neck. His lips on the tender skin caused me to shiver. With strength I didn't know I possessed, I pushed him away.

"Chase."

His eyes opened, looking glassy. He took several deep breaths. "What is it, Sweetheart?"

"This is a little...unexpected."

"Uh huh." He shook himself, as if trying to come to his senses. "I didn't plan this, if that's what you're thinking. I wasn't sure what was going to happen today, but when I saw you, I knew, I mean I've always known, I just didn't know how to handle it, what to do about it..."

"What on earth are you trying to say?"

"That I love you."

I couldn't believe the words. I'd heard them in my dreams so often; I thought my alarm clock would buzz me back into the waking world at any moment.

"My fever must have come back."

"No fever, I promise. I love you, Cassie Roberts, and I've been an idiot." He kissed me again, and I realized my lips were raw. I'd never felt a sensation more wonderful than my chafed, swollen lips.

He paused and continued speaking, "I'll say it again if you want – I've been an idiot. I should have asked you out the day I met you. Because I've loved you since that day in the barn."

My throat closed as tears threatened to choke me, happy tears. "That's the absolute worst line I've ever heard."

He looked at me with his heart in his eyes. "Is it working?"

"Yes. Heck yes." I threw myself at him and tenderly bit his lower lip. I guessed by the way we toppled to the floor that he approved.

Like an unwelcome guest, the question that plagued me before surfaced again. I still needed an answer.

"Chase?"

"Hmmm?" He picked up my arm and kissed my wrist, tracing his lips all the way to the inside of my elbow. I would have rather been kicked in the head by dad's Brangus bull than tell him to stop, but I reminded myself I was the new, improved Cassie. I pushed him away again.

"Chase, what about Shawna?" There, I said it. "She's my friend. Are we cheating? Because I can't, I won't." I tried to get up, but I was locked so tightly in his arms, I wasn't going anywhere.

"Shawna's just a friend."

The words didn't register.

"What? But you proposed?"

"And she told me 'no.' Turned me down flat."

She told him no? She told him no! I felt a spark of joy, which evaporated quickly as I wondered if I was just a consolation prize. He must have read the uncertain look on my face because he grabbed me firmly by the shoulders.

"She told me 'no' because she said the whole town of Summerville knew you and I had it bad for each other, and it was about time we admitted it, to heck with my professional ethics. And she was right. It wasn't fair to any of us to ask her to marry me. And besides all that, your buddy Jeffrey won her over with his moves on the dance floor. They've been dating for a month."

I felt like God had opened all of heaven and dumped it in my lap.

"When you visited me at the hospital, did you say anything about all this?" I remembered my "vision" of his face hovering over me, speaking endearments.

He nodded. "I tried to tell you then, but you were in no shape to listen."

Something still troubled me. "But Chase, why did you ask Shawna in the first place? Did you think you loved her?"

He shook his head. "I was hurt, Cass. Hurt and confused. I thought you'd end up with Deavers and it ate at me like dry-rotted leather. Shawna was sweet and good company; she numbed the hurt a little. I asked her to marry me on a whim. If she hadn't told me no, I'd have set her straight. It was never her I wanted."

I threw myself at him again, with renewed vigor. He kissed me once more, and then this time, *he* pushed *me* gently away.

"We'd better take a break."

"Yeah, okay, you're right. I've lost all feeling in my lips."

He looked at my mouth and smiled. "No, it's not that. I mean, sorry about your lips, but you can't blame a guy for getting carried away." He tilted my chin up so that my eyes met his. "What I meant is that we're going to have to be careful about being alone here."

I looked at him like he'd just landed from another planet.

"Why?"

"I'm not taking any chances." He sat up, pulling me with him. "I want to do this right. We've made so many mistakes, and still here you are, in my arms. If I ever doubted God, I don't anymore."

He held me tight. "I don't intend to dishonor you, your family, or God, by going about this the wrong way and putting my own selfish desires first."

Are you kidding me?

I mean, we were sitting there on his floor tangled up like old Christmas lights. Granted, some pesky layers of clothing stood between us, but I still felt warm from his kisses, and desire pulsed through me. I wanted to do things the right way this time, too, but I couldn't imagine *not* following my current emotions to their logical conclusion.

I drew his face to mine.

"Please, satisfy your selfish desires."

He laughed softly. "You don't ever listen to me, do you? Always testing my limits. I need you to trust me on this one."

I sighed. I knew by the thread of gentle steel in his voice he wasn't budging. "Promise you won't break my heart?"

He ran his fingers through my hair. "I can't promise I'll never disappoint you, but I promise I will never, ever intentionally hurt you. And no, I won't break your heart."

He kissed me again, and I felt the trusting part of my nature, which had been locked tight so long, open up like a flower to the sun.

"I guess that'll do."

chapter

FOURTEEN

"Lesson One, this is a reining horse." Chase pointed to Riata, a beautiful blue-eyed paint with a mane that flowed almost down to her knees. We stood in the middle of his large arena for my "Intro to Reining" course. Before I could assist further with Splash's education, I had to learn the game myself.

"Very funny." I played with the snowy mane, admiring the mare's flashy coloring. "She's gorgeous."

"My cousin Lindsay finished in the top five in Youth Reining at the Paint World Show with her. Won a buckle and trophy saddle." He gave the mare an affectionate pat on the rump. "Up you go."

I took the reins in one hand and swung into the saddle. "You sure I'll be able to do this?"

"I've seen you ride. You've got the seat, legs and light hands. And you've run barrels, so you're used to speed and agility."

I patted Riata's sleek neck. "*Was* used to speed and agility. I haven't turned a barrel in a long time."

Chase rested his hand on my leg. "Trust me, you've got the stuff. And in all the right places." He stared at me with sultry eyes and I felt a burn in the pit of my stomach.

"If you want me to remain chaste, stop making comments like that! Now tell me what you want me to do – with the horse, that is."

"All right, fine. It's always business, business, business with you."

"Don't even!" I popped him across the shoulder with the end of my reins and Riata jumped. "Whoa, girl. Sorry."

"Knew that would get a rise out of you."

"Did someone add testosterone to your cornflakes this morning?"

"No, I think it just naturally elevates when you're around. But you're right, this banter is counter-productive. Back to reining."

He asked me to lope Riata in figure eights, executing flying lead changes in the center of each figure. The pretty mare made the changes easy, a little nudge with my outside heel and poof – switcheroo. I could have really impressed my old East Coast equestrian friends by throwing an English saddle on her and loping along a fence rail switching leads every other stride. So far this was way too simple.

"More speed now!" Chase hollered.

I made some kissing noises and pushed with my heels. Riata surged forward.

"Too obvious, you don't need to do all that. Just use your body and roll forward at the hip to accelerate. To decelerate, roll back."

I tried it and was amazed at how sensitively the well-trained mare reacted to a shift in body position.

"Now comes the fun part. I want you to accelerate when you reach the far turn of the ring. About halfway down the fenceline, I want you to say 'Whoa!' and sit deep in the saddle. Then follow up with a slight pull back on the reins and release."

I never got to the pull back part. I urged the mare forward like Chase said, and as she raced forward, yelled "Whoa!" Nothing could have prepared me for the abruptness of the stop. I nearly lost my seat as the mare sat down on her rear and slid almost twenty feet. My face turned bright red as I grabbed the horn and waited for the ride to come to a complete stop.

"You could have warned me!"

Chase grinned like a naughty schoolboy. "Couldn't resist. Wanna try a spin now?"

"Why the heck not?" I replied in the snottiest tone I could manage.

Spinning proved another lesson in humility. With just a slight twitch of the reins and a nudge of my heel, Riata hunkered down and sent me into a dizzying vortex. The arena flashed before my eyes so quick I thought I was on the egg scrambler at the fair.

"Whoa!" Riata froze. I breathed a sigh of relief. "I don't know about this." I felt definite doubts about my future in reining.

"Are you kidding? You stayed on, which is more than some riders do their first time."

"I guess Splash and I both have a long way to go."

"We'll get you there." He stroked Riata's fine shoulder. "It's just gonna take miles on an auto-pilot horse like her to teach you the ropes."

"Poor Riata," I rubbed her neck. "You've got your work cut out for you."

***

Every muscle in my body ached as Chase soothed me over a good Mexican dinner. Sophia re-filled my tea glass as I dug into my chile relleno. Despite my tired, sore body, I enjoyed this trip to his favorite haunt much better than the last go-round.

"So your brothers aren't into horses at all?" I asked between bites.

"Not Justin. Jethro's another story."

"Will I meet them?"

"Of course, next Thanksgiving or Christmas. Unfortunately they're much older than I am, so we were never that close."

"Do you like them?"

He laughed as he gulped his iced tea. "That's kind of a funny question. They're my family, so I guess I have to. But otherwise, I'd say I'm not really fond of Justin. He's a forty-year-old confirmed bachelor, completely stuck on himself."

I added some hot sauce to my Spanish rice and loaded a mouthful onto my fork. "Now he's the one in Dallas, right?"

"Right. He's a stockbroker for a Dallas firm. He's a forty year old teenager, driving flashy cars and partying at West End."

I thought of Garrison and nodded. "I know the type."

"Even as a kid he never wanted anything to do with the ranch, preferred sports, his friends and girls. He couldn't wait to move to the big city. He's been talking about moving to New York, imagines himself as a Wall Street big shot."

"Okay, so I won't be seeing much of him. What about Jethro?"

He dipped a chip into his guacamole salad.

"You'll like Jethro. He's my middle brother, good guy. He's an engineer, lives in San Antonio with his wife Annabelle. They've got two kids, a boy and girl, the boy's not far from Sam's age. We'll have to go visit them sometime and take Sam to the Riverwalk."

I loved the way Chase talked about the future, including me in it. Ifigured if he wanted to introduce me to the rest of his family, he must be thinking long term.

"But he wasn't into the ranch, either?"

"More than Justin, not as much as me. He enjoys a spin on a tractor now and then to unwind."

We finished our meal and Chase drove us back to his place (we'd driven to the restaurant together this time). He went to the barn and grabbed a bridle, and then slipped it over the ears of a bay stallion in the bachelor paddock. He led the stallion out of the field and closed the gate.

"Come here," he motioned with his hand.

He helped me onto the horse, and then sprang up behind me. I felt like a medieval maiden riding in the front of her knight's charger. Except my knight wore Wranglers. Chase urged the stallion down the gravel driveway, and then took me on a tour of the surrounding acreage. We passed the borders of his pastures and into a wooded area broken by clearings.

"This land is beautiful."

"It all used to belong to my family. This is the part they sold off to the oil company. They gave my brothers lump sums of cash as gifts, but I took the remaining land, which came with the barn. The oil company demolished my parents' old house, which makes me sad, but so far that's all they've tampered with. Oil companies do that a lot from what I understand, buy land intending to drill on it, and then put it on the back burner."

"Works for you." I nestled back against his chest. He groaned softly.

"You make it hard to behave."

"So what are you going to do about it?" I wanted to behave, too, but sometimes my hormones overrode my nobler desires.

"Suffer in silence, I guess. Call me crazy, but I meant what I said. I want to do this right, all in the proper time."

He sounded authoritative, so I replied "Yes, Sir."

The bay bobbed along, navigating the woodland terrain with careful steps. I felt sleepy and content, lulled by the horse's motion and Chase's arms around me. Twilight overtook late afternoon, and lightning bugs began twinkling.

Chase seemed to be in a philosophical mood. "You know, both of our dads are great husbands and fathers," he said.

"Uh huh." I agreed.

"Well," he continued, "if I could only pick one dream, it wouldn't be to become a great horse trainer, but to become a great family man, like them."

I tilted my head back to look at him. "You mean 'old-fashioned.'"

"Exactly."

Chase's commitment to his faith - our faith – and home-spun, down home values filled me with a sense of security, and…familiarity.

"Ugh."

"What is it?" Chase sounded concerned.

"I just realized I'm dating my father."

We both laughed so hard we almost fell off the horse.

***

Splash proved a quick study, smart as a whip and athletically talented, but sometimes unruly and unpredictable. One day he was giving and cooperative, the next day Mr. Fun and Games. Not unlike most teenagers, in particular males.

Chase treated me like an apprentice, coaching me every step of the way, explaining how to train for the different reining maneuvers. We began the process of "fencing," the preliminary exercise for sliding stops. I rode Splash directly toward the rail at a trot, focusing on keeping him straight when he wanted to turn or bend. When he got within twenty feet of the fence, I commanded "Whoa!" asking for a halt. Initially I used my reins, voice and seat, but in a short period of time, I relied on voice and seat alone.

Dad sometimes rode Splash. He wasn't as tall or heavy as Chase, and ever since Splash's training had begun, he'd been itching to ride. He insisted he didn't want to interfere, just to take a spin now and then. I thought it was a shame he wasn't younger, because with Dad aboard, Splash performed his best, as if they shared a deep connection. Which they did, Dad intimately knew Splash's ancestors back three generations.

I hit an impasse while working on spinning. Chase instructed me to work Splash in tight circles at the trot, gradually making the circles smaller and smaller. The problem was that as I tightened my circle, Splash slowed to a walk, refusing to pivot on his haunches at more than a snail's pace. When I asked for more impulsion, he pinned his ears, turned his head and snapped at my foot. I remained patient the first several sessions, but after a couple months of frustration, I begged Chase to take over.

It was actually Dad who got the first spin out of him. Chase worked from the ground while Dad cued from the saddle, and as I watched, the lights came on and Splash began turning 360s. Not pretty at first, but definite spins. I had to give Dad credit; the old boy still had it.

I didn't understand why Chase insisted I had to learn to make Splash spin myself.

"You've got to be able to do this in competition," he said.

"Competition? I thought I was just helping to start him."

"You are. And part of that is starting his competitive career."

"I think I'm going to be sick." Just the thought of riding against the likes of Cliff Kesterson scared me senseless.

"Come on, where's the gutsy woman I love?"

"Don't you dare attempt to flatter me into this."

"Never known you to back down from a challenge."

I scowled.

Just once I'd like to win an argument with my adorable know-it-all boyfriend.

chapter

FIFTEEN

"Here Mom, rub Angus' foot for luck." Sam thrust the giant rabbit towards my perch atop Splash, and I rubbed the fluffy paw.

"Thanks, but prayer would probably do more good. Aside from being the largest 'mini' lop in Texas, I don't think Angus possesses any magic powers."

Truth is, even if he did, it would take more than magic to get me through this competition. Why on earth Chase chose the Dallas Stock Extravaganza for my reining debut, I'll never know. I still wasn't sure how I ended up exhibiting the horse in the first place. I thought I was simply a training assistant until Splash grew solid enough to tote Chase's bulk around, but he insisted that the colt needed experience in the performance environment.

I'd drawn the fourth spot in the Non-Pro roster. Chase had competed against Cliff in the Open on another horse, and as he put it, "got spanked like a bad puppy." In all fairness Chase's mount was a young colt gaining experience, while Cliff rode a performance machine fresh from a three-year-old futurity victory. The colts were the same age, but Cliff's horse displayed a much greater depth of experience. Cliff had ridden by afterwards, flashing a flowing blue ribbon and an enviable check, telling me "I warned you, Cass."

Until then I'd found the Extravaganza entertaining. I'd never attended a reining event of this level, and I enjoyed the electric atmosphere. As horses and riders performed in the gigantic indoor stadium arena, the crowds thrilled at the flashy sliding stops and dizzying spins – the two most recognized maneuvers in reining. The trainers seemed intensely competitive, yet between them was an unmistakable sense of fraternity.

Chase's favorite colleague was Ivan Jenkins, an African-American cowboy from Austin. Ivan rode a stunning black and white stud in the Open against Cliff and came darn close to winning. Only Cliff's polished precision had given him the edge over the more difficult, powerful performance delivered by Ivan and his stallion, Ice Maker. Ivan and Chase ribbed each other about it afterwards.

"You reneged on our deal, Ivan."

"Oh no I didn't, I came closer than you."

"You had a better chance on that powerhouse of yours. My colt's wet behind the ears."

"Excuses, excuses."

"Hey, can one of you let me in on the joke?" I held Splash's reins in one hand as I joined the men's huddle, trying to look like I belonged, but feeling very much the outsider. Chase put his arm around me and pulled me in.

"Sorry, Honey. Ivan and I were joking about the fact that we promised each other one of us would beat Showboat, I mean Kesterson. Unfortunately neither one of us delivered the goods."

"And it's a shame," Ivan added. "That pompous…" he looked at me and grinned, apparently weighing his word selection, "…fellow is unbearable to deal with after he's won."

I later asked Chase why the other trainers got along so well, but ostracized Cliff. Sure, the guy could be smug, but so could all the other hotshot cowboys. I wondered why they all had it in for him.

"You really don't know?"

"Not really."

"Let's grab a sandwich and I'll explain." We purchased a couple burgers and baskets of fries from a snack vendor and sat in the bleachers, watching a reined cowhorse event in the arena while we talked.

"I'm sure you've noticed I live pretty simply, Cass."

I stared at him. What did that have to do with anything? Yeah, Chase lived in a trailer, but he seemed to have plenty to get by.

"I guess."

"Well, I do. Just like all the other guys here." Chase waved his arm, as if encompassing the whole showgrounds. "In fact I'm in better shape than most because at least my land is paid for. I started with a barn and sixty acres, which is right much." He turned to me. "There's no money in horse training. You ought to know that before we go any further. Your dad had cattle and his army pension to supplement what he made as a trainer. I have neither."

"I don't care about money…" I started, and then shut my mouth when I realized what a foolish thing that was to say. I had a son to support; of course I worried about money.

"By the time we care for the livestock and travel to these events trying to win pocket change, there's almost no profit in it. We do this for love of the sport, for love of the horses, but not to get rich and famous."

It made sense. Of course the other trainers resented Cliff, who'd realized his dreams by marrying Mandie. While Cliff lured his clients with expensive facilities and flash, the others struggled to make an honest living. I remembered Chase's initial refusal to pursue a relationship, and wondered if there had been more to the decision than professional ethics. I wondered if he really needed the work. The realization made me feel tender, and I leaned into him and kissed his cheek. He smiled.

"Anyway, your buddy Kesterson bought his status with his wife's money. He bought everything - from the caliber of the stock he trains, to his level of expertise. He didn't scrimp, scrape and strive to earn it like the rest of us."

I bit into a french fry, rubbing my other hand on his leg.

"Isn't that a little unfair? I mean, if I was loaded like Mandie and offered to finance the fanciest reining operation in Texas, wouldn't you take me up on it?"

Chase growled. "Playing devil's advocate? All right, maybe. But I really don't think I'd want success to come that way. I don't know if I'd feel like a man if I couldn't support my family with my own two hands."

He stared at the horse in the arena, hunkered down on its haunches, expertly frustrating the lone calf it had isolated from the herd.

"Cassie?"

"Yes?"

"Another reason I hedged about asking you out is I knew if it went further, if we fell in love and I wanted to marry you, I worried about providing for you and Sam. I live in a trailer. I know how cruel kids can be. I can't afford designer clothes, new cars…"

I put a finger to his lips, and then shushed them with my own. "Stop right there." I loved him so much in that moment, imagining his insecurity about caring for me and my son. "It's true that money's a fact of life, and heaven knows it's always in short supply. But the fact is, more than anything, Sam and I need love. If love happens to come in a double wide on a shoestring budget, that's okay."

That seemed to satisfy him, but I got the impression he still wasn't entirely sure.

I thought about the conversation as I sat on Splash, waiting to be called into the arena. Sam grabbed Angus' foot and "waved" to us. I wondered why I'd let him bring a rabbit to a reining competition, albeit a house-broken, litter-box-trained rabbit.

Before I entered the ring, Dad and Chase arrived near the in-gate to provide some last words of encouragement. I felt sick, wishing they'd let me bail out.

"I'm afraid I'm going to disappoint both of you. I didn't sign up for this."

"You could never disappoint me, Baby Girl. Just get in there and let Splash show his stuff, we can't ask any more."

Chase laid his hand on my thigh, which was covered in leather show chaps.

"He's right. Just pretend we're in the practice arena at home. Whatever happens, happens, and it won't be the first time. Trust me, this is a friendly crowd, they've seen it all before, especially in the Non-Pro."

Nice speeches, but I didn't feel reassured as the announcer called my name and we entered the arena.

I felt a lack of confidence because Splash and I didn't share oneness. I'd had it with Trixie and a few other horses over the years, but Splash and I, despite mutual affection, never quite saw eye to eye. I wasn't sure what to expect, whether he'd perform brilliantly or botch every maneuver.

I nudged him into a walk, proceeding toward the center of the ring. He jigged a little, probably catching my nerves. I twitched the reins, and he slowed to a smoother walk. We halted in the center of the large arena, signifying our readiness to start the pattern.

We began by loping fast circles to the right. Thanks to Chase's endless drills in the round pen, Splash moved with fluid, cadenced grace, bold and steady. After two large, round circles, we moved into a tighter, smaller circle. I tried to slow Splash with my seat, but he wanted to go, so I had to use the reins to check his speed. He collected, but under mild protest.

I loped him to the center of the ring to repeat the maneuvers on the other side. I bumped hard for his flying change and he executed it, curling his neck up like a dressage horse and changing leads with exaggerated animation. *Ugh*. I wondered how many deductions we were racking up.

We ran to the end of the arena and I mouthed "Whoa." In this at least I felt confident; the sliding stop was Splash's glory. Sure enough, he threw the brakes and I braced myself. I grinned as he slid over twenty five feet; whooping and applause broke out in the bleachers. We rolled back beautifully over our tracks, pivoted and charged toward the opposite end of the ring, executing another stop and rollback. We finished the series with a stunning final slide.

A moment later my pleasure evaporated as I over-cued for a spin and found myself riding a whirling dervish. Splash spun in gorgeous rotation, but I couldn't stop him after four turns. After four and an eighth, I became frantic, hollering "Whoa! Whoa!"

I heard the crowd's disappointed "awwww" and my spirits sank. Chase's voice carried over the crowd, encouraging me. "That's okay, Cass." I jabbed Splash with my opposite heel and finally the darn horse stopped short of exceeding a quarter turn, but I was sure we'd incurred a point deduction.

Splash must have sensed my anger, because he finished the rest of the pattern, including the spins to the left, without putting a foot wrong. He backed and stopped four-square, standing after completing the final maneuver. The crowd applauded kindly. I'd never felt so glad to exit a show arena in my life.

Dad, Chase and Sam met me as I left the arena, wreathed in smiles. I didn't see what they were so happy about.

"Gorgeous, Cassie!" Chase seemed elated. "Great job for two first timers. I think you'll finish in the money."

"You seeing straight? You've got to be kidding?"

Dad chimed in. "Nice work. I'm proud of both of you." He rubbed Splash, and the colt butted Dad with his head.

"I felt like an idiot. Did you see that stupid spin?"

They all laughed, except Sam. Still holding his rabbit, he looked grave.

"You're too hard on yourself, Mom. You always are."

When our scores came in, I decided maybe he was right.

"And the total score for Cassie Roberts and Texas Splash O Rein is 217." The announcer called over the loudspeaker. Again, the crowd whooped and hollered.

Many of Chase's trainer buddies came over to inspect us, shaking Chase's hand and offering congratulations. I leaned over and whispered in Dad's ear.

"So we actually did all right?"

Dad laughed. "More than all right, you came in second. That should amount to a $15,000 purse."

I almost choked. According to my agreement with Dad, my share would amount to over three thousand dollars, more money than I'd seen at one time for as long as I could remember. Dad and Chase would split the remainder. I felt glad I'd been able to bank some money for Chase. Certainly he seemed pleased.

We talked later that evening, standing outside Splash's rented stall at the Dallas Equine Complex. Splash's fiery red coat gleamed in the fluorescent lighting as he chomped his hay. He looked fit and muscled, but to me he was still plain Splash.

"I think he's got the stuff, Cassie." Chase looked thoughtful as he stared into the colt's stall.

"You think? After just one performance, and we didn't even finish first?"

"Yeah, I do. I've thought so for a long time, I just didn't dare say it. But now I can. To perform like that his first competition with an amateur on his back, he's got the stuff."

"I'm glad, so glad. For you and Dad, that is."

Chase grabbed my hands and clasped them in his. "For you and Sam too, Cassie. All of our futures are tied to this red spitfire." He nodded to Splash. "I've watched Cliff's crop this year, paying attention to anything old enough to compete in the Games."

"And?"

"Perfection."

"And that's reassuring?"

"You didn't let me finish. Cliff's colts perform like well-oiled, perfectly tuned machines. But they lack that extra something, that spark that separates gold and silver medals."

"And Splash's got that?"

"I know he does. And we have plenty of time to perfect it. Meanwhile Cliff's colts are peaking early. In fact he pulled one today with a hock injury, and last month in Amarillo, one of his horses broke a coffin bone on a bad stop."

"Oh!" I felt genuine grief at the waste of good horseflesh.

"I'm not even blaming Cliff; sometimes it's inevitable when you put this kind of stress on them so young. Look at young gymnasts, or football players. We ask incredible feats of athleticism from these horses."

"But you won't let that happen to Splash."

Chase shook his head. "Not if it's in my power to help it. If all goes right, this colt will reach top form in time for London."

I wrapped my arms around his neck. "You're very sly."

"Oh really?" He wrapped his arms around me and kissed me long and slow.

"So when do I reach perfection?" I couldn't resist the joke, especially when I saw the flicker of confusion on his face. "I mean, you're bringing me along nice and slow too, I gather?"

He swatted me on the butt. "Now you," he scolded, "are a feisty filly. As for when you reach peak performance, I think you'll discover the answer to that question very soon."

***

I discovered a new passion the next day while watching the freestyle exhibitions. Chase didn't compete in freestyle, but I intended to remedy that after watching the beautiful maneuvers set to music. The first horse and rider, decked head-to-toe in red, white and blue, performed a reining pattern to *God Bless the USA.* The crowd packing the stadium cheered wildly. I'd never seen such a gorgeous display of horsemanship mixed with the artistic elements of costume and music. No wonder the event was so popular.

Even Dad the purist, who initially thought the whole thing was hokey, stood with his right arm over his chest like the rest of the crowd as the performance ended. Sam jumped up and down in the bleachers, hollering "USA!" Fortunately he'd left Angus in his cage near Splash's stall, so the rabbit wasn't traumatized by the enthusiastic response of the fans.

After the *God Bless the USA* exhibition, Chase excused himself, mentioning something about checking on Splash. I offered to go with him but he refused, urging me to stay with my family. I felt rebuffed, but the feeling faded as I lost myself in the next performance, two matched palominos interpreting *One Moment in Time.*

Out of nowhere my mother appeared in the bleachers, dressed in jeans and a western shirt.

"Mom? What are you doing here?" We'd left her home at the ranch, and I couldn't imagine how she'd arrived in Dallas or why.

Her response was light and breezy. "Oh, your father made such a fuss over your competition yesterday, thought I'd come check it out. Guy Deavers got an emergency call from one of his clients competing here, so he offered to drive me." Sure enough, Guy approached the bleachers, coming over to give me a bear hug.

"Well isn't this cozy? Got quite the party going."

We sat down and watched more freestyle together, chit-chatting with Mom and Guy. It dawned on me that Chase had been gone over an hour, and I became irritated. He was missing all the fun.

Then the announcer caught my attention. "This next exhibition is accompanied by a dedication. Is there a Cassie Roberts in the audience?"

Mom, Dad, Guy and Sam all exchanged knowing looks. I felt like the victim of a practical joke, and my face flushed hotly.

"What's going on?"

"Wave your hand, Cassie," Mom prodded. At a loss, I raised my hand while the crowd applauded.

"This next performance by trainer Chase Eversoll is dedicated to his girlfriend, Cassie Roberts. Cassie, enjoy!"

Chase entered the arena on Splash; the first time I'd ever seen him ride the colt. I figured he must consider Splash sufficiently conditioned to bear his solid weight. He'd run his stirrups short to compensate for his long legs.

Rascall Flatts played over the loudspeaker, *Broken Road*. I cried like a baby as Chase and Splash performed what looked like a dance, beautifully spinning, backing and sliding to our love song. Mom started crying, too, and Sam gave me a fierce hug, holding my hand until the finale.

When the music ended, Chase rode Splash to the middle of the ring and the colt knelt on one knee in a bow. The fans in the bleachers screamed "Yeah! Say yes!" It took me a moment to realize what they were talking about, until the announcer walked to the middle of the arena and handed Chase a microphone.

"Cassie, sweetheart," he spoke into the mike. "I hope you'll do me the honor of becoming my wife." He held up something that sparkled; I assumed it must be a ring. "If you don't, I'm going to look awfully silly." The crowd roared with laughter.

Sam shoved me forward. "Go on!"

I made my way down the bleacher steps and entered the arena gate. Chase had dismounted from Splash, but the colt held his bowing pose. I ran to my husband-to-be and he swept me up in his arms. Again, the applause thundered, increasing in volume as he slipped the ring on my finger, and then kissed me in front of thousands of onlookers.

No one remembered who won the futurities that day, but everyone remembered the moment Cassie Roberts became Chase Eversoll's fiancée.

chapter

SIXTEEN

Interesting things occurred before the wedding. Dad and Norman, his cousin/neighbor, re-fenced about twenty acres of our property to add to Norman's spread, along with ten head of our cattle. Apparently Dad was serious about parceling out bits of the ranch. Mom and Dad retained the bulk of the acreage, so I supposed he wasn't throwing in the towel yet, but the sale puzzled me. The reason for the dispersal didn't register until three days before the wedding, when Mom and Dad invited Chase over for a pre-nuptial dinner.

Dad cooked burgers for everyone. Few foods compared to the simple goodness of ground beef patties grilled over charcoal in Dad's clay pot. I made Chase study every flip of Dad's spatula, hoping he'd one day be able to duplicate the flame-kissed perfection. We ate them rare, slathering on ketchup, tomato and onion. I mentally scratched "make out session" off the night's to-do list.

After dinner we all sat on the porch, including Sam, since he was involved in whatever announcements Dad wanted to make. With great pomp and circumstance, Dad addressed the family and his future son-in-law.

"I plan on making a sparkling toast at your wedding reception, but what I'm about to say is just for us."

Sam sat on the commercial grade carpet of the screened-in-porch, Mom reclined in one of the rockers, and Chase rocked in the other with me on his lap. Dad stood like a politician addressing a friendly crowd. Chase and I smiled at each other, wondering what he had up his sleeve.

"First of all, I want to welcome Chase to the Roberts clan." He looked at my future husband, and we all clapped. "You've brought joy to Cassie and Sam, and as a father and grandfather, I couldn't be more grateful." He nodded towards Mom, "It's a burden off Peggy and I to know Cassie and Sam'll be cared for after we're gone, not that we plan on checking out any time soon."

Dad wiped some sweat off his forehead with a handkerchief. "Cassie's done a fine job on her own, but God intended for raising a family to be shared by two. I wouldn't have made it without your mother all these years, Cassie. She's the heart of this family. I pray you'll make as fine a wife for Chase." I looked at Mom, stoic in her rocker, knowing Dad's words to be true. I'd underestimated my mother far too often.

Dad picked up his tea glass and took a slug before continuing. "Chase, I've always taken you for a good man and horseman; I don't suppose I can offer a greater compliment. Now I'm proud to have you as a son. The best advice I can give you is to keep your eyes on the Lord, and your family will grow strong. On that note, here's your first wedding present."

Out of nowhere Mom produced a large, rectangular package wrapped in brown paper. She handed it to us, and Sam helped tear the wrap away. Inside was a beautiful framed parchment with scrolled gold lettering that read "I can do all things through Christ which strengtheneth me. Phillipians 4:13."

"It's wonderful," I said. I'd seen similar etchings in the Christian bookstore and knew they cost a fortune. I tried to imagine the grand picture in Chase's humble trailer, and somehow the image didn't seem ridiculous. We'd hang it in the living area, where the verse would dominate the room.

I got off Chase's lap as he rose to hug Mom and shake Dad's hand. "I love that verse, you must have an idea of what it means to me. Thanks so much, it'll always hang in a place of honor in our home."

Dad continued. "That's not all." Chase and I exchanged surprised glances as we sat back down. "I ran into a friend at the feed store a few weeks ago, remember Dude Davis?"

I nodded; my parents had been friends with the Davises for years.

"Well, he had heart bypass two months ago and just can't run his place like he used to. He's selling off livestock and renting his land to a farmer. He asked me if I cared to take a look and see if there was anything I wanted. I didn't expect to find much, Dude never kept more than a few grade ranch horses to work the cows. When I got there I stumbled onto the most beautiful appendix hunter mare you've ever laid eyes on. Dude said she was his daughter's old horse, and his daughter lost interest after she married and had kids. He bred the mare to a big-name hunter stud last year trying to make a little money, but now he's in no shape to raise a foal. I got the mare and her papers for the cost of the stud fee."

Chase and I exchanged confused looks, wondering why Dad had invested in another broodmare.

"She's your next wedding present. The sire's Sky's Blue Dynasty, his foals are worth at least $10,000 the minute they hit the ground, so you can keep the foal or sell it, whichever you see fit."

We shared another round of hugs with a few tears mixed in. Sam wanted to see the mare immediately, but Dad said she'd be waiting in our broodmare pasture after the wedding. I couldn't get over Dad's generosity. Maybe it was relief his wayward daughter had finally found a decent man to make an honest woman of her.

"I'm not through." Dad continued his speech.

"Mr. Roberts – can't wait to call you Dad – this is really too much. You've gone overboard." Chase couldn't seem to take it in.

"Don't steal his thunder," Mom warned, "he's been planning these surprises for weeks."

"Now then, for your last gift, your mother and I want you two to enjoy a real honeymoon, not the weekend trip to San Antonio you planned. You'll get plenty of chances to see your brother, Chase, but you and Cassie should at least enjoy your first few days as man and wife alone. So our final present is a seven-day trip to Grand Bahama Island."

Chase and I jumped out of the rocker and jumped up and down in circles, like we were kids playing ring-around-the-rosie.

"No fair! I wanna go!" Sam pouted.

Chase reassured him. "We'll take you to Disney World in a year or two to make up for it, I promise." Sam brightened, as Chase's word could be trusted.

I hugged Dad and told him I loved him. I whispered in his ear. "So what's twenty acres and ten cows worth these days?"

He replied, "A picture, a broodmare and a honeymoon."

"Just what I thought."

***

Chase and I planned a small wedding, which was a good thing since I couldn't have supplied bridesmaids for a large one. Shawna didn't harbor any ill will about the Chase affair, so I had a maid of honor. She was a real sport about the whole drama, and fortunately her thriving relationship with Jeff helped my cause. I wanted to doll Jeff up in a bridesmaid's gown as well because he was my only other "girlfriend," but my mother and Chase's would've raised a stink. I thought of phoning Dana, but my Virginia Beach days seemed so far removed, I thought it was better to leave Dana and her world behind.

Mom, Shawna and Chase's mother helped me select a spaghetti strapped gown with a gauzy white overlay, a pearl and rhinestone tiara and a pearl-studded veil. We played with my hair until half of it ended up in a pile at the crown, while the rest fell in soft curls halfway down my back. Shawna wore turquoise, floor length satin, and we both carried gardenias, my favorite flower.

Sam made me cry, so grown up in his mini tuxedo with turquoise cumberbund. He was old for a ring bearer, but both Chase and I insisted he take the job anyway. He hovered protectively over our wedding bands, tied to a satin pillow with ribbons. I had no doubt he'd keep them safe until Chase and I placed them on each other's fingers.

I finally met Chase's brothers, who served as ushers. I liked Jethro and his family; Justin was as annoying and self absorbed as Chase described. Chase's father looked jaunty in his best man's tux, his mother elegant in a suit. They gave us a handsome check to deposit in the bank, along with their best wishes and a request for more grandchildren.

Mabel Williams, the church pianist, played "Jesu, Joy of Man's desiring" as Justin and Jethro seated the mothers and Chase's Aunt Clara. I peeked in from behind the church, certain Chase couldn't see me. The little sanctuary looked beautiful. In addition to everything else, Mom and Dad had covered the church in more gardenias to match our bouquets. I caught my breath when I saw Chase in his jacket with white tails; he looked even more handsome than he had the night of the Cattleman's Ball.

Shawna gave me a quick hug before marching the aisle.

"You're a true friend, Shawna. Thanks for sticking with me."

"Hey, I traded up, remember?" We laughed and I spotted Jeff seated in one of the pews, eager to catch a glimpse of his lady.

Thank you, God. For once in my life, everything turned out just perfect.

Dad offered his arm and Mabel concluded her "Jesu" solo, and then launched into a vivacious "Here Comes the Bride." We walked down the aisle to my groom, past family and friends gathered to wish us well. Pastor Barry smiled at me as I joined Chase, but I had eyes only for my soon-to-be husband, whose face shone with all the love in the world. Before Pastor Barry uttered the first word of the ceremony Chase looked at me and said, "I do."

***

"This can't be real."

We splashed in pristine, crystal water, isolated in a cove off Gold Rock Beach. It had taken just a few hours by plane to reach Grand Bahama Island, but we might as well have traveled to the other side of the world. Only then did I appreciate the enormity of my parents' gift of a real honeymoon.

Chase lay with me at the edge of the water, where gentle waves lapped over us. Tiny tropical fish, like the kind you saw in aquariums, flittered around us as they swayed in and out with the tide.

Paradise.

The warm people of Grand Bahama embraced us. As soon as they found out we were newlyweds, we got the finest tables in restaurants, discount taxi rides and tips on secluded romantic spots like the cove we currently enjoyed. Our taxi driver had assured us we wouldn't be disturbed until he returned in a few hours' time. We made the most of it.

I still got a kick out of Chase's farmer's tan, displayed to unfair advantage by his Navy swim trunks. He'd looked really funny when we first got to the island, dark arms and face with tan lines that stopped abruptly at his neck and forearms, forming a dazzling white tee shirt effect. His legs matched the stark white of his chest.

He'd reminded me curtly that horse trainers only rode shirtless on the covers of romance novels, so his farmer's tan was here to stay. By day three, though, the Bahamian sun had worked magic and he looked much better, although the lines weren't completely erased.

Chase grabbed the back of my neck and pulled me towards him for a slow, wonderfully invasive, no-holds-barred kiss. True to his word, he had restrained his "selfish desires" until Pastor Barry pronounced us man and wife. Once the vows were spoken, though, I became fair game. Just the thought of our wedding night made me blush. Chase, unrestrained and uninhibited, had been something to behold. Sometimes playful, other times thunder and lightning and fire.

Quick as a flash he reached behind me and snapped the fastener of my bikini top, casting it aside. I felt like Eve in the Garden of Eden, enjoying the sensation of water and sun on my bare skin.

Chase laughed. "Now who's got tan lines?"

An hour later, both of us dreamy and content, we realized we needed to pack up our things. Our driver would be back soon, and he didn't need to see us in our current state of undress. I slipped on my bikini bottoms and shorts, and then searched for my top. I couldn't find it.

"Chase?"

"Yes?" He wrapped his arms around me and started kissing me again.

"Will you stop that for a minute? This is serious. Where'd you put my top?"

He looked around, confused as I was that it didn't seem to be where he left it. He pointed to the edge of the water where we'd been laying. "I tossed it right there."

I whacked him across the chest. "You goof! The tide must have carried it away!"

He doubled over and fell in the sand laughing. I burst out laughing too, until I remembered I didn't have any other clothes. I'd come in my bikini and a pair of shorts (that's all anyone wore in the Bahamas), bringing only an extra towel.

"What am I going to do? I can't ride back to the hotel topless. We've got to find it." I stripped off my shorts and we both dove into the transparent water, hoping to catch a glimpse of my sparkling blue bathing suit top. We swam for maybe five minutes when Chase surfaced a few feet from me.

"Cass, you're not going to believe it."

"What?"

"I've found your top."

Relief flooded through me.

"Well, toss it over here!"

"I can't. You'd better come look at this."

I swam over and stood next to him.

"Okay, promise you won't freak out. He's not going to hurt you."

"What do you mean, 'he'?"

"The barracuda that's got your top."

"Chase! Will you stop clowning around!"

"I'm not clowning. Hold your breath and go under with me."

Out of curiosity I did as he asked. To my utter shock, just a horse-length away in the water bobbed a great barracuda, clasping my sparkling top in his jagged-edged teeth. I reverse dog-paddled as fast as I could. Chase swam back to the beach, grabbed our disposable underwater camera, dove back under and snapped the barracuda's picture. Strangely enough the beast didn't move, effectively cooperating with my husband's photographic efforts. The photo would later end up in our honeymoon album. Chase joked he was going to send it to *National Geographic.*

We laughed ourselves sick on the beach. My gallant husband gave me his tee shirt to wear on the taxi ride back to the hotel.

"We tell no one about this, right?" I tickled him under his arms, his only vulnerable spot, until he agreed.

"Deal. What happens in Grand Bahama, stays in Grand Bahama."

But it didn't quite stay in Grand Bahama. Besides the picture, the memory of the quirky episode ministered to us in times of trial or tension. Whenever one of us became angry or depressed, the other would smile knowingly and say "it's time to break out the barracuda." Confronted with a sour-faced fish holding my bikini top, it was hard to hold a grudge.

PART II: FOUR YEARS LATER…

chapter SEVENTEEN

My seat bones ached, my back hurt and my head spun as I loped yet another fast circle in the practice arena.

"All right, Sweetie, I wanna see one last textbook sliding stop, then you can quit."

If this is what it takes to be an international competitor, then I'll sit in the stands.

I snarled at my husband, who stood near the gate with a cold Coke in his hand.

"How 'bout I hop down and drink the soda, and you get *your* butt up here and do some work?"

"I'm not going be the first reining gold medalist, you are."

"I've got my doubts about that. You and Dad are crazy to make me ride this horse in the trials."

Chase picked up a dressage whip near the fence and pointed it at me. "Less talk, more work."

More work? Can't you see I'm dying here?

I was in the best shape of my life. The grueling workouts my husband subjected me to had hardened my muscles into a physique Jillian Michaels would envy. Under Chase's tutelage, I'd become a true athlete. Not wanting to let him or Dad down, I trained with all the gumption I could muster and reaped the rewards in terms of physical fitness.

But he'd stepped it up too hard lately. It seemed like every workout I tired sooner than the last, and I thought I ought to be gaining stamina, not losing it. I couldn't keep up with the ridiculous pace Chase set, and I didn't know how to tell him. Every time I complained, he took it as a joke.

"Fine! One last sliding stop and I'm done, perfect or not."

I rolled forward and Splash surged into a gallop. I felt dizzy but fought it, wiping sweat from my forehead with my free hand. *Just one last maneuver, then we quit.*

"Whoa!" I issued the command, but I didn't follow through with my seat to complete the cue. Splash sensed my hesitation and threw the brakes awkwardly; the resulting slide was short and ugly.

"What was that?" Chase slipped through the fence and walked over to Splash and I. "Better do that one more time, end on a good note."

I slid to the ground and handed him the reins. "Do it yourself."

I stalked off, maintaining my dignity until I got inside the trailer, where I collapsed onto the sofa. The room started spinning in a blurry, starry fuzz. I closed my eyes and willed the feeling to pass.

Moments later I heard Chase walk through the door.

"Cass?"

I didn't answer, couldn't if I wanted to. I sensed him kneel beside me, felt him take my hand.

"Sweetheart, I know it's not easy having your trainer for a husband. I've pushed extra hard these past weeks, but you've really met the challenge."

I finally managed to speak. "This is what you call meeting the challenge, lying limp on the couch?"

"Hey, I couldn't handle the workouts I've dished out to you lately. I'm sorry I've pushed so hard, it's just with the trials coming up…"

The trials. I was sick of hearing about the trials. No one could think about anything else, talk about anything else. They were set for late fall at the Kentucky Horse Park, and Dad and Chase spent every moment planning. They'd attended to every detail from making hotel and stall reservations to completing registration forms.

As if my daily sessions with Chase weren't enough, Dad often jumped in as well, offering "constructive criticism." Guy and Jeff visited the ranch to monitor the horse's precious joints, tendons, ligaments and muscles. Our farrier meticulously shod Splash's hooves to promote maximum performance. Sam pitched in with hours of meticulous grooming and rubdowns with Vetrolin liniment. I joked with Dad and Chase about the creation of "Team Splash."

The trials would decide which three horse-rider reining teams deserved to represent the United States in London the following summer. For some reason I couldn't fathom, Chase and Dad wanted me to ride. Splash had performed consistently over the past years with both Chase and I aboard, but the men felt I got the better performance out of him.

I disagreed, and the thought of world-class competition with the possibility of crumbling under pressure made me quiver in my boots. Only the lure of becoming a national heroine persuaded me to go along with the plan. I dreamed of a gold medal strung round my neck, my hand over my heart while the Star Spangled banner played triumphantly.

Of course at this rate I'd pass out on the podium. If I made it there.

Chase treated me to a lingering massage that night. I surrendered to his gentle ministrations, allowing his callused hands to work magic on my sore muscles. He rubbed warm ginger oil into my skin, kneading the knots out of my neck and tailbone. I listened to Josh Groban serenade me from the bedside boom box, enjoying the scent of the lone candle Chase procured to light the room.

"I ought to throw tantrums more often."

Chase laughed deep in his throat.

"I've been more trainer than husband lately. Sorry."

"It's not like I don't want to win, too."

"I know, I just feel guilty about your dad and I dragging you into our 'delusions of grandeur' as you used to call them."

"I've got as much invested in Splash as you two. *I* brought the horse into the world, didn't I? *I* caught the flu running his hind parts around a pen in the dead of winter. *I* rode him in his first competition, even though I was so nervous I couldn't keep my food down for a week. This dream's as much mine as yours and Dad's."

"There's the gritty cowgirl I know and love."

He proceeded to prove it, over and over again, and I forgot about the grueling workout, in fact forgot my own name for a moment or two. Too often we fell in bed exhausted at the end of the day, too tired for any sort of intimate interaction. When we did connect, we became all the more vital and needy, like two thirsty people discovering an oasis. I woke up the next morning soothed and refreshed.

***

Unfortunately my vitality didn't last.

We stood in the middle of the practice arena the next afternoon, having finished an hour-long series of figure eights and slow-fast transitions. In other parts of the country it was Indian summer, but in Texas it was still just plain hot. I wiped sweat from my brow, fighting queasiness.

"Focus will be the key in Kentucky; there'll be riders from all over the US, not to mention the international competitors there to check out the competition…Cassie, are you listening?"

"Hmmm?" I snapped to an erect posture atop Splash. "I'm sorry, Honey, what were you saying?"

Chase looked up at me from his position on the ground, his face expressing concern. He shook his head as if trying to clear it.

"Sweetheart, I'm worried about you. I'm starting to think these excessive workouts are counter- productive, maybe we need to let your body recover."

"Maybe I just don't have the stuff?"

"You've got the stuff, I promise."

"I meant what I said the other night, this dream's as much mine as yours and Dad's."

He threw his head back and laughed. "Okay, Martin Luther King. I hear you. I just want to make sure we're not over-taxing your physical strength. You've been through workouts that would level most men."

I stuck my chin out. "Don't fret over me, pal. I'm tougher than any cowboy."

"I know you are. But you're flesh and blood. Tomorrow I want you to take it easy."

I wanted to refuse, but the promise of a break from the rigorous drills sounded too tempting.

"I'll take you up on it, but only for Splash's sake." I patted the red stallion on the neck. "He needs a day off."

The following morning was Saturday, so I didn't have to worry about waking Sam for school or packing his lunch. Chase fed the horses and worked some of his other prospects, although he'd taken on a very limited number of trainees due to Splash's relentless campaign. I toyed with the idea of reading a book or watching a movie, but found the bliss of just lying in bed, doing absolutely nothing, impossible to resist.

Leila came over to hang out with Sam, and the two of them sustained me on concoctions they'd learned to make in their Family Living class. They brought me cinnamon toast, biscuit pizzas, pigs in blankets and yogurt parfaits. I fought the urge to laugh each time they entered the bedroom with a new dish.

I heard a soft knock at the door. "Come in."

The kids entered with an enormous dome-shaped silver cover over a platter. Leila stifled giggles as Sam struggled under the weight of carrying the plate.

"My goodness. You two must have an entire turkey under there. You've really outdone yourselves."

A pretty pink flush colored Leila's creamy cheeks, still framed by her two strawberry pigtails. Sam stood tall, muscles quivering under the weight of his burden. As I watched I swore the serving platter jumped. Leila's hand shot out to steady the silver cover.

"What are you two up to?"

Sam laid the dish on the bed. "We're proud to present…rabbit salad!"

Leila lifted the dome-shaped cover off the enormous platter to reveal Angus, in his fuzzy bulk, consuming a plate of shredded lettuce, raisins and carrots. We all howled with laughter.

"You two are a mess. How am I supposed to rest with giant rabbit in my bed?"

"Just trying to perk you up, Mom."

"And you have." I petted Angus' lush fur. "Now shoo. You two have spent all morning looking after me, and I appreciate the delicious treats, but it's a gorgeous day, go enjoy."

"We will. Dad's giving Leila a reining lesson on Riata, and then we're going for a ride on her and Belle."

I smiled at Leila. "I started out on Riata myself."

Leila looked pleased at the prospect of riding the mare. "She's so beautiful with those blue eyes. I'm just afraid I'll fall off. Belle's the only horse I've ever ridden, and she's slow as my gramma."

"It's a different experience to be sure, but I've watched you ride. You've got a natural grace. You'll do fine." She smiled at the compliment.

Hours later, I watched the two of them set off down the driveway mounted on horses, laughing and happy. Chase and I were a little uneasy about the seriousness of the friendship between them, but I felt reassured by the fact that Sam, as a teenage boy, displayed more maturity than I had as a grown woman. He seemed to be one of those fortunate people born wise.

I warmed with maternal pride, and then crawled in bed, losing the remainder of the day in deep, dreamless sleep.

***

Chase wanted to sneak in one more competition before the trials to keep Splash sharp, but he didn't want anything requiring long distance travel or much in the way of preparation. We decided on the Watermelon Classic held in Hope, Arkansas, a small event associated with the county fair.

"Now we're like, slumming?" I asked Chase in a snotty, valley girl accent.

I looked around the small fairgrounds and didn't recognize any of the other competitors, which felt strange. Over the years we'd become acquainted with most of the regulars on the circuit, although we'd been careful to keep a low profile, showing mostly in Non-Pro, never competing head to head with Cliff or the other bigwigs in the Open. Chase was saving the little red horse for just the right occasion, namely the trials.

"This is perfect, my reining princess. I just want enough of a competitive atmosphere to give you and Splash one last shot in the arm before Kentucky."

I thought the trip was a little pointless, but over the years I'd learned to trust my husband's instincts. Chase Eversoll rarely did anything without purpose. Besides, it was nice to compete in an atmosphere that held so little pressure.

We drew fourth. I watched the first three runs and felt embarrassed. We had no business at the rinky-dink show. I remembered how as a kid I'd hated it when some big shot trainer descended on a local show and cleaned house, so I felt bad we were about to do that to these kids. Splash could stop and spin circles around the county fair horses ridden by teens.

My husband must have read my mind. "Cassie, we're not here to goof off. We're giving Splash a last tune up. I want you to get a good run out of him."

"Yes, Boss."

We began our pattern with circles. It wasn't a particularly warm day, but I felt clammy in my long-sleeved shirt, jeans and show chaps. *Not now, I don't need this now.* Sliding stop, rollback. The crowd hollered as Splash and I cut through the maneuvers like cake. The accolades fluffed my pride.

Sweat stung my eyes and my vision began to blur. *You've got to be kidding me.* I felt faint, but I was so close to finishing the pattern, I knew I could hang on. I cued Splash for a spin and tried to hold on as the 360s heightened my dizziness. Splash stopped, but I still felt like I was spinning.

I cued Splash for the opposite side, and as he spun out from under me, the world erupted into stars, and then went black.

***

"This hospital needs to open a Roberts-Eversoll wing." Chase for once didn't appreciate my humor. He looked nervous as a turkey on Thanksgiving.

I lay in a hospital bed hooked to an IV. I thought it was funny how quick doctors were to pump fluids into a person, and then realized the sense of it. The fluids would certainly do no harm and might well do some good, especially if I was dehydrated like when I'd had the flu.

Chase sat in a chair next to the bed, his hand in mine. I squeezed it reassuringly.

"Honey, I'm fine. You may have to accept the fact I'm not the tough cowgirl you thought I was. I'm probably just wimping out under pressure."

"There's nothing wimpy about you."

The nurse entered the curtained partition and asked if I needed anything to drink while we waited for the doctor. I asked for a Ginger Ale, which I sipped slowly to avoid provoking my temperamental stomach.

"Where on earth is that fool doctor?"

"Chase, Honey, settle down."

The doctor drew back the curtain, entering the treatment area with a clipboard and a red folder in his hand. I poked Chase in the arm.

"Hello, Dr. Drake. Remember me?"

The doctor looked at me, and then smiled. "Cassie. Well, well, it's a pleasure to see you, but we really have to stop meeting like this." I knew he probably didn't remember me from Adam, but he undoubtedly recognized his own writing in my file.

Chase rolled his eyes in uncharacteristic impatience.

"What's wrong with my wife? Could she be having complications from that round with the flu years back?"

Dr. Drake acquiesced to Chase's mood and sobered, addressing both of us.

"I've reviewed your old chart, as well as your current vitals, Cassie. Your heart rate is slightly elevated, although not as seriously as when you were admitted…" he scanned the clipboard, "…four and a half years ago. Sometimes serious illness can damage the heart, so we're going to be proactive and run a battery of tests, starting with an EKG."

The next several hours involved an exhausting round of blood-letting, peeing in cups, sitting still while hooked to monitors and running while hooked to monitors.

"These hospital people are worse than you," I joked Chase. "You could learn a thing or two from them."

"Yeah, well, I wish they'd stop performing tests long enough to give us some results."

He kissed me absent-mindedly on the forehead; I thought his face looked pale and tired. Men just didn't handle these things as well as women. I found myself wanting my mother.

At last Dr. Drake returned with an armful of paperwork. Chase seemed to be holding his breath.

"Any news? Do you know what's wrong with me?"

"I do have some news. The tests were quite conclusive."

The doctor's face looked grave, and for once my husband appeared to be the one who was going to faint.

I tried to hide my own fear for his sake, but I couldn't help wondering if Chase was right, if maybe the Bangkok flu had damaged my heart, or worse.

God, if it's my time to go, I won't question it. But for my family, would you consider holding off a little longer? Sam still has so much growing up to do, and Dad and Chase, well you know they're hopeless without me. Mom would have to manage all these men by herself…

"Cassie?"

I realized I'd closed my eyes. "I'm sorry, Dr. Drake."

"I think you'd both better listen to what I have to say."

Chase and I clasped hands.

"I've got some disturbing news as well as some pleasant information to relay. The unfortunate news is that you're not going to be able to participate in the International Equestrian Games." He looked pointedly at me, and I felt stricken to my core, but my distress didn't match the crestfallen look on Chase's face.

Dr. Drake quickly delivered the rest of his information. "I can see I'd better tell you the good news. The reason you can't compete is because by next summer you'll be heavy with child. You're pregnant, Cassie." Dr. Drake beamed, pleased with himself and his clever delivery.

I didn't know what to feel. A ray of joy maybe, clouded over by a sharp stab of disappointment. I felt uncertain, fearful of Chase's reaction. I caught the sad look on his face before he turned to me and said, "Praise God, I'm so glad you're okay. A baby, who would have thought?"

Dr. Drake seemed to feel uncomfortable, anxious to make his exit. "Well, I'll leave you two to celebrate. Congratulations. Cassie, you'll want to make an appointment with your OB/GYN as soon as possible for prenatal care. I'll have the nurse come in with your discharge papers."

The doctor exited the room, leaving us in an unnatural silence. Unconsciously I laid a hand over my stomach. *A baby*. I wanted so much for Chase to be happy about it, but I wasn't sure how I felt myself. Of course we wanted another child (Chase had officially adopted Sam shortly after our marriage), but only after the all-important International Equestrian Games. It had been my responsibility to make sure it didn't happen before then.

Chase must have recognized the need to say something. He patted my hand awkwardly. "It's not like we didn't want a baby, Cass, who are we to question God's timing? A baby's a gift." He sounded like he was trying to convince himself as much as me.

"I'm so sorry Chase, I thought everything was okay, I never dreamed this would happen." Tears began streaming down my face, and Chase took me in his arms. For the first time in our married life, I found little comfort in them.

chapter

EIGHTEEN

"You're mad at me."

"Honey, I am not mad at you."

We drove home from the hospital in Chase's pickup. Dad had already deposited Splash back at the ranch after our ill-fated outing at the Watermelon Classic. Sam had accompanied Dad while Chase took me to the hospital. Chase called them and told him I was okay, just over-exerted and dehydrated. We both agreed to hold off on other news.

Chase stared straight ahead at the road, hardly looking at me. I would have given anything to know what he was thinking. I fumbled for something to say to him.

"I know I told you I'd take care of family planning, and I obviously bungled the job. But Chase, I kept track of my cycles on the calendar each month, I told you when I knew it wasn't safe…"

"Cassie, enough!" His voice sounded edgy. "This is not your fault. We've been dealt a surprise and we'll deal with it. In a day or two we'll snap out of this funk and realize how God's blessed us. We're a team, all right? We'll figure this out."

I didn't see how. Chase and I had intended to try for a baby immediately after the Games, or after the trials if things didn't go our way. Chase loved being Sam's dad, the two embraced their father/son relationship, but I knew with absolute certainty Chase didn't want another child until we'd finished chasing our dreams. He wanted to wait until he could focus on our baby without the demands of pursuing such an ambitious goal, especially when the fate of two families depended on the outcome.

We'd shared warmth and happiness over the past four years, the most loving and wonderful I'd ever known, but at the same time those years had been dominated by Splash and the fantasy of a gold medal. We'd traveled all over Texas, Oklahoma, Colorado, Kentucky and nameless other states campaigning the red colt, getting him used to competition, developing finesse, confidence and showmanship. Every aspect of Splash's road to the International Equestrian Games had been carefully, painstakingly plotted. Now the peanut-sized life within me threatened to upset all we'd worked for. Chase could pretend he was okay all he wanted, but I knew better.

On Monday I convinced my OB/GYN, Dr. Hahn, to work me in for an appointment. I held out small hope that the hospital had made a mistake, mixed up my test results with someone else's. Dr. Hahn confirmed the hospital's diagnosis, however, offering congratulations while wreathed in smiles. My baby was due less than a month after the Games.

I drove home in a dismal mood and pulled up to the trailer, grateful Sam was at school. We hadn't told him yet, and it was hard to put on a happy face. I saw Chase dismounting from Splash in the arena, flinging the reins over the stallion's head to lead him into the barn.

Chase and I had barely spoken since the ride home from the hospital. When we were together he acted kind and distant, but he took himself off to the barn more often than necessary. I let him go, hoping after enough time in his man-cave he'd emerge with a game plan. We needed one badly, as our entire strategy required alteration.

We needed some strategy on the homefront as well. We didn't even have a place to put the baby; our trailer only contained two bedrooms. Yet another botched ambition - we'd entertained high hopes of international success, which would have generated enough revenue to build a house with room for a nursery and an extra bedroom.

I scolded myself for the negative thoughts. *Get over yourself, Cass. It's not as if Chase isn't perfectly capable of riding Splash in the trials. Splash's more accurate with Chase riding anyway.*

Splash's behavior under saddle differed with each of his three riders. With me he was still unpredictable, exhibiting both flashes of brilliance and moments of carefree abandon. With Chase he was workmanlike and precise, less flashy but more controlled. With Dad he responded like an expensively crafted instrument in the hands of a master; the two of them moved in glorious harmony.

Too bad about Dad's age and bad back. Chase will just have to ride him, that's all there is to it.

I sat on the sofa in the living room, waiting for my husband to walk in the door. He smiled weakly as he entered the trailer, but he must've read my expression, because he asked "What's wrong?"

"We have to talk, Chase."

He sat down at the opposite end of the sofa, pulling off his hat. He stared at the floor. "I know. I'm sorry I've been avoiding you."

"I think I figured out when it was."

"When what was?"

"The night I got pregnant."

He smiled a half smile. "I hope I was there."

I took what little encouragement I could from his attempt at humor. "It must have been that night Sam slept over at Kevin's, the night we watched *The Notebook* on DVD. The timing was risky but the movie was so sweet I couldn't help myself…" I began sobbing again, another irritating side effect of pregnancy. My emotions ran wild enough without raging hormones.

Chase's eyes widened. "Yeah, that was a good night." He finally turned to me. "I know we shouldn't be moping around here like two people at funeral. What frustrates me more than anything is that this ought to be a blessed event."

"Then why can't it be? Why is it the end of the world? So the baby bunks with us until we figure out a way to get a bigger trailer, or build a house. And you'll just have to ride Splash in the trials. We can make it all work."

"You're absolutely right."

I wanted to deck him for paying me lip service when I knew he felt otherwise.

"Will you please tell me how you really feel? Stop mincing words and catering to me."

"I'm trying to support my pregnant wife. Isn't that what I'm supposed to do?"

"Yes. I mean, I don't know. I know you're upset, and if you don't let it out, it's going to fester and you'll end up resenting me."

He got up and paced our small living room. "I could never resent you..."

"But?"

He looked confused, as if weighing what to say. "Alright, fine. I'm entitled to feel a little crushed, aren't I? Not to mention I'm under a mountain of pressure."

"So it's all about you, then?"

"No, Cass, it's not. But it is on *my* shoulders. Assuming I can get the USHA to let us change riders, I've got less than two weeks to convince that horse to perform for me instead of you, and if I can't, then four years worth of work goes down the tubes. And it won't just affect me, but also you, the children and your parents. Now this baby's future's tied to that horse, too. Do you understand the burden I'm carrying?"

Actually I'm the one carrying the burden, not to put too fine a point on it.

He looked toward the ceiling, as if questioning God. "Why didn't I go into something like business or engineering? Why don't I have a real job?"

"Stop talking like that! Do you know how that makes me feel? I've never asked you to be anything but a horse trainer, because that's the man I love."

"I don't even know where to put the baby, Cassie. I can't even provide a room for my own child. What kind of man can't take care of his family?"

He stormed off to our room and closed the door.

I shook with fright. I'd never seen Chase in such despair, and I was the cause. He'd never admit it, but in that moment I was certain he didn't want the responsibility of me, the baby, Sam, any of us. He was right, we'd put him under too much pressure. Chase had been my rock, so steady and unchanging. Now I didn't know how to deal with this wounded, insecure version of my husband.

I longed for escape. I fled to the barn, grabbing an old bridle off a hook in the tack room, scanning the mare pasture for a likely horse. I caught Gwennie, bridling her as fast as my numb fingers could fasten the buckle on the throat-latch.

Gwennie was the broodmare Dad had given us as a wedding present. She was the most exquisite creature I'd ever seen, possessing refinement, strength and grace. She also possessed seventeen hands. I led her out of the pasture and closed the gate, then used the rails to launch myself onto her back. Despite my haste and nerves, the good-tempered animal stood quietly as I mounted.

Chase emerged from the house just as I nudged the mare with my heels.

"Cassie!" His voice sounded like thunder.

I urged Gwennie down the driveway in a madcap gallop. I passed the school bus as it stopped to deliver Sam, turning my head to avoid the curious looks of the kids aboard. We clattered out of the drive and onto the dirt road, Gwennie valiantly running but stumbling over rocks and ruts. For a second I considered the folly of my actions. Like most of the broodmares, Gwennie wore no shoes. The road was certain to tear up her hooves, and if she stumbled and went down…

I pulled the elegant mare into a clearing where the footing proved softer. She flew across the field and into some nearby woods. Once into the woods, we picked our way more carefully, losing ourselves in the arborous acreage.

I didn't know what I hoped to achieve by my flight. I guess the general idea was to run away, leaving Chase stricken with guilt and remorse. At the same time, galloping a giant mare bareback and pregnant did little but highlight my own immaturity. Already I felt guilty about the foolish chance I was taking with the baby's life.

I sobbed into Gwennie's neck. *How can this be happening? Everything was right with the world just a week ago.* It dawned on me disasters were like that, everything was normal and pleasant until something intervened and changed life forever. I patted my stomach apologetically. *I'm sorry. You aren't a disaster.*

I lost track of time, roaming the woods in a wounded daze for at least an hour. Twilight fell and patient Gwennie must have longed for her pasture. I sighed and decided to start home, feeling childish. Then I realized I didn't know which way home was.

I tried to retrace our steps, but I was no tracker. The woods all looked the same, filled with green pines and hickory trees colored by autumn leaves, the meadows dull and brown. Nothing clued me to our position, what direction I should turn. I must have wasted another half-hour attempting to blunder our way back.

Darkness closed in as I dropped the reins and let the mare have her head. She stood a much better chance of getting us home than I did. She began to turn when a rustling noise in the trees startled us both. The tree limbs shook violently, too much commotion for a mere bird or squirrel. My heart caught in my throat as Gwennie tensed beneath me.

Dear God, please don't let that be some wild, hungry animal or a lunatic with a chain saw.

I braced for confrontation, but then Gwennie nickered so I thought it must be all right. In the moonlight a horse and rider emerged from the foliage. The magnificent black horse, shining blue in the pale light, also stood seventeen hands tall. Gwennie recognized her offspring, Sky. Chase rode him bareback, closing the gap between us, a murderous look on his face.

I considered running and started to nudge Gwennie, but Chase caught her bridle before I could flee.

"Cassie Eversoll, if you ever do a fool thing like this again, God help me."

"How could I stay in the trailer after you stormed out?" I couldn't form coherent thoughts and the words just sort of spewed. "I know you need time to process all this, but you made me feel horrible. I'm used to you being my rock, and instead you sounded like you were giving up." I began sobbing again, cursing the out-of-control emotions that robbed me of my last scrap of pride.

Chase released the reins and grabbed my hand, pulling it to his lips and kissing it over and over again. He laid it tenderly against his cheek, and to my surprise, I felt his wet tears on my fingers.

"I've hated myself every second since you left the house. If anything had happened to your or our baby, I'd have died inside, Cassie. Died."

I wasn't quite ready to forgive him yet, but I felt relieved. "You're still a jerk," I said between sniffles.

"My being a jerk doesn't excuse you from putting yourself and the baby in danger. That makes you a jerk, too. I ought to tan your hide."

"I'd like to see you try."

"I will when we get home. But right now we've got about an hour of riding before we reach the house."

"An hour? I had no idea we were that far out. I guess I lost track."

"We're maybe thirty minutes away at a lope, but you're not loping bareback in the dark."

We rode in silence. Although I still felt wounded, Chases's heartfelt apology had comforted me, and I thought everything might turn out okay. I figured once we reached home, we'd hash things out and move on.

As we approached another meadow, Sky began dancing and snorting. Chase tried to steady him, but the long-legged horse pranced, clearly upset.

We smelled a stench as we approached the clearing, and then the horses nearly tripped over two large vultures feasting on the carcass of some small, woodland animal. We must have frightened them, because they flapped their enormous wings and hopped a few feet away.

Gwennie planted her feet in fear and refused to move, but Sky plunged into a series of wild bucks. Despite his expertise as a horseman, with seventeen hands of thrashing bronc beneath him and no saddle to grab, my husband sailed over Sky's head, crashing to the ground with an audible thump. Lord only knows what he hit – rock, tree stump? Sky galloped for home, full tilt, as Chase lay still as death.

I jumped from Gwennie's back, keeping a tight hold of her reins, leading her to where my husband lay fallen.

"Chase!"

He remained silent and motionless.

"Chase!" I screamed like a woman possessed, knowing that if the man on the ground lay dead, the fault was all mine. I sobbed over his inert body, praying in wails and moans for God to breathe life back into his lungs.

"Chase!" I chanted his name, willing him to answer me, but the meadow was silent except for my ranting. I dropped Gwennie's reins, letting her go, crawling into a fetal position next to the man I loved.

If he's gone, Lord, take me too.

chapter

NINETEEN

I sat in the dark and cold for an eternity, cradling my husband's body. Gwennie could have fled home like her errant colt, but instead the valiant mare stayed with me, standing over us, keeping watch. I felt grateful for her company as my fear and loneliness grew unbearable.

I imagined that Chase stirred. Afraid to hope, I watched him in the moonlight, praying for so much as a twitch, some flicker of life. Just when I thought I'd imagined it, I saw his fist clench and unclench, and his eyes winced in pain. He began gurgling from his mouth, and I could have screamed for joy, except for his obvious distress.

"Ugh, aaahh, oh, uh."

"Chase! Sweetheart!"

"Aaahh!" He moaned and thrashed.

"Chase! Lie still, I'm here."

He tried to brace himself with his arms and sit upright, but fell back down.

"Chase, lie down. It's Cassie, honey."

He looked right through me, struggling and groaning. I would have given anything for some water, aspirin, anything to help, but I had nothing of any use. I felt his forehead and it seemed cool to the touch, which was something.

"Chase, look at me. Eyes to me." He forced his eyes open and stared at me. I felt relief as recognition dawned on his face.

"Cass."

"I'm here, Sweetheart. Try not to move, lie back. There, that's good." I tried to soothe him in the same tones he used with the horses. "Help will come soon, I promise."

I hoped I wasn't spinning fairy tales. I felt certain Sam would have assembled a posse hours ago; surely it was just a matter of time before they found us.

"What hurts?"

His voice was barely audible. "Everything."

"What hurts the most?"

"Leg."

"Which leg."

"Left."

I stopped asking him questions because it pained him too much to answer. Instead I sang to him – hymns, lullabies, country tunes.

He tried to say something.

"Don't talk. Save your strength."

But he insisted. "I guess…now…would be the time to…break out the barra…cuda." It took him forever to get it out, but I felt cheered at his joke. His humor was still intact.

"I think this is going to take a lot more than a scary-looking fish with a fetish for swimsuits. I wish you'd grabbed a cell phone before coming after me."

"Last thing…on my mind."

"It's okay. Sam surely knows something's wrong by now. Sky must have made it home ages ago."

We sat in the clearing with Gwennie, the vultures and the stench of the dead carcass for at least two hours, trying to keep Chase's mind off the pain by profusely apologizing to each other. It became a contest to see who could offer the most pitiful, heartfelt atonement.

"I want this…baby…so much, Cassie. I'm…so proud."

"I know you do. This baby does complicate things, but God knows what He's doing, we're gonna trust Him on this one."

"You bet. He brought us…together, didn't he?" Chase's breath sounded shallow.

"Shush. No more talk."

A slight rustle in the trees nearby caused the hairs on the back of my neck to stand on end. Gwennie jumped as a dark form bounded into the clearing, and I stifled a scream. Only when I recognized Hank's soft whine did my terror turn to relief.

"Hank!"

Moments later our cattle dog shoved his cold, wet nose into my face and assaulted me with sloppy dog kisses. I put my arms around him and relished the feeling of warm fur.

"Chase, it's Hank. That means Sam's here somewhere. We're almost rescued."

Gwennie neighed. Flashlight beams shone on us as three riders – Sam on Belle, Leila on Riata and Dad on Splash – entered the meadow.

"We found them!" called Sam.

"Who's hurt?" asked Dad.

"Chase!" I called back.

Dad hopped down from Splash, eyeing the two of us, and the way Chase's leg bent at an unnatural angle. He scratched his head as if perplexed. "Now this is quite a fix."

Leave it to Dad to make the understatement of the night.

***

We debated the wisdom of moving Chase, but given the situation, we had little choice. No ambulance could make it that deep into the woods. Dad called 911 to see if they had any suggestions. Since Chase was conscious, cognizant and able to move his arms, hands and right leg, the operator asked if we could get him close enough to a road for ambulance pickup. Sam untied something sticking out from behind his saddle and held it up. I realized it was a wooden skim board, the one he took to the lake in summer. Dad gave the operator our address, along with directions, and hung up the cell.

"With God's grace they'll be waiting at the trailer when we get you out of here. Hang on, Son."

We rigged a crude contraption with the skim board, a sleeping bag and some rope, strapping Chase to the board like a papoose. He clutched my hand and I saw fear flash in his eyes, pain etched in his features.

"Hold on, Honey. Help's waiting at home; we've just got to get you there."

We stabilized his body position the best we could, trying not to move the injured leg, but it was impossible to avoid jostling. Chase cringed but didn't cry out.

Splash proved the hero of the night. We hooked the main rope to the D-rings on his saddle so he could pull the contraption back to the house. Leila and I walked alongside the board to steady and ease it over rough ground, while Sam led Gwennie and Riata home. Splash had never pulled anything in his life, but Chase had used driving lines on him as a foal, so at least the ropes along his sides didn't frighten him. He never once spooked or balked at his strange burden, but plunged ahead steady as a tractor.

We saw the lights of the ambulance as we neared the house, and I thanked God and Dad's good directions. Four paramedics ran to meet us, swarming around Chase, loading him onto a real stretcher. I rode in the ambulance with my husband, relieved he was now in the hands of competent medical professionals as opposed to stranded alone in the woods with his wife.

***

We spent two nights at the hospital, a now familiar home away from home. I asked one of the nurses if they offered frequent-customer specials, hoping this constituted our last visit for awhile. Fortunately the hospital staff refrained from lecturing us on the perils of horseback activities or questioning the wisdom of riding in the woods at night.

After his long, exhausting ordeal, Chase escaped with a mild concussion and a broken leg fractured in two places below the knee. The breaks were clean and the doctors predicted they'd heal, but they required significant surgery to repair. Riding in the trials was out, a total no-go. He'd be in a cast for weeks. I could have cared less about the International Equestrian Games right then, I was just thrilled my husband lived and breathed. Back in the woods I hadn't been so sure.

Chase enjoyed his hospital meds, which rendered him pain-free and euphoric, but his level of pain and irritability increased exponentially upon returning home. I eyed his bottle of painkiller, thinking the stuff they sent home must not be as potent as the version doled out at Summerville General. Sam and I made him as comfortable as possible, propping his leg up with pillows on the sofa, urging him to forget about everything but getting well. Of course he refused, insisting that we invite Dad over to talk about the trials. I agreed because he was right, some sort of decision had to be made.

The next evening we sat around the card table that served as our dining area, Chase's cast-bound leg propped in an extra chair. An open box of pizza remained untouched, at least by everyone except Sam.

"Hey, a guy's gotta eat," he said, and he was right. Even under dire circumstances, a teenage boy was a teenage boy. Besides, Sam was thrilled at the idea of having a little brother or sister and felt he had reason to celebrate. We'd broken the news about the baby to everyone at the hospital. When Sam found out he'd shouted, "I'm not an only anymore!" Then he'd thrown his arms around me.

My parents came over after dinner. Mom was thrilled about the baby as well. She lectured the men to focus on the positive and stop brooding about the darn horse. At her rebuke Dad instantly shaped up, offering warm congratulations and assurances of his sincere delight. For an hour or so we celebrated the new addition like a normal, happy family. But when Mom and Sam adjourned to the living room to watch an Animal Cops re-run so Dad, Chase and I could figure out what to do about the trials, the mood again grew somber.

"Well, I guess this is the end of it, then." Dad sounded like he was trying not to feel bitter and failing miserably.

"It can't be. We've worked too hard, spent too many years dreaming. There has to be a way." Despite Chase's determination, the facts weren't in our favor.

Dad scratched his chin. "I don't guess Cassie could ride him the trials, and then you ride him in the Games?"

Chase shook his head. "The same rider has to be the one to qualify. I don't think even our extenuating circumstances would buy us leniency from the IEG committee."

"What about your cousin Lindsay?" I asked.

He thought a moment. "Not a bad idea, but she'd have to give up two weeks of grad school to come out here and get used to Splash. There's no guarantee he'd take to her. Then she'd have to give up more time going to Kentucky for the trials. If it all went bust, she'd blow the whole semester for nothing. We can't afford to reimburse her if it goes wrong."

"Would she be willing to take the risk?"

"I don't know." Chase didn't look hopeful. "My Aunt Donna and Uncle Tom are awfully proud to have a daughter in grad school. I think they'd kill me."

I turned to Dad, who sat with his head resting in his hands.

"Any ideas?"

He shook his head.

"Well, then I guess I'll be the one to say it. We could see if Cliff would put one of his rookie trainers on him. I'm sure he'd do it, he's got nothing to lose."

Chase's face paled, but he nodded. "That's the best solution, much as it pains me. Marvin," he looked straight at Dad, "Don't blow this opportunity just to spare my feelings. Cliff's a showoff, but he's got a soft spot for you and Cassie. He'd probably jump at the chance to play hero and bail you out of a jam. You can't afford not to ask him."

Dad sat without speaking for long moments, and then quietly said, "No."

I looked at Chase and shrugged my shoulders.

Dad continued, "We pursued this as a team, the Roberts and Eversoll families. We're gonna finish it as a team. Even if it ends here."

Dad spoke in a tone that meant his decision was final. There was no talking him out of it. We shared a long, sad silence.

When I couldn't stand it anymore, I said the first thing that came to mind. "It's too bad you aren't twenty years younger, Dad. Splash does better for you than anyone else. You ought to be the one to ride him."

"Hmmmfff." Dad blew off my comment, but Chase sat up straight in his folding chair.

"That's the best idea anyone's had all night."

Dad waved his hand dismissively. "You kids are crazy. Chase, those meds have affected your brain."

"It's not crazy, Dad. She's right. You get more out of that horse than anyone."

"I'm almost seventy years old."

I picked up on Chase's excitement. "Dad, don't you remember that guy on *Good Morning America*, the ninety-year-old who's still competing in water skiing competitions and winning? Why, you're twenty years younger than him!"

"Oh no, my back would never…"

"Dad, your back's held up since your surgery. It only gives you trouble now and then, and I bet your doctors would help you manage it so you could compete."

Chase's eyes widened with possibilities. "Think about it, you'd take the world by storm. The oldest International Equestrian Games competitor in history."

"You'd be on cereal boxes."

Dad looked deep in thought, as if he was actually considering the incredible idea. Chase and I pressed hard.

"I don't know if I can do this at my age," Dad sounded doubtful.

Chase pointed towards our living room, to the framed parchment that read "I can do all things through Christ which strengtheneth me."

"When you gave us that picture, did you mean it? Or were they just words on a plaque?"

Dad laughed. "Are you joking? You two don't really consider this a possibility?"

Chase nodded gravely. "It's not just a possibility, Sir; it's our last, best hope."

chapter

TWENTY

The atmosphere at the gorgeous Kentucky Horse Park in Lexington felt more like a festival than a high-end reining event. Despite the fact we were at the United States' Reining Team trials, competitors from all over the globe, particularly Canada, Italy and Germany, flooded the horse park en masse, presumably to preview the competition. The beautiful equine facility overflowed with riders, spectators, horses and media.

"It's like an equine world's fair," I told Chase as I walked by a vendor selling German sausage and sauerkraut next door to an Italian calzone cart. The smells didn't mingle well and I fought back nausea. The accents floating around the park sounded as varied, everything from British cockney to velvety French to Australian "G'day." Dad, Chase and I felt like Dorothy, the scarecrow and the tin man in Oz. I half expected a munchkin quartet to welcome us to World-Class-Equestrian Land.

The media coverage amazed me. "Chase, did you have any idea it would be like this?"

We made our way to a reserved section of seating for exhibitors in the 6,000 capacity covered arena. I tugged at my husband's sleeve as he hobbled along in his cast, pointing him toward a flurry of reporters and cameramen descending on Cliff Kesterson.

Cliff, astride a stunning buckskin sired by his prized Locomotion, appeared at ease with the cameras, smiling and gesturing broadly with his hands. We caught part of the interview over the noise of the crowd.

"Reining's an American sport, so we should dominate, but we've got strong competition from Germany and other countries. The United States' Team needs a strong captain with a proven record of excellence and consistency."

An attractive female reporter inched her way closer to Cliff. "And that would be you, Mr. Kesterson." It was a statement, not a question. "With your track record, many in the sport feel your competing today is purely ceremonial."

Cliff made an "aw, shucks" shrug of his shoulders. The reporter pressed on.

"It's also rumored that your toughest competition here at the trials will come from your own horses and apprentice trainers. What can you tell us about that?" She stood on tiptoe and thrust her microphone in his face.

"Besides Diamond Engine here," he patted his buckskin, "I've brought two other fine stallions, Thunderstar and Smokin Fire, ridden by two of my best men, Clint Keeton and Steve Gunner. They're sure to give me a run for my money. We promise to do y'all proud in London." Cliff lifted his finger to symbolize "number one."

An older male reporter threw in a last question. "Mr. Kesterson, is there anyone at this competition you're worried about, any potential long shots?"

"There's a difference between home-grown competition and world class horses, friend. I'll let you be the judge."

Cliff posed for more shots.

"Macbeth." Chase spoke quietly, and I could hardly hear him.

"What?"

"Macbeth."

"I don't get it."

"Act V, Scene V. Had to memorize it in high school."

"Wouldn't have pegged you for a Shakespeare fan. I still don't get it."

"…it is a tale told by an idiot, full of sound and fury, signifying nothing."

I spoke in my best fake British. "How apropos."

We dissolved into laugher, releasing some of the tension we both felt in the high stakes environment. Dad seemed oblivious, almost like a lost child, wandering through this strange world in which we found ourselves. We reached our seats and watched some of the early runs, trying to get a feel for the arena and the judges.

In contrast to the media frenzy surrounding Cliff, no one noticed "Team Splash," for which I felt grateful. The reporters ignored us, an unremarkable stallion with his unremarkable staff. No one knew Dad was riding. If our quest fell short of the mark, the last thing he needed was a national spectacle made of it. We allowed ourselves to be referred to as "Number Seventy Two."

My cell phone rang, and I picked up the call. Both Dad and Chase looked at me. "Mom," I told them. I spoke to her briefly and hung up the phone.

"What did your mother have to say?" Dad asked.

"They're getting close; she's pretty sure they'll make it in time to see you run."

"I was afraid you'd say that."

We'd been at the horse park for over a week, resting Splash from the long trailer trip and getting him used to the environment. When it came time for competition, we wanted him relaxed and ready. Mom had stayed home with a protesting Sam.

"You need my help! I really don't mind missing school," he'd insisted. And we'd insisted just as fervently that we did mind, although we could have used the extra pair of hands. Now they were on their way from Texas to join us. Chase and I would be glad for their company, but I knew Dad would just as soon not have an audience. I'd never seen him so nervous.

We watched a few other runs, mostly by unknowns like us. The horses performed well, but without the panache and level of difficulty we'd see from Kesterson's horses, and hopefully, Splash. Scores ranged between 210 and 220. Admirable, but not contenders.

I tugged on Dad's arm.

"What do you think?"

He cut me a sideways cowboy grin. "I think our horse's got the talent to waltz away with this thing if the old man riding him doesn't choke with stage fright. Nothing like coming out of a thirty year retirement to compete in an International Equestrian Games trial."

Chase gave him a sympathetic look. "Better you than me. I'm actually thanking God for this ugly cast on my leg." He thumped the cast for emphasis. "I've been to my share of reining events, but this beats anything I've ever seen.

This isn't just cowboys strutting their stuff. One of the favorites is a Canadian-born American riding a borrowed horse from Ohio."

Clusters of people left their seats and congregated along the arena railing. We consulted the event program to look at the next draw.

"Cliff?" I asked.

"The one and only." None of us admitted it, but we all wanted to see Cliff's run. Chase closed his program and pointed at Cliff's horse.

"That's the same colt we saw him run at Congress. Cliff's campaigned that horse since the ripe age of two. Horse's smooth as silk."

Cliff's reins dangled as he ran his pattern, the attractive buckskin apparently requiring no guidance from his rider's hand. He collected beautifully for his slower circles, and I didn't see Cliff so much as shift in the saddle.

"I guess he's figured out how to use mental telepathy." I sounded disgusted.

"All right now," Dad scolded, "whatever you two think of Kesterson, look at the rapport he has with that animal. Give a little credit where it's due. He reflects well on the sport."

I expected Chase to argue, but he conceded. "You're right, I'll give him that. Cliff's maneuvers are textbook, and that's a decent horse."

The buckskin spun like a ballet dancer executing a pirouette. Stunning. The throngs in the seats and at the arena rail cheered him on with shouts of "Woo-hoo!" and "Get 'er done!"

When Cliff completed his performance, the spectators who weren't already standing rose to their feet. We joined them and stood, Dad even hollering accolades. Chase and I couldn't dispute the fact they were well earned.

The crowd waited impatiently for the scores, then shook the complex with applause and foot stomping when he received a 227.

I whispered in Chase's ear. "The judges didn't leave much room at the top."

"They didn't intend to," he whispered back.

Cliff's protégés and their stallions, along with some of the others we wanted to see, had drawn later spots. We left the stands, making our way to the stabling area to check on Splash. The accommodations for the horses bordered on luxurious, and we'd splurged for a paddock for the weekend at no small cost. We ambled slowly, accommodating Chase and his crutches. He amazed me at how agile he was with the giant cast.

As we entered the barn, we noticed a small group congregated around a bay colt. One man examined the horse's legs, feeling along the cannon bone and fetlock. The handler spoke with a clear Midwestern dialect, but the others talked with German accents, asking questions about the horse's earnings and bloodlines. We couldn't squeeze by them gracefully with Chase's impediments, so we blundered through, apologizing for interrupting. They smiled and bid us "Guten tag."

After we passed them, Chase told us that we'd most likely stumbled onto a sales transaction. "I'm telling y'all, the American Quarter Horse is becoming a hot commodity. Whether that's good or bad remains to be seen, but foreign competitors are always on the lookout for champions to import."

As we made our way to Splash's stall, we ran into a familiar face walking down the center aisle between rows of bored horses.

"Ivan!" I ran to him and threw my arms around his neck. He picked me up and swung me, looked as happy to see us as we were to see him.

"Not sure what I did to deserve a greeting like that, but I'll take it. How are y'all doing?"

"Better now that we've run into you." Chase waved his hand. "Have you seen anything like this in all your life? It's a blessing to spot a friendly face."

"Guess you saw Showboat's run?"

"Yeah, we all watched it."

Ivan gave Dad a friendly fake punch to the shoulder. "So you know what we're up against, Marvin? I think the US Reining Team was selected before the first entrant ever made his run."

"There's no doubt some truth to that," Dad admitted, "but that doesn't mean the judges won't give us all a fair shake."

"I 'spose your right. I'm just gonna go out there and ride my horse."

"Who'd you decide on?" Dad asked.

"Come here and I'll show you."

Ivan walked us about two stalls back and pointed to the occupant. "This is Fria."

"Your mare?" Chase sounded surprised. The mare in the stall munched hay from her net, rattling it with her nose to shake more loose. The horse looked blue-gray in the barn light, her coat glossy, her steel-colored mane and tail long and thick.

"Hey gorgeous girl." I tried to coax her over to the stall door, but she focused on eating the rich alfalfa.

"Don't knock my mare, now," Ivan warned Chase, "this filly can spin circles around the boys. She's a knockout."

"Girl power." I nodded. "You get 'em, Fria."

"I noticed you drew sixty four, guess we all have awhile to wait."

"Yeah, I was gonna find my wife and decide if I want a turkey leg, **spätzle or parmigiana for lunch.**"

"Ha! We'll see you later, buddy. We'll be cheering you on."

We found a restless Splash gnawing at the wood of his fine stall. I gasped. "Will we have to pay for that?"

Dad grabbed a halter. "We've probably got hours yet. Why don't we let him enjoy the fancy paddock we sprang for?" Chase agreed and Dad led Splash out of the stall and out to his private paddock. He took off at a run, bucking and enjoying the sunshine after his stall confinement.

Dad put his arm around me as we watched his antics. "Can you believe your old man is about to run a pattern in the trials? We never would have imagined this seven years ago, me flat on my back and you in the middle of that storm, trying to bring him into the world."

"You'll make history, Dad."

"I never wanted to make history by being the most geriatric participant in a televised athletic event."

"Then make history by becoming the most geriatric participant ever to kick butt and take names later in a televised athletic event."

Dad looked me in the eye, and only then did I realize how scared he was. "I don't think it's going to be that easy. I'll settle for not looking like a fool."

***

Chase and I watched more runs while Dad and Splash schooled in a warm up ring. Both of Cliff's flunkies performed well, one scoring 224 and the other a 225 ½. The Canadian-turned-American national Chase mentioned created a stir on his borrowed horse, outscoring one of Cliff's riders by a half point to move into the top three. I felt happy that at least the US team wouldn't consist entirely of Cliff, Cliff and Cliff.

We cheered as Ivan took the arena on his pretty gray Fria. If anyone doubted his wisdom in pitting a mare against the stallions and geldings, they changed their tune when she began tearing up the arena floor. The mare ran her pattern with the energy of a supernova, creating spark and energy with every maneuver. The startled crowd screamed with excitement. I jumped up and down calling "Ivan! Ivan! Ivan!" The stadium exploded again when Ivan's score of 226 posted.

"Ivan just made the team," Chase spoke in my ear. That score placed Ivan second behind Cliff. Unless the remaining roster contained a huge upset, Ivan wasn't likely to lose his spot.

Very few runs now separated Dad from his turn at the trials. We looked for him near the outdoor schooling rings, and found him by an in-gate surrounded by Mom and Sam. I saw a suspicious looking bundle in Sam's arms.

"Sam Eversoll, I told you to leave that rabbit at home." Sam looked sheepishly toward the sound of my voice.

"No way, Mom. He's here to bring Grandpa luck."

Dad reached down from the saddle and reached for Sam's bunny. "Don't listen to your mother, Sam. You bring that rabbit's foot over here; I'll take all the luck I can get."

"Glad y'all got here in time. Did you have a good trip?" I asked Mom.

"We did not." Mom folded her arms. "Sam didn't want to waste time eating real meals or making long stops, so we stuck to gas stations and fast food. The restrooms were fil-thy! On the way back we're stopping at Cracker Barrel, young man. My travel guide rates their bathrooms four-star." Mom looked crossly at my son, who shrugged, still holding the monster rabbit.

"Well, the important thing is you made it here," Chase added. "Now I expect Dad better get ready for his date with destiny. How about we all pray?"

We circled and bowed our heads, holding hands like we were saying grace. Dad took both hands off the reins and reached down to Chase and Sam, who stood on either side of him. I ended up holding hands with Mom and Angus the rabbit.

"God," Chase began, "despite all the odds you've brought us here today as a family. This dream began thirty years ago for Cassie's dad, the rest of us joined in along the way. We don't know what eternal significance might be attached to today's outcome, so we just pray Your perfect will be done. Protect Dad and Splash from harm, and whatever happens, we promise to give you the glory."

"Amen."

"Amen."

"Amen."

"and Amen."

The Roberts-Eversolls entered the stadium as one. When "Number Seventy-Two" was called, however, Dad alone rode into the arena on his red stallion. The rest of us held hands near the arena railing.

By this point in the trials, many of the spectators had politely wearied of the competition. Their enthusiastic "yeahs" and "wows" had diminished in volume as their fervor waned. The favored contenders had all finished their runs, and in the crowd's minds, the IEG team was decided. Their attitude reeked of ho-hum. Dad received a mild, weak round of applause as he entered the ring.

Dad's pattern began with a stop/rollback series. He and Splash charged around the arena, accelerating fluidly with each stride. Dad's reins hung loose as he approached the first rollback and mouthed "Whoa!" With his usual flair, Splash sat down and slid. The sleepy crowd, stunned out of their monotony, began hollering. Splash rolled back and took off like a rocket in the opposite direction, executing another flawless stop and rollback. Chase and I exchanged high fives as the crowd continued to wake up, offering applause and shouts of approval.

Mom turned to Chase and I. "So he's doing well, then?"

I laughed at her. "Yes, Mom, he's doing well."

"He does look handsome out there, doesn't he?"

I put an arm around Mom's shoulders. "He sure does."

Dad picked up a right lead canter and circled, first ground covering and fast, then collected and elegant. I thrilled as I watched the performance.

"Chase, are you seeing this? Splash never runs like that for you and me."

"It's their chemistry, Cass. Same as with people."

Splash changed leads with a beautiful economy of movement, and then completed his left-lead circles. He stopped and backed in a perfect straight line, then stopped a moment before spinning to the left like a child's toy top. The crowd jumped to their feet, wondering where on earth the fiery red colt and his mature rider had come from. Chase and I giggled as we overheard explanations.

"That's Marvin Roberts…*the* Marvin Roberts from like…thirty years ago?"

"You're off your rocker!"

"No I'm not, look at the program."

"Can't be the same guy."

"Can and is."

"Where'd the horse come from?"

"His daughter's been showing the horse in Non-Pro, can you believe it?"

Chase and I wished Dad could have heard the stir he was causing. But his attention was all on Splash. The two finished and stood humbly, indicating their completion of the pattern. Then Dad dismounted and dropped Splash's bridle for the judges' inspection. Meanwhile the crowd went nuts.

"He's got it, Cassie." Chase whispered excitedly. "That run smoked Cliff Kesterson. Your Dad should have this sewn up."

We began cheering with the crowd, a wave of euphoria washing over us. Until the judges posted their score.

224 ½.

The crowd complained loudly, outraged. Like most fans, they were well versed in their sport and knew Dad's run should've knocked the pants off the others. 224 ½ placed Dad in fifth, behind Cliff, Ivan, Cliff's flunky and the Canadian.

"What happened?" Mom looked disoriented as Chase explained. We converged around Dad as he exited the arena. People approached us, offering Dad compliments on the brilliant run and consolation regarding the judges' lousy scoring. Dad smiled but made a hasty exit with Splash toward the barn. I thought I caught a glint of tears in his eyes.

We walked to the stable like zombies, unable to process our turbulent emotions. For Dad to succeed so brilliantly only to get slapped in the face, well, it hurt.

"But why?" Sam asked, depositing his rabbit into a cage near Splash's stall. "Why?"

"I wish I knew, Sam." Chase answered Sam but looked at Dad. "That run was the stuff of dreams, you did us all proud. I guess the judges just thought twice about sending a seventy-year-old to the Games."

Dad dealt with the disappointment better than the rest of us. He patted Splash, then stripped off the saddle and began grooming the stallion. "We did what we set out to do, didn't we? All I wanted was to not make a fool out of myself, so we came out ahead. Now I guess it's time to go home."

Ivan came to congratulate Dad. "Marvin, I've never seen anything like that. I'm so sorry you got a bum deal. You could register a complaint."

"Absolutely not." Dad was emphatic. "The judges' decision is the judges' decision. But congratulations Mr. Jenkins, you'll do our sport justice in London."

We emerged from our gloom to congratulate Ivan, but our hearts weren't in it. They weren't in it hours later when we sat around a steak dinner at a restaurant, supposedly to celebrate Dad's brilliant performance at the trials. No one touched their food, not even Sam. After a while, Dad took Mom by the hand. "Come on, Honey. We've got a long trip ahead tomorrow, best get some shut eye."

Chase held me in bed at the hotel that night. We cuddled together as best we could with his cast in the way. I cried silent tears into the scratchy, rough linen pillowcase.

"It's really over now. What are we going to do?"

"There, Sweetheart. It's all right. We said we'd trust God whatever happens, right? Maybe He's telling us it's time to let go of this dream. We'll spend more time as a family now. I can probably make good money training Amateur and Non-Pro horses. God'll give us a new vision, an even greater dream."

I nodded my head. "You're right. We've trusted Him this far, we're gonna trust Him all the way. There's better and brighter things ahead."

We were silent for a moment, and I thought Chase had drifted off to sleep.

"Chase?"

"Hmmm?"

"I trust God, but my heart still hurts."

"I know. Mine does too."

***

We looked for Ivan to say goodbye, but he was in the competition arena performing an exhibition. None of us felt like watching. We left him a note on Fria's stall and loaded the trailer. As I fastened the velcro on Splash's shipping boots, shouts and commotion rang throughout the barn.

"Diamond Engine's down! He's down!"

"What?" I stood up and looked at Dad and Chase; they seemed as confused as I was.

People began leaving the barn, heading for the covered arena.

"What's going on?"

We stopped a passer-by, a home-spun American in cowboy boots and Wranglers. To our chagrin he spoke with an Italian accent.

"Sigor Kesterson's stallion, there'sa been some sort of accident. Scusi." He bustled by us, eager to investigate the source of the drama.

Chase grabbed his crutches. "We'd better get over there and see what's going on. Sam, you and your grandma stay here with Splash."

"But..." Sam started to protest but shushed at a stern look from Chase. Chase, Dad and I made our way to the arena. It proved almost impossible forcing our way through the crowd. We ended up climbing to the mezzanine level of seats, Dad and I supporting Chase, to view what was going on.

Cliff's beautiful buckskin lay on the arena floor broadside, surrounded by Cliff and several other horsemen, some wearing "Event Staff" jackets. A few of them cleared the arena entrance so a waiting Blue Cross equine ambulance could drive into the ring. A man, presumably a veterinarian, injected something into Diamond Engine's neck, while two others encased the stallion's left rear leg in a type of brace.

Dad, Chase and I watched the expert equine paramedics load the horse into the ambulance. Fortunately, in the heart of Kentucky racehorse country, Cliff's horse would find the best treatment available.

"I wish someone would tell us what happened."

A girl in a rhinestone studded belt and bling jeans sitting nearby must've overheard me. She scooted over to where we sat, eager to enlighten us.

"The horse was doing a sliding stop and his haunches just crumbled beneath him. People close to the arena swear they heard a crack. Cliff jumped off and the stud tried to get up, but that left hind leg just sort of dangled."

"Oh, no." My eyes welled with tears, grieved at the animal's suffering. At least the men in the arena made him comfortable with anesthetic. We watched the ambulance leave, and onlookers began dispersing.

I turned to Dad and Cliff. "What could have happened?"

"Stifle?" Dad suggested.

"Possible," Chase agreed, "although the fact the spectators heard a crack is a bad sign. He could have come down wrong on the left hind and broken a cannon bone. Or it could have been a combination, sore stifle led to a bad landing on the leg."

"It's a shame, whatever the case." Dad shook his head.

An announcement came over the loudspeaker. "Ladies and gentlemen, our exhibitions will resume in approximately thirty minutes. Throughout the afternoon we'll keep you updated on the condition of Diamond Engine. Thank you for your concern and patience."

The lady in the sparkly outfit rose to leave. "Guess that's it for Kesterson and the International Equestrian Games. At least his rookie made the team so he's still got a horse in."

I looked at Dad. "I didn't even think about that. Dad, do you realize what this means? With Cliff out, that makes the team Ivan, Steve Gunner and the Canadian guy, and you the alternate."

Dad seemed puzzled, unable to take it in.

Chase raised his hand. "Whoa, whoa, whoa. Don't jump to conclusions. Better wait until the vet examines Cliff's horse. If it's a minor fracture or a slipped stifle, he might still be in it. Let's wait until we hear from the USHA."

"There you are!" A breathless Ivan spotted us from ground level and took the stairs two at a time to reach our perch. "I've been looking all over for you."

"It's terrible, isn't it? That gorgeous horse…"

"That's not all. All 'H-E-Double Hockey Sticks' has broken loose. I've been trying to find you, Marvin, a USHA representative is looking for you. Have you heard about the Canadian, Girard?"

We all shook our heads.

"His horse drug tested positive for stimulants."

"What?" Our jaws all dropped.

"He was selected for random testing and the horse came up positive. He's out."

"How can anyone be that stupid?"

Ivan shrugged his shoulders. "He claims he knew nothing about it, and he might be telling the truth. Word is the owners needed a big win and might have tried to stack the deck."

I slumped into my seat, dumbfounded. Dad and Chase shook their heads, just as confused.

Dad looked wide-eyed and incredulous. "So does this mean what I think it does?"

Ivan nodded. "Yep. You better develop an appetite for mutton and Earl Grey. You're going to London."

chapter

TWENTY ONE

Dad became a media sensation. The storyline proved impossible to resist – the crushing injury suffered by Diamond Engine, the scandal over the positive drug test and the seventy-year-old hero emerging from the shadows to become part of the three-man team. A country-themed satellite network featured the story on one of their reality shows, and the American public, previously unaware the sport of reining even existed, became enthralled.

Summerville didn't know what to do with its living legend. Tourists visited our small town hoping to catch a glimpse of Dad or get an autograph. His five seconds of fame forced us to hire security for our spread, as well as the Rocking R. Chase gave interviews while Dad became inundated with offers to endorse products. "Team Splash" was out from under the radar, whether we liked it or not.

We sat around Mom and Dad's table one Sunday after church as Jeff and Shawna joined us for a fried chicken dinner. They'd married a year after we did and Shawna was seven months' pregnant. We exchanged gestational woes, sympathizing with one another's gravid ailments.

"I'd forgotten about the heartburn." I complained, when after only two bites of chicken and a dollop of potatoes, my throat filled with noxious gas. "I just want to eat already!"

Shawna patted her swollen belly. "I know what you mean. I'm so sick of bland food and antacid. I told Jeff he'd better bring me the biggest burrito he can find the moment I pop this baby out."

We all laughed.

"I'd take her up on that, if all she wants is a burrito." Chase advised. "Cassie's informed me she expects a pair of diamond earrings for bearing our child."

I jumped in to defend myself. "Only because he'll miss the last month of my pregnancy. He'll be in London with the rock star here." I nodded to Dad.

Dad looked cross and pointed his fork at me. "Don't start with me, young lady."

Jeff couldn't resist stirring the pot. "C'mon now, Mr. Roberts, you're the hottest ticket around. I could probably swipe a pair of your skivvies from your bedroom and make a fortune auctioning them on EBay."

"Jeff Deavers, I'm big enough to turn you over my knee." Dad growled.

"And man enough to do it, Sir. Still, might be worth the risk."

Even Mom nearly choked on her chicken trying to stifle giggles.

***

Months passed, everything eclipsed by the coming competition and Dad's rise to stardom. He accepted a few endorsement offers, only for products he'd used all his life and truly believed in. The money poured in like a welcome rain. None of us ran out and bought new trucks or 80" televisions, but we repaired old fences, spruced up our barns and Chase and I began designing a house with an architect. Dad squirreled away a nest egg for himself and Mom. His one concession to frivolous spending was a booked trip to Hawaii for the two of them after the Games and birth of the baby.

I worried about Dad's health under the strain and pressure. He sat astride Splash in our practice arena on a late spring afternoon, visibly sore in the back. He hunched over and winced as he wrapped his arms around himself in a self-massage.

"You okay, Dad?" I brought two iced teas, one for him and one for Chase. "You don't look so good."

"I can't live up to this 'ironman' reputation the media's slapped me with. Heck, I'm starting to wonder if the US Horse Association's gonna fail *me* for illegal drug use. I've popped more painkiller lately than that guy on *Celebrity Rehab*."

"Just a few more months, no quitting now." Chase looked more worried than he sounded. "I do think we can lighten up on the practice. You two have this down, and there is such a thing as excessive training. You'd better mention that back to your doc."

"Trust me, he knows. Since I've had weekly visits over the past months, we've gotten to know each other intimately. I've done wonders for his practice."

"You're the most famous seventy-year-old in the world, or at least the horse world. How does it feel?"

He took a long slurp of his tea.

"I'd be lying if I said it wasn't kinda fun. The money's a blessing, and it's a hoot folks want the autograph of an old guy like me. But I never expected this kind of attention. I didn't intend to become the poster boy for the geriatric set."

Dad pointed to the security van at the edge of our property. "And I'll be glad when we can be done with all that. I'm afraid to take a pee when I need to, they might catch it on camera."

Chase and I agreed. "Us, too. But just think, soon this particular journey'll be over."

Chase raised his tea glass to Dad. "One thing we can say, we took it all the way."

They clinked their tea glasses together. "That we did, Son, that we did."

***

Cliff's Star Maker ranch sent out a press release that Diamond Engine was recovering well. They thanked the public for its support and concern, and announced the stallion would be available for breeding next season. In the meanwhile, they felt confident Smokin Fire and Steve Gunner would take top honors at the Games, chalking one up for the Kesterson team as well as Team USA. They also wished Clint Keeton and Thunderstar the best as alternates.

We actually sent Cliff a card offering sympathy for his injured horse, but we never heard back.

Jeff made plans to accompany Dad, Chase, Sam and Splash to London. Dad and Chase didn't trust Splash to the hands of unfamiliar veterinarians, and Jeff jumped at the chance to attend the most important reining event of all time. Sam pleaded to come along as a groom, and we couldn't deny him the opportunity to watch his grandpa make history.

When the time came I watched them leave with a heavy heart. They'd drive our trailer to Dallas and board a specially equipped plane there, along with Ivan and Fria, Cliff and his entourage. Mom and I thought about driving to Dallas to see them off, but I was so emotional and heavily pregnant, we decided against it.

I hugged Dad and Sam, bawling like a calf, and kissed Chase through the salt of my tears.

"I want to go with you."

Dad tried to comfort me. "Of course you do, Baby Girl, and you'll be there. You'll be right here in my heart as I ride that pattern."

Chase wrapped his arms around me one last time. "And you'll be in heart every minute. And on my cell." He held up his phone with my picture on it. "We'll talk all the time, I promise."

"Make Sam shower and brush his teeth. He forgets, you know."

"I know."

"Oh, Mom." But Sam hugged me one last time anyway.

Splash whinnied from the trailer, probably confused as to why none of the other horses accompanied him. I reached through the escape door on the side to give him a final pat.

"Take care of my boys, fella. They're everything I love in this life."

The horse looked at me with chocolate eyes, nickering softly as if to say "I will."

chapter

TWENTY TWO

Mom and I thought about hosting daily viewing parties, inviting Shawna and Chase's parents, but decided against it. We wanted to treasure the experience in private, and if things didn't go well, didn't need for anyone else to witness our suffering. So I camped out at Mom's for the duration of the coverage since they'd bought a new satellite system, and we could tune into the event in its entirety. We set the recorder to capture everything, starting with the Opening Ceremony.

"There they are! There they are!" I squealed as Team USA entered in the Parade of Nations, each rider leading his/her horse. Dad walked next to a tiny girl leading a large warmblood, tacked in an English saddle. Splash looked miniature in comparison.

"Look at your father in that hat." Mother laughed and shook her head. Like all the other reining competitors, Dad wore a white cowboy hat with a leather red, white and blue Team USA jacket.

"It doesn't seem real."

It didn't seem any more real three days later when the reining competition began. I wrote all the scores in a notebook as we watched each competitor, keeping track of individual and team records. Canada and Germany provided the chief competition, consistently scoring high marks. Ivan was the first American to compete, and I tingled with excitement as I watched him.

"C'mon Fria! Show those studs what you're made of!" She did. The gray filly drew the crowds to their feet as Ivan rode her through their pattern. The pair chalked up a 228 ½, placing them second behind the top German rider.

"That'll get Team USA off to a good start, won't it, Cassie?"

"It's a great start. But to medal they'll need Dad and Kesterson's rider to turn in good scores, too, although I hope Dad beats the pants off Steve Gunner."

"So do I."

Long hours passed watching all the draws and foreign competitors. Oddly enough, Steve Gunner had drawn second to last, and Dad, dead last. At least he'd enter the arena knowing what he had to beat.

We grew tense waiting for Gunner's turn. As Americans we hoped for a good score, but as Roberts women, we wanted the gold for Dad. *I don't think I can stand him playing second fiddle to Cliff's flunky.*

Just before Gunner took the ring, a passing thunderstorm, accompanied by hail and howling wind, knocked out our satellite. The baby kicked hard inside my swollen belly as a bolt of lightning illuminated the sky outside the ranch house windows. I felt like retching, so I gripped the sofa cushion with all my might as the television screen flickered, then turned to snowy static. Mother scowled at me as I jumped from the couch and paced her den in frustration.

"Cassie, you'll go into labor if you don't settle down! The storm'll pass in a minute, the satellite'll pick back up."

"We don't have a minute, Mom! They just went to commercial break. Cliff Kesterson's colt's up next. You'd think with all Dad's endorsement money we could afford a decent satellite system!"

I wrung my hands as if the motion would help move the storm along. The baby kicked again, and I watched my stomach shake beneath my maternity dress. Thump, thump, thump. I placed my hand over the source of the motion and felt the outline of the little foot beating against my insides.

Mom patted the seat next to her on the sofa, and I sat down again. She squeezed my shoulders, pulling me towards her in a quick embrace.

"Sorry I snapped at you. The suspense is maddening, isn't it?"

We laughed like two nervous schoolgirls. Mom uttered a passionate prayer to restore our television reception. Whether in answer to prayer or simply the typical pattern of East Texas thunderstorms, the bad weather rumbled through in the span of five minutes. More importantly, our satellite dish found its signal again, and the picture returned to the screen. We caught the female sports announcer with big hair and a southern drawl in mid-sentence.

"...here in London, England, in this groundbreaking event for western riding, no horse is favored more than Smokin' Fire, trained by Cliff Kesterson of Star Maker Ranch, ridden by Cliff's protégé, Steve Gunner." Mom and I exchanged disgusted looks across the sofa. The camera panned to Cliff's spectacular bay colt. Cliff smiled a cheesy grin and gave a 'thumbs up' as his horse and apprentice entered the show pen.

The colt exploded across the arena like he'd been smacked on the behind with a bullwhip. I moaned. *Come on, make a mistake. Just a little one, enough to leave room for Dad.* "Screw up, darn you!"

"Cassie!" Mother's tone was sharp, but she didn't fool me. American or not, she hoped the darn horse tripped over his own hooves, too.

Cliff's protégé hardly moved in the saddle, making the ride seem effortless. Which it probably was. We knew Cliff's work well enough to know a trained monkey could likely navigate that horse through the pattern. As the colt rolled back and exploded again, I watched for a flaw in the performance, hoping for a slight stumble, a hesitation, an over-spin. I couldn't spot one.

"Cassie?" Mom's voice trembled. "Tell me this isn't as good as it looks."

"It is, Mom. Oh, it is." I choked back tears, telling myself to take the high road. "At least it'll be a good score for the US Team. If Cliff's horse medals, Dad medals." That didn't change the fact I wanted Dad to kick some hiney.

The crowd didn't content itself with mild applause. Every gorgeous maneuver merited whistles and screams of "Yeah!" After loping, spinning and sliding a beautiful pattern, the bay finished by backing ten feet prettier than a high-end sports car in reverse. Even through the television, I sensed the wildness of the crowd and heard the thunderous applause.

"How will they score?" Mom's face, drained of color, looked pinched.

"High." I growled, not at Mom but at Cliff's hotshot rookie and the robotic colt. Sure enough, the judges posted a score of 229 ½ and the crowd erupted in cheers. *One giant step for Team USA, one backward leap for Marvin Roberts.* Dad and Splash would be hard pressed to top that, particularly if the IEG judges shared the American bias against seniors.

I slammed a sofa pillow to the floor. The baby kicked again, hard, probably influenced by my adrenaline. As the rider exited the arena, the camera caught Cliff and his minion exchanging a high five. *The arrogant jerk, he knows he's won.*

"Well, that's it, then. Your father can't beat that." *Mom, ever the optimist.* I fought the urge to tell her to shut up. The hokey announcer popped back on the screen.

"What a fantastic ride for Steve Gunner! Cliff Kesterson must be thrilled. That score just assured them a medal." At least they didn't break out the gold then and there. If nothing else, Dad deserved his moment in the spotlight.

"...and now, fans, here's some real history in the making. Seventy year-old Marvin Roberts, the oldest International Equestrian Games competitor in history, riding the seven-year-old 'Texas Splash O Rein.'"

The camera focused on Dad; Mom and I swelled with pride. He looked so handsome sitting atop Splash in his simple western shirt and leather chaps, his ancient black Resistol crowning his head. He looked like an icon, the epitome of a dying breed of gentleman rancher. *Whatever happens, I'm so proud of you, Dad.* The crowd kindly offered an enthusiastic round of applause. I wanted to hug each one of them.

Splash looked, well, like Splash. Compared to the muscle-bound Kesterson colt he appeared almost skinny. His hind leg cocked in repose, as if he were half-asleep in the round pen at home instead of the IEG arena in London. His ears twitched nonchalantly back and forth. Dad nudged him ever so slightly and they made their way to the arena.

"Just look at him!" Mom exclaimed. I watched Mom, transfixed, as she stared at Dad on screen with all the love in the world shining in her eyes. I realized I must look the same way when I stared at Chase.

I held my breath in anticipation, clutching Mom's hand, straining to see an air of destiny surrounding the pair on the TV screen. The camera revealed only a dignified senior mounted on a plain red horse. Truth is, Splash looked as ordinary as he had the night he was born, some seven years before, in the middle of another thunderstorm.

"Come on, Splash, you can at least wake up." I sat on the edge of the sofa as Dad nudged the stallion forward.

Splash moved into a steady lope after entering the arena, accelerating confidently until he stopped, smooth as oil on a baby's bottom, and then rolled back over his own tracks. He ran the length of the arena again, fluid and flowing, executing another stop and rollback. Splash's mane rippled like red fire as he flew through the pattern.

I clutched my stomach and Mom reminded me to breathe.

"How are they doing?"

I waved my hand for her to be quiet. "Shhhh! I don't want to miss anything! So far so good."

I held my breath as Dad and Splash approached their first sliding stop. I could almost feel Splash surging beneath me, as if I was riding the pattern instead of Dad. I super-imposed myself on the red colt, feeling the strength of his lengthening stride. Yet where I would have hitched back on the reins to ask for the stop, Dad's reins remained completely slack. Splash surged forward with incredible speed, and then appeared to melt into the arena floor. I gasped.

"Good or bad?" Mom asked fearfully.

I was too enraptured to answer. The little red fireball must have slid thirty feet. Fans in the arena jumped to their feet and even through the television we could hear screams of "Woo-hoo! Get 'em Marvin! Yeah!" I whooped out loud in the living room.

"Very good!" I finally answered.

Splash backed ten feet, stopping with his hind legs neatly tucked beneath himself. I caught Dad ever-so slightly lay his reins along the stallion's neck, and Splash crossed his forelegs, spinning on his haunches four precise spins to the right. I closed my eyes and imagined the vertigo Dad felt while the arena flashed before his eyes as Splash turned 360 degrees in less than a second. An opposite flick of the reins, and Splash spun four and a quarter spins to the left. Dad's movements were so imperceptible, it seemed like he and Splash exchanged mental telepathy. If the crowd had been excited about Cliff's colt's performance, this fervor now completely eclipsed it.

Splash began loping circles, first large and fast, then small and slow. He loped in perfect balance, power under control, extending for the faster circles, executing an effortless flying change in the middle of the arena. Again, in my mind I bumped Splash slightly with my heel, asking for the change, expecting flawless execution.

I watched for anything that might cause a deduction, cursing the cameraman when I couldn't get a good enough view of the performance. What I could see was beyond good. Maybe even beyond darned good. The two moved in such harmony, I dared label it greatness. The crowd thundered through the television screen. I longed to be there so bad I could taste it.

Circles complete, Dad and Splash finished with one final maneuver, another sliding stop. Again, no reins. This time the camera captured a better angle and actually I saw Dad mouth "Whoa." Splash again threw the brakes, this time delivering a slide so long people later joked that the little horse slid the length of London, not stopping until he fell into the Thames.

The fans rose to their feet and the announcer, who'd had the courtesy to remain silent throughout Dad's magnificent performance, began chattering like an excited squirrel.

"What a way to end the first ever International Equestrian Games Reining Competition! What an incredible performance by Marvin Roberts and Texas Splash O Rein! The fans here in the arena stadium are out of control!"

Mom and I jumped up and down in the living room, holding each other's arms and circling in some sort of ridiculous dance.

"...and the scores from the judges are in!"

Mom and I clung together, and my heart leapt to my throat.

"I'm going to be sick!" I told Mom.

Instead of scolding, she said, "Me too."

Finally, the announcer relayed the score. "You're not going to believe this, folks! Marvin Roberts, our seventy-year old competitor, and the seven year-old Texas Splash O Rein, have just won the gold medal with a score of 237!"

Mom and I jumped up and down, yelling hysterically, no more idiotic than the fans in the London arena. No one seemed able to take it in. I pointed wildly to the television as the camera panned to Dad, who'd exited the arena and dismounted near Chase and Sam. The three of them took turns hugging each other and the horse.

As the world went wild, Splash yawned, licked his lips, and snuffled Sam's hair.

I laughed, tears streaming down my face.

"What is it?" Mom asked.

"He still looks like an ordinary colt."

***

A thousand things happened at once.

The house phone answering machine began picking up (we'd had the sense to silence the ringer for the competition), and a slew of congratulations filled the recorder. Shawna, Guy, Chase's parents, countless others. We only heard bits and pieces because our cell phones started ringing as well. In fact as we watched Dad on camera, Sam handed him a cell phone and seconds later, Mom's phone rang. Surreal. Then my phone whinnied with a horse ring tone.

"Chase!"

"He did it, Cass! We all did it." Simple words for a miracle none of us could fathom. The humble colt from the humble ranch with the humble trainer had just fired the imagination, as well as the hearts, of the entire horse world.

In my emotional state I began sobbing. "I miss you so much! I just want you all home. Or I want to be there with you."

Chase's voice sounded raw with emotion. "I know, Baby. You should have been here, but I promise we'll leave jolly old England real soon. Now that your Dad's got that shiny ornament for his collection, we've got more important things to think about, like little Lucy."

"You mean little Luke." We argued about whether the squirming mass in my abdomen was a boy or girl.

Mom motioned toward her phone as Chase and I swapped endearments, and then we switched phones so I could talk to Dad, and she could talk to Chase and Sam.

"Hey, Baby Girl." Dad's voice sounded like he was at the store in town picking up groceries, calling to see if he'd forgotten anything.

"You were right, Dad. You were right all along."

It seemed ridiculous to watch Dad on television, talking to me on his cell phone as he stroked Splash's neck with his free hand. I could still hear the crowd roaring both through the television and his phone. I saw Sam speaking into a microphone thrust in front of his face by a reporter.

"I better let you go. Your demanding public awaits. But I love you Dad, and I've never been so proud."

"You make me proud too, Baby Girl, every day."

The phone clicked off as they ushered Dad to the podium hastily set up in the arena for the medal ceremony. Chase and Sam led Splash into the arena to stand by the tallest podium while Dad stood at the top, removing his hat from his head. Steve Gunner stood next to him on the second highest podium, while Cliff held Smokin Fire nearby. As I watched, Cliff extended his hand to Chase, Sam and Dad, and the smile that accompanied it seemed surprisingly genuine. The German rider, claiming the bronze, stood at Dad's other side, while someone held his dun. They all lowered their heads to accept their gleaming medals.

As the gold was hung around Dad's neck, Mom and I held each other again, dissolving into hopeless buckets of tears. I'd never cried so much during a happy occasion. When the enormous American flag was displayed, flanked by another American flag in Steve's honor and the German flag for the other rider, Mom and I stood at attention in the living room, hands over our hearts as our national anthem played.

Dad won an additional gold medal for the USA Team victory, and he, Steve and Ivan shared the podium for that ceremony. I found myself as proud for Cliff and his protégé as I was for Dad and Ivan. Mom and I stood again, hands over our hearts, singing the anthem at the top of our lungs.

***

At last the pageantry, pomp and circumstance came to a close. The hokey announcer signed off, and the coverage turned to show jumping. But the media frenzy over the seventy-year-old athlete had just begun.

Calls streamed in until our voicemails ran out of memory. Mixed in with congratulations from family and friends were product representatives from everything from corn flakes to vitamin supplements to pickup trucks. If Dad was popular before the Games, he had definitely escalated to man of the hour.

Later that night I talked to Sam, wishing I could wrap my arms around his bony shoulders. He loved the attention and celebration going on in England. "You should see my autograph book - you won't believe who I met! But the person everyone wants to see is Grandpa. It's one big party..."

Before bed I talked to Chase again. By then the initial euphoria had worn off and given way to plain exhaustion. I also felt lonely and left out, the three most important men in my life an ocean away, riding the crest of victory. Chase talked so fast and so excitedly I only half listened to what he said.

"...what surprised me the most was the reaction of the dressage and three-day event riders. Do you know they actually came to the reining competition to support us? I figured they'd turn up their noses. Several of the dressage riders said your dad's ride was the most beautiful display of partnership between a horse and rider they'd ever seen. Can you believe it?"

"No, that's amazing." My voice sounded flat.

"You all right, Honey?" From a world away, Chase knew something was wrong.

"Yeah, I just miss you all so much. And I'm thrilled beyond words, but I wanted to be part of this with you, not stuck at home."

I felt so ashamed of myself, here I was on the night of our finest hour sulking and miserable.

"Cassie Roberts Eversoll, none of this would have happened without you. And your Dad's making sure everyone knows that. Do you know how many interviews he's done in the past few hours? And he starts every one out by telling the reporters how Splash would have drowned the night he was born if it weren't for his hero daughter."

My heart ached with tenderness. "Really? He's telling everyone that?"

Chase laughed. "Don't take my word for it, just turn on your television and you're bound to see it live. Your dad's the most popular guy here, and the whole world's caught reining fever."

"Don't I know it. You'll die when you find out who's been calling the house, trying to appoint Dad their new product spokesman…aaahhh!"

Something warm and wet gushed from my body.

"Cassie, what is it?"

"Oh no!"

"Cassie!"

"I think my water just broke!"

"Please tell me you're joking! The OB said you had a couple more weeks."

"I've had mild contractions all day, but I thought they were Braxton-Hicks."

I grabbed a dirty towel from the floor and tried to mop up the wet spill, but a contraction gripped me and I howled into the phone again.

"Cassie!"

"Chase, I better get my mom. Come home soon." I hung up the receiver and yelled for mother.

She arrived in seconds, instantly assessing the wet carpet and pained expression on my face.

"I'll take your bag to the car, and then I'll come back to help you into some dry clothes."

"But Mom, Chase was supposed to be here. I can't have his baby without him!"

"Cassie Jayne, we're leaving for the hospital this instant!"

And we did.

chapter TWENTY THREE

Contractions assaulted my body in painful, explosive waves.

"This can't be happening!"

I looked first to Mom, who sat in a chair next to the hospital bed, then to the delivery room nurse who had just examined my nether-regions and proclaimed me seven centimeters dilated. They exchanged motherly, knowing looks, and then Mom spoke up.

"It can and it is. You're having this baby today."

"But Dr. Hahn promised! She said…"

The nurse laid a reassuring hand on my shoulder and bubbled with humor.

"We'll let your baby argue due dates with Dr. Hahn when he or she pops out, which'll probably happen within the next hour or so."

My eyes welled with tears. Mom at least understood my predicament.

"I want Chase." I sounded like a five-year-old kid whining for a lollipop. Mom's face softened.

"I know you do. He's moving heaven and earth to get out of London, and after that gold medal win, I'm sure everyone's doing everything possible to help him. But the fact is you're gonna have to settle for me."

I cried until the next contraction broke over me and twisted my entire body into a knot, causing too much pain for tears.

"Aaarrrgghh. Help me." I appealed to Mom, the nurse and the anesthesiologist who'd just walked into the room. Certain parts of my body felt like they'd been set on fire.

"How do you feel? The epidural helping?" The doctor asked the question with a straight face but I assumed he must be joking.

"Well, my left leg is completely numb, so I feel absolutely nothing in my left leg. Unfortunately, I don't think that's where this baby's going to come out! And believe me, I feel *everything* going on down there!"

"Cassie!" Mother tried to shush me by shoving an ice chip in my mouth. The monitor next to my bed indicated a big wave of red, and I gripped the hospital bed for dear life.

"AAAAAAAHHHHHHHH!"

"Take it easy, Mrs. Eversoll." The anesthesiologist needed lessons from my husband on soothing frightened animals. His timid voice didn't produce near the calming effect Chase's did. He checked the site where the epidural needle entered my spine, and told me to press the button on the control he'd given me to supply more medication. I'd already pressed the darn thing three times.

The nurse, Eileen, ushered the doctor from the room. "It's all right, Dr. Steinmetz, I think I'd better call Dr. Hahn. Best thing for Mrs. Eversoll now is to get this baby out." Dr. Steinmetz quickly took the offered escape route. Nurse Eileen left to call my OB. I turned to Mom with trembling voice.

"I'm having this baby by myself, aren't I?"

"You are not. I'm not chopped liver, you know. And just think how that husband of yours is going to melt when he rushes into this hospital room tomorrow and finds you holding his newborn."

Mom painted a pretty image, and I clung to it as another contraction racked my body. Moments later nurse Eileen rushed into the room and checked my monitors. She wasn't laughing or joking anymore.

"Is something wrong?" Mom's voice became anxious.

"Dr. Hahn's on the way, she'll be here any minute." She tried to sound calm, but Mom and I both sensed something wasn't right. "Cassie, can you roll more toward your side?"

I did as I was told. "Is my baby okay?"

Another contraction pulsed through me, and along with it, a strong impulse to push. I told the nurse.

"Don't push! Not until Dr. Hahn gets here. Pant like a dog, quick breaths." She turned to Mom. "I'll be back in just a minute. Don't let her lie on her back, and don't let her push!"

I felt too frightened to cry. Mom hovered next to me, doing her dead-level best to coach. "Pant, Cassie, pant!"

We panted together, making a "hoo, hoo, hoo" sound. Any other time it would have been funny. Mom showed visible relief when my doctor and Nurse Eileen returned.

"Hi Cassie." Dr. Hahn smiled brightly, looking immaculate in her black spectacles and pristine scrubs. Her air of competence soothed me where the anesthesiologist's meek attempt had not.

"Is everything all right, Dr. Hahn?"

She affected a professional, matter-of-fact tone with me.

"The baby's showing signs of stress from the labor. The best thing we can do for both of you is to deliver as quickly as possible. We're going to try naturally first, but if you don't progress fast enough, we'll perform a c-section."

I looked at my mother in horror. *This can't be happening!* Mom bowed her head in a quick prayer and I did the same. *Lord, please let my baby be all right! I'm so scared. How can I get through this without my husband?*

Dr. Hahn put on a pair of latex gloves and rolled me onto my back, pushing my legs apart. Nurse Eileen held one hand and Mom held the other.

"All right Cassie, no more screaming, no more panting. I want all that energy funneled into pushing. Next time you feel a contraction, PUSH!"

She no sooner spoke the words than I felt another wave of pain. I bore down with all my might. The pressure felt so intense I thought my head would explode.

"Good Cassie! The baby's crowning!"

A terrible, ripping, burning sensation overwhelmed me. I whimpered. Mom rubbed my arm.

"Hang in there, Cass. I'm so proud of you."

I felt sweat dripping down my face in spite of the cold hospital room.

"You are?" I asked weakly.

"Of course I am. You've got more gumption and guts than I ever did, I could never do what you're doing right now. Back in my day, they put us to sleep for this."

"That's so not fair! I want them to put me under. Aaaaaaaahhhhhh!" Another contraction. Dr. Hahn scolded.

"Don't scream, Cassie! Let that energy out by pushing! You have to push harder next time, we have to get this baby out." I felt the sudden urge to smash Dr. Hahn's black designer eyeglasses, make them a permanent part of her face.

Mom continued murmuring encouragement.

"You can do this, Cassie. You're strong as ten women. You're Texan."

The next contraction I pushed with everything in me. Mom, Dr. Hahn, and Nurse Eileen praised.

"Good job! The baby's head's out!"

Dr. Hahn seemed to be working furiously at something. Mom turned in her direction and gasped.

"It's okay, Mrs. Roberts."

"What is it?" I shrieked.

Dr. Hahn addressed me in her matter-of-fact tone again.

"It's okay, Cassie. The umbilical cord's wrapped around the baby's neck, it happens sometimes. I've got it loose." Before the words could register, the monitor showed a monster wave rising.

I pushed with the last bit of strength I possessed. I felt a slippery sensation, and then the pain subsided. For some reason I squinted my eyes shut.

"Cassie, look!"

I opened my eyes. Mom pointed to the tiny, messy human bundle in Dr. Hahn's arms. The trio of women grinned at me. I felt like I was going to pass out.

"Good girl, Cassie!" The three of them praised simultaneously. Dr. Hahn and Nurse Eileen took the baby to a nearby table for a quick examination.

Out of breath, I still tried to rise from my hospital bed. "Is my baby okay?" I felt frantic.

Dr. Hahn turned and smiled, then nodded.

"He looks good. The cord was causing the fetal distress, but his vitals are fine now. You can hold him in just a moment."

Tremendous relief washed over me. I looked at Mom. "She said 'he!'"

"Uh huh. You and Chase have a son. I have another grandson."

She stroked my hair and held my hand. "I've never seen anyone or anything so brave."

"You were great too, Mom. You've got more gumption than you get credit for. You're always there for my bloody moments." We laughed, which made my insides ache.

Moments later, Dr. Hahn handed me Luke Marvin Eversoll, wrapped in soft hospital-issue blanket. He stared at me with serene blue eyes, a peaceful expression on his tiny face. Mom cried, "ooohing" and "awwwing" over him.

I hardly noticed as Dr. Hahn stitched me up. Despite the trauma of birth, little Luke's head was perfect and round, his color healthy pink. Nurse Eileen helped me start him nursing, and he took to the idea greedily. We all admired him.

"Forget the men and their silly medal. Yours is the greater accomplishment." Mom's voice still rang with pride, and I loved the sound.

"I think you're right, Mom. I think you're right."

***

I couldn't remember a time I'd been so lavishly cared for. Word spread throughout the hospital that Marvin Roberts, International Equestrian Games Champion, had just become a second-time grandfather, his grandbaby delivered right here at Summerville General. Flowers and stuffed animals poured into my room, and the nursing staff outdid themselves making me comfortable. If I wanted ice cream in the middle of the night, it was delivered. Extra pillows? Not a problem. My whim was their command. The only catch is Dad had a lot of autographs to sign when he arrived to visit his grandson.

I treasured the sensation of cradling Luke Marvin. It had been so long since Sam's birth, and such different circumstances. I'd forgotten the downy wisps of fine hair, the silky skin, the scent of baby powder. I got to know my baby in those first hours, a content, confident newborn who rarely cried. I kept him swaddled in the hospital bassinet next to my bed while I dozed, and then picked him up and nursed him when he fretted. I laughed at him as he aggressively latched on. This was one baby in no danger of missing those nourishing first days of mother's milk.

Luke happened to be nursing when Chase, after twenty-four hours nonstop aboard three different airplanes, unshaven and in need of a shower, at last stumbled into the hospital room. He entered the room with a bright, eager smile, but as Mom had envisioned, his whole countenance melted at the sight of his son. He washed his hands in the room sink, and then gently stroked Luke's head. The moment felt too poignant for words.

Luke's abrupt burp broke both the silence and the mood, and we erupted into giggles. My husband kissed me, and then I held Luke so that Chase could see his face.

"Let me introduce you to Luke Marvin Eversoll."

A tear rolled down my husband's cheek as he picked up his son for the first time.

"How does it feel?" I asked.

"To be a father?"

"Yes."

"I was already a father. Little Luke just makes it times two."

He couldn't have given a better answer.

"Speaking of Sam," he continued, "he and your Dad are waiting very impatiently outside."

"Dad and Sam?" I asked, puzzled. "They flew home with you? How on earth did you all manage that? And what about Splash? You didn't just leave him, did you?"

"Settle down! You'll upset our son." He raised a finger to caress Luke's cheek. "Yes, they flew home with me. Your dad arranged it all; the airlines were only too happy to help the famous new gold medalist in his hour of need. As for Splash, Ivan and our buddy Cliff Kesterson are taking care of him and flying him home with Fria, Smokin Fire and Thunderstar."

My mouth must have dropped to the floor. "You've got to be kidding me."

"Not at all. Believe it or not, no one was more congratulatory than Cliff. I think he might be an all-right guy after all. Not to mention I'm sure he'll get some 'good guy' press out the story."

"So all's well that ends well?"

"I don't think the story's ending; I think it's just begun."

We heard a light tapping on the door and answered "come in."

Mom, Dad and Sam converged on us, or rather Chase, since he was holding the new addition. Sam proclaimed "He's so cute!" with delight; tears poured down Dad's face.

Chase handed Dad his grandson.

"Well, I'll be." Dad seemed too choked up to speak, but finally gathered himself together.

"And to think I used to dread growing old. If I'd only known seventy was going to be the best year of my life."

Epilogue

I closed my eyes and listened to the sound of quiet, broken only by the German clock ticking rhythmically in the living room. I treasured the rare sensation, as it wasn't often the Eversoll house enjoyed such tranquility. I tiptoed past the nursery and peeked at the rosy-cheeked cherub resting in his crib. Little Luke looked so angelic in his sleep, you'd never guess that when awake, the toddler roamed the ranch like a turbo-charged action figure. If I turned my back for a moment, he'd be halfway to Texarkana in his pint-sized, battery-powered John Deere. Corraling the spirited miniature cowboy proved a full-time job.

Chase had gone to town for a supply run with Sam and his ball gear in tow. Sam had made the varsity team, and the practice field wasn't far from the Feed and Seed. So for the moment the silent house belonged only to me. I poured a glass of iced tea, pampering myself with a garnish of fresh mint and a lemon wedge. Wandering out to the porch, I settled into an antique rocking chair and sipped my aromatic refreshment. *I am a blessed woman.*

The pastures blazed with yellow, blue and orange wildflowers; I never tired of the porch view overlooking the pond and fields. The horses' coats shone from rich grass and glowing health. The entire Eversoll ranch enjoyed a spring of contentment.

Belle must have sensed my presence because she approached the fence and nickered, enticing me to join her for a pet or treat.

"Later, girl, I promise." I would have loved to share the moment with her, but the chair cradled me comfortably, and it felt good just to sit still.

A neigh rang out from the bachelor pasture, and I smiled, turning toward the sound. The "boys" in the stallion field always made some ruckus or another; we laughed at their antics as much as Luke's. Sure enough, Sky and Victory fought a mock battle near the water tank, rearing up on their hind legs and squealing as they pawed. The display of masculinity lasted only a moment or two, and then they settled down, shook themselves off, and began grooming one another.

I marveled at Sky. The six-year old stallion looked magnificent, from his beautifully shaped head to his mile-long legs. So black he gleamed blue, the colt measured at least seventeen hands tall. I took enormous pride in him; he looked the part of a champion more than Splash ever had, but I'd learned looks can be deceiving. Only time would tell what kind of heart resided in Sky's broad chest.

My thoughts turned to Splash. I still missed the sight of the red horse in our stallion pasture, but I knew Dad spoiled him shamefully at the Rocking R. Splash could have continued competing, but Dad saw no point in it, they'd claimed their victory and retired. Splash now stood at stud at Dad's ranch for an unbelievable fee, which set Mom and Dad nicely and I'm sure suited Splash just fine.

I heard the sound of tires on the dirt and gravel drive, and Chase's truck, loaded with sweet feed bags and shavings, pulled up to the house. I waved and he must have spotted me, because he jumped out of the truck and sauntered up to the porch.

"Master Luke asleep?"

"If he wasn't, do you think I'd be out here sipping tea?"

"Good point." He grinned and bent over to kiss me. "How long's he been down?"

"Maybe fifteen minutes."

"Then we might have some time." I caught the gleam in his eyes as he motioned toward the door, and I wasn't unwilling, but I didn't want to go in just yet.

"In a minute." I promised.

"Wow, I must be losing my touch." He sat in the chair next to mine.

"Never. It's just when you run on a never-ending hamster wheel, it's nice to step off for a moment."

He reached for my hand and we rocked there like two old people, savoring the peacefulness. Another neigh rang from the stallion field and we both turned.

"Bet you it's Sky and Victory again. They were at it earlier."

As I spoke Sky reared and pawed the air, and then streaked across the pasture like a blue flame. Victory followed at a mad gallop, but couldn't come close to catching him.

"Wow, have you ever seen anything like him, Chase?" My husband shook his head and gave me an odd look.

"Wish you still mooned over me like that. And you forget I still limp because of that animal."

"Oh, stop it. You do not limp." I slapped him on the arm. "It's just Sky has this promise of greatness about him, so it makes me wonder."

"Are you ever sorry it wasn't you in that arena?"

"What?" The question caught me off guard.

"You heard me."

"Of course not. I wouldn't trade Luke for the world, and it was right for Dad to be there. It was his moment, his horse."

"But Sky is your horse."

"What on earth are you getting at?"

"I'm just saying maybe there's room for two champions in the family."

"Sky's not a reining horse, he's hunter bred."

"Last time I checked there were hunter/jumper events in the International Equestrian Games." I looked at Chase like he'd lost his mind.

"What happened with Dad was incredible, something we'll remember forever. But it was a one-shot deal, unless you want to ride and train another champion reining horse. Any fool knows quarter horses don't make the jumping team, and certainly not cowgirls from Texas."

Chase pointed to Sky, who stopped his wild gallop and stood at the far end of the field, his mane blowing poetically in the breeze.

"He's big as a warmblood and fast as a full Thoroughbred."

"And I couldn't pass for an amateur hunt seat rider, much less a jumper. Chase Eversoll, I think that gold medal went straight to your head." I picked a piece of ice out of my tea glass and threw it at him, bringing him back to earth.

"Hey!" He rose from his chair and extended a hand. "All right, then, if you're not going to entertain my delusions, then come entertain me some other way."

I couldn't resist the plea, so I left my cozy chair to follow him, taking a last, lingering look at Sky.

Could he...?

No, I'd ridden the roller coaster of Dad's aspirations. I was done with global equine competition, and I wanted nothing more than to be a rancher's wife and mother.

Still, if the horse has the stuff...

Enough! I couldn't let my thoughts wander down that path.

Then again, I had to admit it wouldn't be the strangest miracle ever to happen in Texas.

About The Author

Born in the Lone Star State, Becky grew up riding & showing quarter horses and paints. In college she combined her love of riding with a love of writing, working for a publisher penning articles on horses and riding. Today, she writes equine adventure stories for children and adults.

Becky is the author of *Texas Rein,* a contemporary western romance; its sequels, *Tropic Rein* and *Christmas Rein*; *Ribbon Chasers,* an inspirational story for young barn girls, and *The Stallion and the Serpent,* a high fantasy novel written with co-author L.R. Giles.

Becky lives in the Shenandoah Valley, Virginia with her husband, James, her children, Austin, Wesley, and Arielle, and various four-legged family.

Visit her website: http://brboyette.com/

Made in the USA
San Bernardino, CA
27 March 2017